DEAD DELICIOUS

ADIE STURM MYSTERY

ANASTASIA AMOR

BRODT PUBLISHING

Brodt Publishing
AnastasiaAmor.com
Anastasia.Amor@hotmail.com

Copyright ©2012 by Anna Brodt
ISBN-978-0-9918062-3-2
Cover Art by Anna Brodt

ACKNOWLEDGEMENTS

I'd like to thank Jane for her input and Kristen for her portrait photo. *Besitos* to Vita and Laura for introducing me to the popular cantinas in San Miguel. Great big hugs to the dive masters who kept me safe in the crystal clear waters of Cozumel. Special thanks to Bruce for his edits.

.

By **ANASTASIA AMOR**

ADIE STURM MYSTERIES

Corpse for Cozumel
Days of the Dead
The Curse of the Carnaval
Dead Delicious

PARANORMAL FANTASY SERIES

Havana Heat

EROTIC ROMANCE

Exploring Irresistible

Praise for ANASTASIA AMOR

ADIE STURM MYSTERIES

A CORPSE FOR COZUMEL!
"The suspense starts in the first few pages and continues until the very end. The strong, sexy characters and intense sexual tension keep you wanting more...great read that's hard to put down." —*Two Lips Reviews*

"I had no idea who the murderer was until the end ...expanse of detail of the locations and the plot, creating a vivid world for all who read her work!"—*Enchanting Reviews*

"...hot sexy men... thrilling suspense. Hold on and keep looking over your shoulder. You won't guess who the killer is until it's too late." —*Night Owl Romance Reviews*

"**5 Stars**! Gripping story, hot characters, realistic dialogue and fantastic action." —*Reader' Favorite*

DAYS OF THE DEAD! "...murder, hot romance, intrigue, and
suspense....Adie is a modern-day, sexy Agatha Christie...charming and quite captivating...put together well!" —*ReviewYourBook*

"You never can tell just what will crop up...Funny – or maybe just weird situations abound. This is a fun read, and will be very welcomed by fans of the series." —*Long And Short Reviews*

THE CURSE OF THE CARNAVAL: *Epic Award Nominee*

DEAD DELICIOUS...*Global Nominee*

"An exciting story filled with great descriptions of the exotic locale Cozumel and the lifestyle of the area's rich and famous, delivers on the intrigue surrounding the unexpected increase in wealth of the key players as well as the sexual tension between Adie and the men who are competing for her affections. There are plenty of surprises and the mystery does not stop until the very last page – if it is even done there! *a great book for a day on the beach or a night in front of the fire – any time you are ready for some hot action and steamy sex.*" —*Readers' Favorite*

"… *Dead Delicious* made me a huge Adie Sturm fan, and now I find myself hankering to read the first books in the series. Adie Sturm is a liberated woman—strong, sexy, and independent … Amor has incredible skill in how she unfolds the element of mystery while keeping the sensual atmosphere alive. Her sexy voice rings loud throughout, making us yearn for our slice of sun, sea, sand, and irresistible male company.

I absolutely loved this book! I sympathized with Adie's dilemma while dealing with three sexy men who all vie for her attentions. To pick the hottest hero, you must read this book and trust me, it is worth your while. …the colorful band of tour group members will have you laughing one minute and tearing your hair out the next…fun, fast-paced, drop dead sexy, and keeps your pulse racing in more ways than one. *Highly Recommended!* **Anastasia Amor is truly the queen of steamy mysteries."**
—— Natalie G. Owens, *An Eternity of Roses.*

"Once again I lost myself in Adie's descriptions of Cozumel, her eclectic group of tourists, her men (oh you're so not going to believe what happens here) and let's not forget murder… "Entertaining!…This standalone story weaves through its own mystery while tying in past emotions and moving us in new possibilities…"—*ChrisChatReviews*

1

Trapped. From under the overhang, a creature struggled. The predator hung on. I swam in closer. Religiously, a monstrous green eel guarded its prey. But the current was too strong. From the deep ridges of the coral, the powerful ocean current released the victim. Freed, it shot straight out. A large knuckled hand attached to a thick forearm swept by, brushing my leg. Vomit rose in my throat and spilled into my regulator. The moray's tiny eye blinked.

****

Deeko's was rockin'—a heavy down-beat blasting from the speakers. It was Saturday night, a few minutes to midnight, and the place was packed like a can of sardines. The dance was a dirty version of salsa with serious body contact. Crazy Toronto club? Sure, but even in a place like Kitchener, grind was everywhere.

Before leaving the restaurant with my tour group, I had asked the waiter where the club was. He'd waved in the direction of a building two doors down and winked conspiratorially. A wicked place like Toronto provided a thrill for the small town vacationers but not my dance partner. Brock Laval had been around the block more than once. His kind of thrill would be hooking up with bad-girl, Adie Sturm.

Let me set the record straight. Brock was wrong. I wasn't really…bad. That was for my time off. I grinned. If I planned it right, there would be lots of that. I pushed Brock away. He lifted his arm to spin me clockwise and then counterclockwise. He was Hollywood attractive, a real hottie, but I had another man burned in my brain.

The way Brock rubbed his butt against mine reminded me to step it up. He was a client, not my next conquest, and definitely not my type. No matter how much I was tempted, I couldn't walk off this dance floor. I'm a tour guide and it was up to me to make this trip outstanding even for players like Brock.

It was Deeko's tonight. Tomorrow we'd be in Cozumel, Mexico for a bit of diving, drinking and a huge dose of Mexican culture. The perk was to travel and get paid for it. But the downside were the jerks in every tour group. If I could get them to happily connect, I'd be home free.

Out of the corner of my eye, I watched a willowy blonde bobbing up and down like a chicken in crisis. So far, she seemed to be having a good time. If she wasn't, I'd be sure to hear about it sooner rather than later.

Irmgard, the petulant owner of Fleisher's Travel, came from money. Short on brains and long on capital, she had bought the agency on impulse. Glancing over to the bar, I saw her eyes flit in my direction. My shoulders tensed but when I saw her focus on Brock, I relaxed. I should have known. Irmgard Fleischer was on the prowl and Brock was the next victim.

My partner pulled me in close and spoke into my ear, but the music drowned it all except for, "So-oo hot." Did he mean he was hot? I frowned. The place was packed and most people were sweating up a storm. Or was he referring to me?

When he had booked, he told me about his friend in Cozumel who would join us for a dive. Did that mean a girl friend? But if this man was in love you wouldn't have known it from the way he inserted his leg between mine, and moved suggestively. When the hem of my red dress rode up dangerously high, I twisted his hands away, jerked my skirt down and spun him around in front, rocking him from side to side. He looked over his shoulder and grinned admiringly at my maneuver.

I'm a martial artist. Although a light-weight and take note I'm speaking about my build not my brain matter, I counteract my petite size by keeping fit. Don't get me wrong, karate doesn't depend on height or weight. It's all about surprise and altering the opponent's balance to take him down. But staying trim does help me move fast. In this case, there was no need to go ninja but Brock's chance to lead was over.

At a nearby table, a sturdy mama in a leather dress scanned the dance floor frowning at the crowd before her beady browns lit on me. Mary Battrock was a technician for Spider Vac, a Canadian company dealing with central vacuums. Apparently, she did house calls to check out hoses and suction power. Right now, her evil stare could have zapped billions of dust mites in one sweep. I turned away but not fast enough.

"Adie Sturm!" shouting through the heavy downbeats of the music, her booming voice resounded miraculously loud and clear.

I pretended not to hear.

Three manly strides and she was in my face. Mary was a far cry from her saintly namesake.

"Adie Sturm!" she hissed, gripping my arm tightly to propel me away from Brock. "Geez Louise, lady. We need to talk. Your tour group is full of flippin' losers! Especially that one." She jerked her chin towards the bar where the object of her disgust stood.

Legs spread hip width, hands behind his back in an at-ease soldier stance, Larry T read military to me. I'd been surprised to hear he was a firefighter. Built like a bulldozer, he was capable of carrying Mary from a burning building in a flash but from the look in his eyes, he would likely have charged straight to the nearest motel room.

"That redneck thinks he's God's gift." With a thick index finger, she poked her significant cleavage. "Can't take his eyes off these puppies. Where'd he learn his manners?"

I thought she was kind of over-reacting for someone whose pushups were so loaded, they could have been packed with NFL shoulder pads. Her chest rivaled Pamela Anderson's and then some.

"All of me is reserved."

There was a story in this but I didn't want to hear it. Sure, it was my job to make them happy but there were limits.

A shiny shaved head was all I could see of Larry as he headed onto the dance floor, zigzagging his way in and out of the crowd like a linebacker about to make a touchdown. Beer in both hands, he shoved through the dancers straight to us.

A wide grin stretched across his face. "Hiya, ladies!"

At least that's what I think he said. With the music blasting so

3

loud and my ears muffled, I could only guess.

"Wanna dance, babe?" His question was directed to Mary.

I don't know why he bothered. It was obvious she had her back up.

Over the din Mary shouted, "No way!" and flipped him the finger.

The rest of her words were lost with a burst of lively salsa music, followed by the appearance of a statuesque blonde announcing the start of the show.

I motioned to Larry T and Mary to move back behind the yellow line where people gathered. They could stand and see the show, both of them a head taller than the average Torontonian. I wasn't so lucky. I plopped down on the floor with some college girls seated cross-legged.

In a form-fitting pink sequined gown, our hostess majestically waved a gloved hand as she purred seductively into the microphone. "Good evening and welcome to our show. My name is Mimi." Twisting her hips, she sauntered forward and back in a snappy salsa step. The audience broke out into applause and a man whooped loudly in anticipation.

Her heavily made-up eyes sparkled with excitement. "We have the very best dancers here tonight ready to perform the salsa. Should you be so inclined, they would appreciate tips." At that, a pale boy in tight jeans sprang up and pushed a ten down the deep vee of her neckline.

After giving his cheek a quick tweak, she peered past the crowd and spotted the first performer. "Put your hands together to welcome the salacious Delilah. She has the moves you want to know better!"

A brunette with bouncy shoulder length hair, in a skin-tight blue satin mini dress shimmied her way across the floor. Unlike the hostess with the rather large chin, Delilah had delicate features and looked ultra-feminine. After gyrating seductively in a circuitous route before the audience, she stopped and blew kisses until a few bills were thrust into her garter. Then, with a big smile, she wiggled out as her replacement, a curvaceous auburn beauty, sashayed in. The audience hooted in appreciation.

At that point, I'd had enough. The mixture of heat and stale body odor was making me nauseous. Back up on my feet, I wove my way through the crowd to the washroom.

By the time I stepped out of the stall and to the mirror, the place was packed.

From above, a husky voice murmured close to my ear. "Nice dress."

I looked up to the hostess from the show. "Thank you. My eyes flicked to the mirror nervously. "My hair's a mess."

"No-oo." With a careful finger, Mimi swept aside a damp strand from my brow and checked me out. "You look lovely. Red is a great color on you."

I was getting purely male vibes and it was weirding me out.

The blonde bent down to whisper in my ear. "Adie, relax. It's me, Ronny."

From my tour group? My jaw dropped. Cocking my head, I examined him closer. This guy in the four inch platforms was Ronald? A transvestite salsa dancer? "It's really you?"

"Yup...part time job. Don't worry, when the tour group meets me, I'll look just like any other dude."

I breathed a sigh of relief. If Irmgard got wind of this, she would be furious. She had little tolerance for those types. That's what she'd say about Ronald if she found out. Being from a stringent religious background, Irmgard and her friends pretended gays did not exist.

"Ronald..."

"No, Adie, please call me Ronny," he said in a husky voice. "My friends do."

"You've put me in an awkward position."

Ronny pressed his index finger over my lips and smiled. "No worries, sugar. I'm a lawyer. I know how to keep things confidential. By tomorrow morning's departure, I'll be a manly man in jeans and a T-shirt. No one will ever guess."

****

San Miguel was baking under a cloudless February sky. Sweat trickled down into my cleavage. It was the start of a bad hair day but I wasn't complaining. I'd take heat any day over ice pellets plummeting Southern Ontario. When active weather hit hard last night, we were lucky North Jet de-iced and left on schedule.

With the La Vida Hotel sign thrown in the back of the shuttle with the luggage, I climbed on board and sat next to the driver. A passenger list in hand, I counted heads and formed a circle with my forefinger and thumb to signal Roberto we were ready to roll.

Driving through San Miguel was a culture shock. A busy obstacle course of scooters, pedestrians and vintage Volkswagens competing for road space. Luckily, I wasn't driving.

The bus passed the museum and headed down Rafael Melgar. Shops, jewelry stores and the landmarks of Las Palmaras and Pepe's Grill lined up on the left with the view of the Caribbean and cruise ships on the right. The ferry pier was first before the major cruise ship hangout, Carlos'n Charlie's. Though this town hummed once in a while, no one could call San Miguel a party place.

On the way south, we spotted road construction. We detoured around the Chedraui Plaza until the shuttle eventually made it back onto the main street.

For me, Cozumel and its only town, San Miguel, was like a second home. A curious mixture of Mayans, Mexicans and expats made up a population of seventy thousand. Situated on the Caribbean side of Mexico, the island was a laid-back paradise.

As Cozumel boasted the second largest coral reef in the world off the coast, most visitors and residents were divers. The island depended on tourism and did everything to build a positive image for the visitors. But not all had gone well. Hurricanes had struck repeatedly, destroying coral and flooding the town.

But the islanders were amazing. Residents had pulled together after the last big one and cleaned up the devastating mess left behind. Palms burnt by the salt from building-high waves had been replaced and today, along our route, one could note new condos and hotels springing up along Melgar.

With the shuttle parked at the entrance Roberto helped everyone out before he deposited the luggage in front of the La Vida. The soft ting of a text had me rummaging inside the pocket of my purse. I dug out my cell and looked.

xx W

It brought a smile to my lips and sent tingles to my core. The second text sent by D had me curious. I visualized brandy eyes in a handsome face. Before I could read the text, a tremendously powerful whiff of floral perfume assaulted my nostrils. Unpleasant didn't describe it. It was like a giant Hyacinth garden in spring. Sweet, clingy sinus poison. Substantial hips pressed me back as Mary Battrock reached in to haul out a zebra print suitcase.

I threw my cell into my purse and grabbed the luggage from Roberto. Eyes averted, I rapidly pulled the case up to the door of the La Vida, hoping to escape.

"Adie, there's something you need to do." Mary's square face was rosy with the heat and effort.

"Yes?"

"Larry T. What a stupid name. As if there is any other Larry on this trip. That man's a moron and ugly," she growled. "I want you to make sure his room is as far away from mine as possible or I'll have to do somethin' I hadn't ought to."

The woman needed to seriously chill but what she said made sense. Avoiding trouble is smart. In this case, trouble was Mary Battrock.

Over six feet and built like a Sherman tank, Larry T was massive. In fact, everything about him spoke Afghanistan. He was seriously solid.

I'm kind of a fashionista and if ever a man looked wrong, this one did. First, the tan shirt tucked into belted dress pants with the practical black rent-a-cop-boots. It was as if he'd never been a civilian or worn regular clothes. I had to agree with Mary Battrock on this one. Second, the ridges and knobs on his shaved head were right off the space channel. A hat, or better yet, hair should have covered that landscape. And what was up with him? His curiously small eyes under bushy brows flitted around, inspecting everything and everyone.

Then there was the lust thing. It didn't make sense. Why was Larry hitting on Battrock? The man wasn't anywhere close to being a chick magnet but Mary was no Heidi Klum. Her square face held slinty brown eyes framed by thinly arched brows, a pert nose and blowfish lips—a mouth exaggerated and sadly misshapen by collagen injections. The beauty she had was in the wild expanse of auburn curls falling to her shoulders.

She wore high-end Walmutts. Accessories were a must this year but her jewelry was Halloween scary. A necklace resembling a collage of M&M candies was wound several times around her thick neck before it draped into the deep valley between white freckled breasts. The strappy green tent dress flowed loosely over rounded hips ending a few inches above the knees. By the size of her muscular biceps and calves, I guessed Mary worked out with heavy weights. I couldn't get an accurate reading on her age by either her clothing or body but the lack of age lines drew my estimate closer to thirty rather than forty.

"Well?" Her voice grated on my ears.

"Sure, Mary. No problem. I'll check it out," I said soothingly.

Somewhat mollified, she turned to the bell hop and barked out an order before gesturing to the Samsonite suitcases a few feet away. Hurriedly, the trim man in the gray uniform maneuvered the pyramid of suitcases towards the elevator and waited for Mary Battrock at the doors.

I glanced around the lobby. Open air with marble flooring and a high ceiling. Impressive. Ornately painted Mayan figures bordered the trim. Gold paint edged the Romanesque pillars. To complement this theme, a gold lion statue sat majestically on a huge slab of cement. Water spurted out of his mouth into a shallow pond inhabited by a school of red-splotched koi.

Wicker couches with plush floral pillows and a few heavy cherry tables were arranged in a grouping near the stairs where a gray-haired couple sat engrossed in a conversation.

I glanced at the desk manager's badge. "*Buenos dias, Luis.* I have reservations under the name Adie Sturm. Fleisher Travel."

"*Si.* We have them." He flipped a page of his ledger before handing over envelopes. "The room card keys are inside as requested. You can sign for them all."

That was a relief. No time consuming personal information forms to fill out. I checked to make sure Larry T was not assigned a room close to the formidable Queen Mary. He was in 208. The room was far enough away, but as I ran my finger over the other names, I was not happy to see that Brock and Irmgard were my neighbors.

As I passed out the envelopes, I glimpsed an arched doorway framed with bright fuchsia bougainvillea opening to a free-form swimming pool. Alongside the sparkling blue water was a row of white chaise lounges and small resin tables topped by striped blue and white umbrellas. With a film of perspiration coating my skin, the swimming pool was looking more inviting by the second. It took an effort to pick up the chalk and list the schedule of events on the board next to the stairs. Done at last, I nodded to Luis and headed to the elevator, dragging my luggage.

Just as I pressed the floor button, Irmgard shoved her bag forward and stepped in. When she saw me, she looked relieved.

"Thank God you got us out of the usual front desk disaster. But honestly, Adie, you could have warned me. I had no idea this place would be so hot." She glanced down to her armpit where a wet stain had appeared on her blouse.

"It's the tropics. Mexico is like this. You haven't had a winter vacation for a while, have you?"

"Too many deals." Irmgard murmured, brushing her wispy blonde hair away from her forehead. "Some of us work for a living, Adie Sturm."

Behind her, a tall lean man with a large blue suitcase squeezed in as I pressed the door button. When the elevator started up I noticed his steely eyes examining me. "Hey, hun. Nice hotel. Good choice."

I don't know if it's me but I find endearments from strangers condescending. It takes away from the positive remark.

"Mm-mm. Glad you like it." From what he'd told me, Daniel was a successful Toronto film editor. "The hotel's close to town. Take a walk to the square. Lots of shops and restaurants."

Daniel nodded. "Will do. Schedule says they're getting ready for a carnival."

"Yes, at the square you can." Before I could say more, the elevator opened. Apparently, Daniel wasn't that interested in my answer. With a parting grunt, he tugged on his suitcase and trekked down the corridor to the left. The numbers on the wall at the corner read 200-220. My room was 210. I tugged on my suitcase and started after him.

"Hey, Adie, wait," Irmgard yelled out, as I headed down the corridor. "For dinner tonight, make sure I sit beside George Clooney."

"Brock?"

Irmgard rolled her eyes. "Duh. You're oblivious to the sexiest man on our tour? What the hell is up with you? It's as if you don't notice men anymore."

I picked up speed. The sooner I reached the sanctity of my room, the better. At the next corner, I pointed to the 211 plate above the oak door. "That's your room." The woman was in my face enough. Work is one thing but my personal life was strictly my business.

Irmgard was not a quitter when it came to digging up dirt. "Cat caught your tongue?" Strangely, at my silence she gave up. "Oh, well. Your celibacy is my gain but," she paused significantly, pointing her finger, "in case you're reconsidering, don't! Brock is mine. Remember who owns the agency, Adie Sturm, and it's not you. " She grinned happily, much like a dog eyeing a steak on a barbeque. "Besides, if you make this easy for me, there might be a bonus in it for you."

"Oh?"

She smirked. "I've got this gut feeling you wouldn't mind a couple of weeks' expense paid vacation right back here in sunny Cozumel in, let's say, March?"

A vision of those sensuous lips lowering slowly on mine made me tingle to my core.

"Deal?" Irmgard probed.

"I think I could help you out but you'll have to do something, too."

"Like?"

"Flirt with the guy. Wear something sexy."

"I may not be gorgeous like you but I've got experience. You think I don't know how to turn a man on? Just watch me."

"Alright." I grinned. "I'll set the trap. You'll need to snare him though. Let me think," I said, mulling over the situation. "I've got it. I'll seat you beside Brock and to make it easy, I'll put Battrock on his other side."

"Great. That manatee will flounder in the wide open sea long enough for this barracuda to ease in and snap up some delicious Brock tuna."

"Listen to me. Your big hook comes later at Moray's Eel. It won't be hard for you to move in for the kill. The trick is to make sure you impress him with your knowledge of cigars and tequila. He told me there's nothing like a good cigar with a Don Julio. He thinks women who know cigars are cool."

"You must be kiddin'? I don't know dick about that."

"Follow my lead and you'll be laughing."

"Okay." Irmgard's eyes darted like a cat spotting a mouse. If she'd had a tail it would have been swishing rapidly back and forth. "I'm counting on you." She fumbled around in her purse before she turned back to me. "By the way do you know anything about him? What kind of work does he do?"

"He's an accountant."

"Oh, so not rich?"

I sighed. "You need money?"

Irmgard pursed her lips thoughtfully. "No, I guess not, but I like a guy that takes me to nice places."

"This is long term?"

Muttering under her breath she turned back to the door and inserted the key card.

I didn't think so. Relieved, I swung around the corner, to the door lettered 210. The plastic card pushed into the slot triggered a tiny green light near the handle. With an elbow nudge, the door opened wide enough for me to pull the suitcase into a mid-sized room.

The air conditioner had been turned off but the patio doors were open, causing the curtains to billow with the breeze. In the center of the queen sized bed, a towel swan had been arranged to decorate the bed. I loved that about the hotels in Mexico. The maids tried so hard to make the room attractive and welcoming.

As I scanned the room, something caught my eye. Near the patio doors, a couch faced a coffee table. Nothing unusual about that but on the table top lay a small tissue-wrapped package. I was about to see what it was when hands gripped me from behind.

2

I screamed. Like in a dance sequence, I side-stepped, swung my hips over to the left and with my right hand back-fisted hard into the groin. The grunt I heard confirmed I was on the mark and I was dealing with a male. From there, it was all muscle memory. My right foot positioned outside the intruder's foot, I twisted around and, with one hand on his left side and the other under his right arm, I grabbed and pushed, taking him down. A familiar whiff of soap and balmy ocean breeze filtered to my brain. Too late. My assailant fell hard, hitting the corner of the coffee table.

A knock on the door. "Is everything alright in there?" a man's voice shouted from the corridor.

I looked down at the tall sea god sprawled on the floor. But seeing the bright blues blink open, I yelled, "It's okay. Everything is fine. Just an accident." Naked apart from a bath towel wrapped around his waist, he sat up, a hand on his forehead.

"Didn't know I was an accident."

"Omigod, I'm so sorry." I bit my lip. "Honestly, Wolf, I didn't mean to do this. It was instinct... you know."

A wiry grin. "Yeah, karate woman, my fault. It was stupid of me to try to surprise you."

"Let me help you." I extended my hand but he staggered up on his own, still pressing his temple before sinking back down on the couch. He looked a little pale under the deep tan.

Now I was worried. Wolf Du Lac was made of tough stock. French-German from the Alsace-Lorraine region where generations of ethnic animosity had been forgiven between the sheets. Years ago our parents had met at Kitchener's Oktoberfest and kept in touch ever since. Had I been of Indian origin, they might have traditionally selected Wolf for my husband. Looking down at those irregular features combined in such a way that oozed sexuality, I would have jumped at that opportunity or at least jumped him. But marriage? No, not now. Too many of my friends had been caught in that web only to be divorced a few years later.

Ten years ago it might have been different. Young and

innocent, I'd fallen hard. In our teens, there had been a serious spark between us, but nothing had come of it. Wolf's mother, the protective she-lion, had silently manipulated us like pieces on a chessboard. Dating was doomed from the start. It was pure chance I recently met up with my teen crush and connected in a big way.

When I saw the blood running between Wolf's fingers I rushed to the bathroom, grabbed a wash cloth, and wet it under the tap before returning. "Here. Let me help," I said slowly, as the heavy-lidded sapphire blues caught me off guard. "I can't believe what I did." I pushed his fingers away from the wound and dabbed at the cut.

He winced with the contact. "Never mind that, babe. Come here," he murmured, pushing the cloth away and pulling me to him. The full sensuous lips were like sugar to a hungry fly. A kiss that landed so lightly yet ignited an intense flame. My core tingled magically as he pressed his mouth on mine once more.

It took extreme will power to withdraw my lips and take another look. Wide powerful shoulders, firm chest and taut abs were those of Neptune, God of the Sea. Although a long fluffy towel covered some of his masculine glory, what I saw of his legs confirmed they were as muscular as ever. Not much had changed, at least on the surface.

"What is it, princess?"

"It's been awhile. I just wanted to take a look at you."

His voice was a husky whisper. "Yeah? What do you see?" Blue eyes gleamed like a tiger's in the dark.

Every inch of him was crying out to be touched. My lips felt suddenly dry. "A man wearing a towel."

He smirked. "It was a very wet shower."

"And you had to do this here?"

"Didn't have time to go to my place if I wanted to surprise you."

I leaned back and studied the smokin' hot man with the streaky blond hair. "How'd you get in?"

"The maid appreciated the tip."

"You mean you bribed her?"

Wolf shrugged. "She needed the money but it was the story that did the trick."

"Which was?"

"I haven't seen my *novia* for two months. My heart's aching with sadness."

"Ah-hh. Achy-breaky heart syndrome?" I ran a finger down his cheek, while gazing into eyes as clear and bright as a fresh-water stream. "Really?"

"Just as much as yours does."

That could be true. Irmgard, the cynic, might be right. Only a love-sick sap would be so oblivious to a sexy guy like Brock. But could it really be true that Wolf missed me? A thud on the door interrupted my thoughts.

"I'd better see who that is. It could be someone from my tour group." I padded over, and squinted out the peephole. A man in a gray uniform stood impatiently tapping his foot.

When I opened up, I saw he had brought a cart. "*Hola.*"

"*Buenos dias,* Señorita."

"I didn't order anything."

Determinedly, he pushed the cart laden with several covered plates through the door. "Where would you like it?"

"But," I protested. "It's a mistake!"

Wolf's deep voice called out. "No worries, Adie. I ordered. Thought you needed a treat after the airplane food."

I beamed. "In that case," I said to the server, "please bring it over to the couch."

The waiter shoved the cart forward and stopped, gesturing grandly. "It is truly a feast, Señor... Señorita!"

"Anything to make my *novia* happy." Wolf grinned like the Cheshire Cat before it disappeared into thin air.

"Would you like to sign for it, Señor?"

Wolf adjusted his towel before he pulled himself up, his hand on the couch for support. "Wait. *Un momento,*" he said, going into the bathroom and reappearing with his wallet. He shoved some bills in the man's hand.

The tip must have been good. The waiter's grin reached his ears. After clicking the door shut, Wolf sat down and patted the couch.

I plopped down beside the sea god and stared at the mysterious object in gold tissue lying on the nearby coffee table. Wolf's eyes twinkled. With one foot, he shoved the table away.

"Wait! That's for me, isn't it?"

"Later."

I could be civilized even if the curiosity was killing me. "Alright, have it your way. What's for dinner?"

"Mayan, but it's the dessert that will have you salivating," Wolf whispered, lips curled in a bad boy grin.

I poked my finger into his chest.

He flinched. "Hey! Take it easy, Adie. Keep all that pent-up frustration for later, eh?"

"Me? You are so full of yourself, as usual."

"What I've got," Wolf leaned in to my ear and licked, "you want."

"Mm-mm." Crazy endorphins in my brain battled hunger pangs in my stomach. Pleasure versus food? A tough decision.

Wolf lifted a lid and a spicy aroma filled the air.

A red mixture in a serving dish. "Looks interesting. Chicken?"

"Just an appetizer of *porc a la diabla*. For my devilish Adie Sturm." With a spoon, he scooped some onto a plate and handed it to me.

The flavors of tomatoes and chilies spiked the fried pork to a favorable peak I'd never experienced before. "Wow!" I breathed in appreciation.

"And to drink, I thought my little princess would like a bit of vino." From behind the couch, Wolf pulled out a bottle of wine.

"Shiraz?"

"Would I bring anything but?" He filled two glasses from the open bottle. "This one is called Faith."

"You let it breathe?"

Wolf nodded. "Should be just right by now."

The magenta wine with the vibrant purple hue shimmered in the glass. "What should we drink to?"

"Well, let's see. Hot sex?"

"Wolf," I warned, but I had to purse my lips not to laugh.

Hand held up in defense, he flashed even whites. "Seriously, we've come a long way and I've enjoyed every inch of the journey. Let's drink to Faith."

Glasses clicked but before I could lift mine, Wolf curled an arm around my hand and in the French manner brought the glass up to his mouth before he whispered the word "faith" almost as a pledge. His eyes gleamed with passion. If ever I questioned the reason I kept getting involved with this man, I had my answer now.

The berry bouquet was soft in my mouth.

"What do you think?"

"A full body with a spicy finish and," I smiled, stroking his arm, "a hint of chocolate."

"Perfect for my spicy woman." His fingertips stroked my cheek. "Missed you."

I lifted my finger and lightly drew a line down his chest. "Really? What happened to your women?"

Wolf lifted an eyebrow. "I think you have me mixed up with another one of your fans."

"Oh?" I said casually as I sampled some shrimp.

"You know there's nothing goin' on."

If there's anything I've learned, it's let sleeping dogs lie. That doesn't mean I wouldn't try to find out but to keep probing was beneath me.

"Adie," Wolf said, picking up the lid on the next dish. "There is something I need to talk to you about."

"Oh?" Was he going to break up? I clenched my teeth, waiting for the other shoe to drop.

"You could help me out with something. Here, try this."

With a toothpick, I speared a crispy piece. "Fish?" Not waiting for an answer, I slipped it into my mouth. "Crab." I shot him a look. "What game are you playing?"

Wolf laughed. "No cards up my sleeve."

I glanced at his hard biceps. "No place to put them."

His eyes crinkled at the corners. "There's always the towel. Want a peek?"

I rolled my eyes. "Explain. What's this all about?"

"Bolivar Imports and Exports International."

"Diego's dad's company?"

Wolf filled his glass. "Francisco died last month."

"Oh!" I was surprised at the news. "Carmelita and Diego. How are they?"

"The funeral was in Mexico City. Your buddy Alvarez was his usual self. Carmelita was a little withdrawn."

"I should see her."

"She may not be back yet. Alvarez said Carm was staying on with her mom when we talked at the funeral."

"So you went to Mexico City?"

"I have company shares and there was a stockholders meeting right after the funeral."

"I thought it was private."

"There was talk of going public three years ago, around the time the older brother died."

"Amancio?"

Wolf nodded.

"Diving accident, wasn't it?"

"Right."

"And the company?"

"It stayed private with your buddy Alvarez at the helm."

"I thought the dad was training Federico to run Imports and Exports."

Wolf drank deeply of the wine before he answered. "As Carmelita's husband they gave him a job but I doubt if Francisco Bolivar regarded him as the heir apparent. An Alvarez is always CEO. For a Bolivar Alvarez, family is blood only."

"So Federico loses out."

He scratched his chin reflectively. "Looks like it. I've met the guy at parties but I can't say I know him very well. Do you?"

"My first impression was loser. I wish Carmelita would find someone else."

"Well, whatever his personal life, he has a share of the company according to the will. Although it may really be Carmelita's."

"So why did it go public after the dad died?"

"Alvarez. It was his concept of the company. He's thinking expansion."

"And you bought shares. How much of the company is public?"

"Not more than ten percent, of which I have five. The rest are small shareholders."

I brushed a strand of hair from his forehead. "And? You have regrets?"

"No. But something's not right."

"Have you asked Diego?"

Wolf laughed. "You think I haven't tried? He's secretive. Of course it may be nothing. I might be jumping the gun."

"But you're not convinced?"

"No."

"Why me?"

"This is right up your alley, beautiful. Alvarez has a thing for you, remember?"

I hate to admit it but he made my mouth water. If Wolf was like creamy milk chocolate, Diego was definitely the smooth dark variety. And I was a chocoholic.

"But be subtle when you ask, Adie." Wolf leaned over and gently kissed my shoulder, sending tingles down to my nipples. With Wolf I melted like an ice cube under a sizzling hot sun. It was pitiful.

"Remember who you're dealing with. Santiago Bolivar Alvarez owns this island."

Another whiff of soap and ocean breeze. It took an effort to focus. "So you're telling me this could be dangerous."

Wolf nodded. "Ask Alvarez about his products, where he ships to, who is involved, but don't make him suspicious. He's a fox, remember?"

The chilies on the pork burned. Reflectively, I ran a finger over my lips. Dry. The lip gloss I'd applied earlier was gone. With Wolf's intense stare on me, I wondered if I looked a mess.

"This won't be a walk in the park, Adie."

I fluffed up my hair and met his eyes. "Diego is my friend. He trusts me."

"All that I'm asking is for you to find out what you can. There might be a simple explanation for the transfers." Taking my hand, Wolf stroked it gently. "I wouldn't normally ask, princess, but, the man working on this is not too sure what to make of it. I should tell you something else."

"What?"

"You know the man I hired to investigate the company."

"I do?"

He brought my hand to his lips and kissed the fingertips, gazing into my eyes. "I can trust you to keep this a secret from Alvarez?"

"Of course."

"If his guard is down, he might let something drop."

This was all a bit strange for Wolf. Usually it was me who got him involved. "Who's the investigator?"

"Brock Laval."

My eyes widened. "My tour group guy?"

"Yup. I asked him if he could check on the money trail. The stockholder report was somewhat vague."

"How was he able to get access to company records? It couldn't be that easy."

"You're right there. Brock knows the ropes. He got himself a job at Bolivar Imports Exports International in Toronto. That was his ticket to see the books. It may not be so easy to check out the offices here in Cozumel."

"So you think I can come up with more?"

Wolf looked at me from over the rim of his glass. "Brock's figures show income going to miscellaneous." He shrugged. "Although he has another plan. The man is very skilled with the computer. Just thought you might be able to get something else out of Alvarez. You have a way with him. Must be your feminine charm."

I laughed. "That's a first. Usually you want me to stay away from Diego." At the sound of my cell, I dug it out of my purse. It was a text.

R u here? Will be wonderful to see you. Come to my party 2morrow. Sending the car 4 u @ 8? Wear something sexy. Besitos! D

That was opportune.

"Alvarez?"

"Um-mm. He wants me at his party tomorrow." I frowned. "This could work as long as I can take my group."

I messaged back. *Love to. Can I bring my tour group?*

"Why do you need to take them?"

"It's on their schedule to see some entertainment." I shrugged. "Any party of Diego's would qualify as entertainment, right?" I glanced at my phone as a melody announced an incoming text.

You can bring anyone you want as long as I get to see you alone.

Quickly, I turned the cell away from Wolf. "He said yes."

Wolf grinned. "This will work."

My finger slid over the cell screen as I checked the time. Five-thirty! I needed to hurry. But the gift in gold tissue wrapping beckoned. I reached over and picked it up hesitantly.

"Go ahead. Open it. It's just something I saw in a shop." Wolf watched me in amusement.

After carefully peeling the tissue off the object, I was intrigued to see a white candle in the shape of a woman. "Ixchel?"

"Yeah," Wolf drawled. "Your Mayan deity. Light it and find peace. I thought it might be good for destressing my favorite goddess."

I shot him a glance. "You mean you have more than one?"

Wolf shook his head. "The only woman on my mind is you, Adie. Want to go out?"

"Can't." I jumped up, remembering the time. "I have to prepare a table for my group and get them seated before seven." I'd nearly forgotten about the bargain I'd made with Irmgard. If I wanted a trip back to paradise, I'd have to make that love connection happen. I set my glass on the cart. "Got to shower and change. Why don't you join me?"

"In the shower?"

I felt my cheeks flush. "I meant for dinner."

"We just ate. Not that my appetite is gone." The glint of his eyes gave away his intentions.

This was the Wolf I knew and would never forget.

A trifle unsteadily, Wolf stood up and took hold of my shoulders. "How about after dinner?" He brushed my hair from my neck and brought his lips to the curve of my throat.

A flash of heat fired my core. It took an effort to speak. "I'm taking them to Moray's Eel around eight. Want to come?"

Wolf had a smile that would have charmed a snake. "I have to go home first. Make some calls. Why don't I meet you at the bar downstairs?"

I imagined his strong hard body pressed against mine. "Sounds like a plan."

3

In a slinky black dress, Irmgard sat silently tipping back a margarita. It wouldn't be easy to erase that sulky expression but I was up for the challenge.

It was Mexican night at the pool. Three bottles of champagne were open and chilling in buckets of ice on our table. By the time I had set the last place card in position, Ronny tripped in wearing a pink polo shirt, skinny jeans, and fuchsia flip-flops.

"Hey, ladies!" With his boy-next-door face and toothy grin, he would have made the perfect toothpaste model. No one would have guessed the six foot guy with blond spiked-highlights was Deecko's lead salsa dancer. There wasn't a hint of that mincing step that sets gays apart. I'm not saying that every gay man has that walk but it takes a split second for me to clue in. I have this infallible gay detector.

"Hi, Ronny." I pointed to the spot beside me. "How are you?" Oddly, nothing was showing up on my radar. I glanced sidelong at Ronny as he sat down. Had I missed something? If he wasn't gay, why was he so pink?

At the lobby entrance, tall, lanky Daniel appeared. He stood for a few seconds looking around as if he studied everything for a possible movie shoot until I waved to get his attention. He sauntered over unhurriedly. "Evening, Adie."

"Daniel, have you met Irmgard and Ronny?"

The film editor thrust his hand out in a guy handshake and grunted.

"You ladies sure look lovely," Ronny said enthusiastically. All men should be such gentlemen. Irmgard smiled and almost managed to look pleasant. Silently, I blessed him.

"Thank you. You look great."

"Really? I was wondering if my floral shirt would be more *apropos*?"

"Not at all. The color is just right for the tropics." I gestured to the bucket. "Would you mind pouring?"

As Ronny started filling glasses, I looked around for the missing tour members. From the direction of the bar, his face as bright red as the T-shirt he wore, Larry T lurched forward like a sailor on a rocking boat navigating his way unsteadily in snakeskin boots. My guess was he'd been hitting the tequila hard.

"Right here." I pulled out the chair on my left.

"Well, thank-ee kindly, ma'am." A whiff of boozy breath nearly knocked me flat. If I'd had any doubts, Larry's dopey smile and glazed eyes pushed the reading past the legal limit.

From behind I heard a shout. "Hey, Señor, bring that margarita over here when she's ready," Mary bellowed out to a waiter. Decked out in a frothy green halter dress, the vacuum consultant sashayed over to our table. "Got me a good seat, Adie Sturm?" Her eyes shot to the place card with Brock's name. "Who-hoo! I'm aimin' to have me some fun tonight."

Larry T nudged me. "Ain't she somethin'?" His mouth was slightly open, drool at the corner. "Yer one helluva party mama!"

It didn't surprise me when those misshapen inflated lips curled back, baring a set of dangerously sharp teeth. I half expected Mary to growl in warning.

But before she could bite his head off, Brock Laval strolled in wearing a yellow muscle-shirt, distracting the pit bull. Sailboats, dragons, anchors and octopi tats combated for space on the muscular arms. The rest of him was toned, athletic and fit.

So Wolf hired him, I mused. They must have met at the gym doing dead lifts. Workouts did more than build muscles. I saw that from the zoned out expressions on the women. He interested me too, but not in that way.

I was more curious to find out what Brock knew. Bolivar Import Export was a huge company. The CEO was Santiago Francisco Bolivar Alvarez. Quite the mouthful. The Bolivar part was the paternal name while Alvarez was Diego's mother's name. Both parents were from Spain originally but he and his sister Carmelita were Mexican citizens. Rich and arrogant, they were hated more than loved. Yet I liked them. The last thing I wanted to find out was something illegal to incriminate them. I needed to corner Brock tonight but discreetly. With Irmgard ready to make her move, this wouldn't be a walk in the park.

Swaggering over to the table, Brock took the seat between Irmgard Fleischer and Mary Battrock. "Good evening, folks. Great night, eh?" He glanced at the band tuning up and then back to me. "Can't wait to dance."

"Is your friend Larissa joining us tonight?"

"I think so." Just as he spoke, a melody sounded. Reaching in his pocket, he pulled out his Blackberry and read the text. He frowned. "Damn. She has to deal with something at the hotel. But, we'll see her later at the bar." He explained to the group, "Larissa is the manager at Moray's Eel. We had plans but she has to bartend tonight." He winked at Larry T. "She's one hot tamale."

Then, noting the glares from the women, Brock came back smooth as glass. "Ladies," he wrapped his arms around Irmgard and Mary's shoulders, "you are especially sexy tonight."

Quick as a wink, I raised my glass. "*Salud!*"

With a steamy glance at Brock, Irmgard lifted her glass. "To love."

"I'm all for that," Larry T boomed. "Cheers!'

"*Muchos amores!*" Daniel toasted.

He sure was a man full of surprises. Spanish and now a toast to love? I wouldn't have taken him for a romantic but who could blame him with our first night here by the pool transformed into a fairy-tale fantasy. With dusk setting, the lights illuminated the orange hibiscus reflecting into the shimmering pool water.

With the zing of violins, a group of musicians clad in tight black trousers, short jackets and wide brimmed hats appeared on the stage. Trumpets and guitars joined in and the atmosphere was filled with happy music.

Mariachi originated in the state of Jalisco but was popular everywhere. It was the spirit of Mexico. Tonight it emanated from every crevice starting with the string instruments and ending with the spicy scents of Mayan cuisine.

I waited until they finished an upbeat guitar solo to tap my glass. "Folks, it looks like dinner is ready. The plan is an hour and a half here and then off to Moray's Eel for some cigar and tequila tasting. What do you say? Everyone ready for some food?"

An enthusiastic hoot from Larry reminded me that this guy was steadily getting wasted. Not much I could do about that. When drinks are included, it happens more often than not.

But it was no use getting negative. I considered the sexual energy at the table. Mary was staring at the buff investigator like he was an éclair with extra cream though if I were a betting woman, I'd say Irmgard had the winning hand.

Usually in a conservative suit, the boss had wisely left that persona behind in the cold Canadian winter. Tonight, she was dressed to kill. Close to six foot and model slim, she easily pulled off the jet black mini-dress slashed to the waist.

Tamales, tacos, fajitas, chicken, refried beans, rice. Everything was hot and steamy as was Irmgard, not to mention experienced, from the way she steered Brock over to the buffet subtly asking him all about himself. A man like Brock would find that topic extremely stimulating. I'd no idea she was a hunter of that caliber. If she got lucky and fertilized this romance, she wouldn't be the only winner. I would be the lucky recipient of her generous trip offer.

As I headed back to the table with a plateful of Mayan tidbits, I kept thinking of how I could help this game along. On the plane, Brock had mentioned the importance of a good cigar with a shot of tequila. I didn't know how knowledgeable he was but it was imperative I give Irmgard the right cards.

By the time I sat down, Daniel and Mary had headed off to dance and Larry T was gone. I decided not to let it bother me. If he wanted to get drunk, that was his business. It wouldn't ruin anything with Irmgard.

I took a bite out of a tamale and let my mind wander to the Mayan appetizers I'd had two hours ago. More than an appetizer, Wolf was entrée material. The man made my pulse race. That didn't happen enough in my life. I'd imagined us together so much I was beginning to think I was as stupid as a teenager with a crush. I ate a tamale reflectively. Would he be waiting at the bar by now? Quickly, I reached into my purse for my cell. When I checked the time, I found there was a text.

Meeting running late. C u at Moray's Eel. xxoo W

It might be better that way. Curious minds kept away from my love life. Was it love? On my last trip I had thought it might be but I had no idea what the sea god was thinking.

"Great food, Adie," Ronny commented, taking the seat beside me. His eyes on my dress, he whispered, "You look fantastic in red. You must have a collection of red dresses."

"I kind of do. Red's my favorite color." Taking up a forkful of fajita, my gaze swept over him from his blond highlights his shirt. "It sure is a change seeing you in a pink polo shirt. I like it."

Ronny grinned. "Thank-you. Say, beautiful, do you have a boyfriend?"

Startled, I shot him a look. "Mm-mm."

"Anything serious?" he persisted.

"Um-mm."

"Just because I appear on stage in costume doesn't mean I'm not into women, especially you." He whispered in my ear. "Don't be afraid to let loose with me. I'm just your average übersexual guy, Adie."

"Oh-hh." My instincts had been right on. "Ronny, you are by no means average. In German über means better than the rest."

Ronny looked pleased as punch and was about to say something when the boss lady returned empty handed, that is without her prey. She did have a plateful of tamales, which she promptly placed on the table in front of her before taking her seat. I hoped she hadn't screwed up our plan. If she had, I would deal with that later.

Irmgard stuffed her mouth with an oversized tamale. "God, these are good," she mumbled between bites.

I filled her glass with bubbly. "Finish that. It's a shame to waste quality champagne, isn't it?" Turning to my new admirer I said, "We'll talk later, Ronny. Alright?"

When I got up, the salsa dancer looked disappointed but, hey, my job description did not include romance provider for the needy.

Just past the buffet, the drinkers around the curved bar were buzzing like a swarm of yellow jackets. The narrow area by the pool teemed with people. Stepping back into a soft pillow, I hurriedly apologized to a six footer's plus-sized paunch. I hastily moved forward, inching myself into line.

It was hard to tell where it started. I crept past a couple of partiers and took a spot behind Brock. Tapping him lightly on the back, I noted he was waiting for two drinks in progress.

"Hey, sweetheart. Nice outfit." His eyes drifted down.

I snapped my fingers. "We don't have much time, Brock, so I'll get right to the point. Wolf told me you were the investigator. Did you find out anything I should know before I see Diego?"

"And they call Alvarez the fox." He chortled. "Du Lac is a sly devil recruiting a hot chick to dig up dirt."

Trumpets took over the chorus drowning out his words. "Pardon?" I shouted.

Brock leaned in. "Skulls. Somehow I couldn't see…"

The violins hit the high notes and his voice was swallowed up. I had no idea what he said. Did this have something to do with Days of the Dead? Mexico did a lot of celebrating for the festival and skulls could be part of it.

Brock pushed away a strand of hair covering my ear and shouted. "Crystal skulls." He cut off abruptly as Irmgard wedged herself between us.

"Thought you might need a hand with the drinks, seeing as they are so large," she purred sweetly. She looked over my shoulder. "I think the bartender wants your order, Adie."

"Water, *por favor*. Lots of ice." I turned back to Irmgard. "Having a good time? You two should try dancing."

Irmgard sneered."To this? You must be kiddin'."

I grabbed my glass. "Well save your energy for tomorrow night's costume party. You can't miss the Bolivar Alvarez Carnaval party."

"Bolivar Alvarez? I saw a street with that name on our way to the hotel. Is there some connection?"

"It's named after my friend Diego Alvarez for his contribution during the hurricane."

"Oh-hh. So he's famous and rich?"

"Right," I mumbled. Something about Irmgard made my stomach cramp. "Excuse me." I took my glass and headed to the hotel entrance to book some cabs before returning to my seat. Now that Brock was with her, that part of my mission was almost accomplished. Soon she'd have him hooked and I'd have a return ticket to Cozumel.

It had been a long lonely winter in Canada. Although I liked my work, it didn't fulfill all my needs. Short visits from two exciting men had spiced it up but when they'd left for Cozumel, I was faced with being alone again. It was just as well. Those two hotties were like chocolate—creamy-rich, sinfully delicious and highly addictive. I bit my lip ruefully. Unfortunately, I wasn't sure about either of them.

Back at the table, I managed to plaster a smile on my face even though my mood was steadily spiraling downwards. A while ago, Jay had broken my heart and taken my savings before I gave him the giant kiss-off. After a few months, I'd womanedup and put him on the backburner. Time heals wounds, they say, but I was still a little gun-shy dealing with that bittersweet thing called love.

When the band took a break, I announced the taxis had been booked for Moray's Eel. Thinking about seeing the sea god again, I raced out to the washroom for a makeup touch up. In the mirror, I saw a woman in need of color. I didn't have a tan. Not yet. I quickly flecked on some sun-kissed rose blush and coated my lips with gloss before racing out to join the group at the entrance.

In the back seat Daniel and Ronny happily squeezed me in. At least these two smelled fresh enough. Larry T, on the other hand, seated by the driver, reeked of a putrid mixture of body odor and booze. I could see why Mary found him such a turnoff. It was wrong to criticize her. I mean, what sane woman would want Larry T?

As the cab took off with the windows down, a balmy breeze blew in. That was the extent of the air conditioning. The sea air kept my fine hair poker straight. I wore it shoulder length, the sides cut jagged for an edgy style. Not that I couldn't jack up the heat factor with a straightener and hair spray if I had to.

Ronnie turned to me. "So Adie, why are we going to Moray's Eel?"

"It's a cigar and tequila bar. Very unique. You can try rare types of tequilas and imported cigars. This way you'll know what to buy when you go shopping for souvenirs or buy them there."

He nodded. "Good thinking. I'm interested if there's someone to teach me."

"The owner knows her merchandise."

"That's the woman Brock is excited to see?"

I opened my wallet to check for cash. "Right. And Larissa will be joining us on our dive. I haven't met her yet but I hear she's dived for years."

Tomorrow's dive. I had mixed feelings about that. I'm not a morning person but that wasn't the problem. A fear of drowning had almost stopped me from getting my certification. But I persevered, knowing Wolf would be my dive buddy. A romantic vision of us holding hands underwater would be worth the classes that were nothing less than torture.

When we arrived, I handed the driver a few bills for the ride. I wasn't about to pay him five for a couple of blocks. I know tips are important to a taxi driver who barely got time off but tourists were fair game and with several Cozumel trips under my belt, I knew the ropes. Two dollars would do.

Moray's Eel had changed since my last visit. Renovated in an eclectic mixture, leather couches and low glass coffee tables were scattered about the long rectangular room. As we walked in, I saw the rest of my group seated at the round bar in the corner.

Tequila shots and beer flashed from sink to counter. The bartender's brunette waves bounced around like a L'Oreal model debuting the latest hair color. In front of her, a tall broad-shouldered man dressed in a white cotton shirt and tan dress pants leaned back in the leather bar stool, his arm casually slung over the low back. His hair was dark brown, curling to his collar, and when he turned, his aristocratic nose completed a perfect symmetrical profile. Drop dead sexy.

My eyes widened in shock. Before I could say anything, he swiveled about and saw me.

"Adelina, what a surprise." Getting off the stool, he was considerably taller even though I wore four inch gold stilettos. His slanted hazel eyes shimmered green with the lamp light. "That spicy scent you wear. Mm-mm, *mi amor*, you take my breath away." This was all said in husky tones as he pulled me in to lightly kiss my lips.

"Diego." The word came out slowly as a whiff of citron made its way from the receptors in my nose to the neurons of my brain.

Every man had his scent, usually a mixture of sweat and cologne. Diego's was delicious. "What a surprise."

"I had a meeting here with Federico, you know, Carmelita's husband. When he left, I stayed." He laughed derisively. "You know how that swine irritates me. Leaves an unpleasant taste in my mouth. Needed something to wash it away." He waved his hand dismissively. "But no more of that unpleasantness. Let me get you a drink. How about the *100 Años*? No, I know something more suitable." He paused, reflectively stroking his lower lip. "Pour us," he said to the bartender with a grin, "the *Don Julio Anejo 1942*. A perfect tequila with those precious notes of chocolate that this lady craves. Adelina, have you met Larissa?"

A bottle in hand, the Latina swung around. Black eyes surrounded by long curled lashes in a heart-shaped face. She was a petite package. Her body was a classic pear, small breasts, wide hips. The white taffeta mini, flared at the waist, disguised and flattered.

"*Hola*. I'm Adie Sturm."

"*Si,* so I was told." Her eyes, a few degrees cooler than her smile, flicked down the length of my dress. "I shall meet you at the pier. Brock will be my dive partner."

I nodded. "Sure, no problem. Be there by eight."

"Do you know where we stop?"

"Tormentos."

Larissa frowned. "And the other dive?"

I shrugged my shoulders.

"Enough dive talk," Diego said to Larissa impatiently. "Adelina is waiting for her tequila." His changeable eyes flicked to the men standing behind me. "You are no longer with Du Lac?"

Before I could answer, Ronny parked himself in front of Diego and extended his hand. "Hey, I'm Ronny Slater. I'm takin' the tour with Adie. Nice ta meetcha."

"A pleasure I'm sure. I am Santiago Francisco Bolivar Alvarez. But call me Diego." He did a guy hand shake. "Enjoying your stay?"

"Shit, yeah. Can't wait to wear a getup for your costume party."

Omigod, he was wearing his salsa outfit! I massaged my

temple where a headache was starting to pulse.

Irmgard and Mary squeezed past Ronny and planted themselves in front of the godfather of Cozumel.

"*Buenas noches,* Señoritas. You are friends of Adelina?"

I answered for them. "Members of my tour group. May I present Irmgard and Mary."

"Diego. A pleasure to meet you both."

Like a raccoon beamed by a headlight, Irmgard froze, seemingly incapable of speech. But it was battleship Mary that surprised me with a sudden tic developing in her left eye. I pursed my lips tightly but a snort escaped. Eyes shot to me.

"Excuse me." I faked a dry cough. "Something caught in my throat."

Diego snapped his fingers and Larissa filled a glass with ice water, setting it on the bar. I took a sip, observing the "Diego effect".

There was good reason for their flushed faces. Diego was a fine specimen of manhood. Not only was he broad shouldered and slim but his face was as perfect as any Armani model's. Apparently, I wasn't the only woman that thought so. Even Larissa couldn't help subtly checking him out between washing beer glasses.

"You are having the party tomorrow, Mr. Alvarez?" Irmgard recovered her speech, swiping her forehead as a trickle of perspiration wet her brow.

"Please, call me Diego. I'm not sure I caught your name?"

"Irmgard Fleischer." Shoulders back, chest thrust out, she smiled in a superior fashion. "Adie works for me. I own Fleischer Travel Agency."

"What a lucky woman indeed to have the amazing Adelina help you." He gazed around, a hint of a smile on his full lips. "It is a privilege to have the presence of all you beautiful ladies at my party tomorrow night."

Mary tittered. "I can't wait to see a Mexican costume party. You *are* Mexican?"

Diego flashed his pearly whites. "Mm-mm. Although my family is from Spain originally, my sister and I have been residents for many years."

Irmgard stroked his arm, pushing herself against him. "Oh, my! You speak perfect English."

"Thank you. I attribute that to my British education." The square cut diamond pinky ring flashed as Diego gestured to the Latina bartender. "A round of drinks for my friends, *por favor, cariño.*" What he added in rapid Spanish I couldn't pick up.

Mr. Hollywood didn't have a chance with Diego's seething hot looks. Brock's ego took a beating but he was an investigator after all, first and foremost. It was a job demanding a low profile. Smiling pleasantly, he took it all in stride, letting the others ask the questions while he sat back and observed.

And I had to follow up on my promise to Wolf. Somehow Brock needed to be cornered for some information. Time was running out. The break came when Diego started relating the history of San Miguel to the women. A discreet motion to Brock and a finger point to the hallway and I left.

Outside of the washroom door, I waited. A creak on a floor board made me whirl about but when I scanned the hallway, there was nobody. When Brock didn't appear, I adjusted my hair in the mirror in the corridor, worried he wasn't coming. After another few minutes, I started to get anxious, impatiently tapping my foot until a shadowy figure appeared. I let out a sigh of relief when I realized it was Brock.

"Finally! You took long enough."

"Yeah, well, I need to be cool about this." Suddenly, Brock touched my arm and spun his head.

"What?"

"Ss-sh. Thought I heard something."

"You're being a bit paranoid, aren't you?" But I looked around. It could have been the ocean wind blowing hard against the outside door. At the end of the corridor, more doors. "What are those? Storage rooms?"

Brock put his finger to my lips. Voices from the bar carried in. After a moment, he drew me close and whispered, "This investigation could be dangerous."

"Alright. I get it. Tell me about the skulls."

"Alvarez is exporting them."

"I've heard of a lady in Kitchener who found one of the

twelve crystal skulls on an archeological expedition in Mexico but this couldn't have anything to do with those, could it?"

He shrugged. "Naw, all made locally in Mayan villages."

"Why export them?"

"Senergy they call it." Brock laughed. "One of those new age words. The Mayans associated skulls with healing powers and energy. Stupid, eh?"

"Mm-mm." I'd had experience with that. There was something to it. My jade and turquoise jewelry had protected me from danger and given me all kinds of sexual energy. Crystal had power. I was sure of it. But then, maybe I was as superstitious as the Mayans.

Brock scratched his head. "What's puzzling is why exporting skulls could be so lucrative."

"New Age spirituality gone viral?"

"Sure, there is that."

"But you don't think so?"

"Millions have been sold and the number keeps building. Nothing adds up. Damn." He frowned. "Haven't been into the office here or the warehouse but I have a gut feeling that something is off. I accessed Alvarez's account."

"You hacked in?"

"Had to." He grinned. "No chance to go over much but I downloaded a document on my laptop. Interested? You're right next door."

Brock was such a sleaze. "That wouldn't be my area of expertise."

"No? You sure?" He eyed me. "You're looking really hot tonight. Why don't we head over to Time Toc for some dancing and then later, who knows?" He wrapped his arm around my waist.

A little pressure on the web and thumb of his hand and I picked off his grip lickety-split.

"Shit, girl!" Brock shook his hand in the air. "No need to get violent."

"Sorry." I grinned. "I do get carried away sometimes. No hard feelings, eh?" Stepping around him, I headed back into the Tequila-Cigar Bar.

Diego was standing between the women talking. I felt

momentarily guilty. Besides rivaling Wolf in the heat department, Diego had always been a sweetheart. It was deceitful to dig into his business. Even doing this as a favor to Wolf was wrong. I shook my head, angry at myself. When Wolf came in tonight I'd make sure he knew I wouldn't go through with it.

As I glanced around looking for the guys from my group, I spotted them at the pool table in the corner of the bar. Two massive hulks, arms like gorillas and bodies like sumo wrestlers, holding their cues, patiently waited for Daniel to make his shot. Their concentrated expressions were scary. With faces so identical, it was impossible to think they were anything but twins. It had been awhile but I knew them. The giants took their eyes away to bare their teeth in a smile. I grinned back. In a crunch, it was better to be on their good side.

"So you remember Churo and Luis?" Diego whispered in my ear. "Loyal as dogs but not very sociable fellows. I had to encourage them to play." I felt Diego's hand slide to the small of my back. "Please take my chair, Adelina." His eyes flicked down my legs and sighed. "Lovely, as always. Perhaps your feet need a rest?"

I couldn't deny that invitation. Stilettos are not Birkenstocks.

The women were not happy with that development but brightened considerably when Brock took a seat.

Diego waved his hand majestically. "More drinks for the Señoritas, Larissa. And your best cohiba, *por favor*." He chuckled. "Remember when we shared one, *mi amor*?"

I did and realized Diego had given me the perfect opening. "Oh, yes. If it wasn't for Irmgard, I probably wouldn't have tried it."

"Really?" Diego eyed the startled blonde.

I grinned widely. "Irmgard enjoys a cohiba with her Don Julio, don't you?"

Brock broke in. "In that case, please allow me to purchase cohibas for the ladies. Larissa, two or," he lifted a questioning eyebrow at Mary, who shook her head quickly, "and also for this gentleman and myself. Sorry, we weren't introduced." "I'm Santiago Francisco Bolivar Alvarez."

"Pretentious." The investigator chortled. "Brock Laval. Short and simple."

The millionaire's eyes slowly swept over the man. "I see what you mean. Short and simple."

" Five foot ten and I'd guess you're a six-footer." He shrugged. "Two inches. But we both know height is not where it counts, is it?"

Irmgard giggled.

Diego looked amused. "No one would say you're a man without *cojones* or are you really just plain simple?"

"Simple, but not the stupid kind. A man of few needs." Brock lifted his glass. "You wouldn't be the Bolivar Alvarez of Import Exports, would you?"

"You're interested in imports?"

Brock smiled slowly. "When I need to be."

4

The rocking of the boat hit me like a kick to the gut. No, it wasn't the after effects of the tequila from last night. This was serious ocean motion. When an El Norte blows in, the Caribbean is a dark, threatening force. Small talk and laughter broke out between showers of salt water spray. Glancing around, I saw the group, ten in total, being sociable. Irmgard caught my eye and winked. Besides Brock's flirtatious smiles, Daniel was visibly courting the queen. Things were looking up. A sexually satisfied Irmgard meant two more weeks in Cozumel with the sea god. By then, hopefully, the El Norte would have blown back to Texas.

Meanwhile, Adie Sturm, strong leader, needed to get a grip. Question was how to overcome the queasy-sick feeling and get back on the saddle.

We were with Snuba-Snork. On the internet, it had as good a rep as any. Our thirty-five footer had an awning covering mid-deck. Usiel was the dive master. With a Mayan name, he looked the part. Square-faced, a wide pierced nose and heavy lips. The dive master's silver cross swung from his thick neck as he threw some masks into a pail to soak. He was naked and hairless from the top of his round head to the roll at his waist, where a gray bathing suit gathered to drape over tree-trunk legs. Surprisingly, diving did not go hand in hand with athletic trim bodies. In fact, excess body weight was an advantage for staying comfortably warm under the sea.

As I studied him, he looked back with brown eyes creased at the corners, peering into the deep recesses of my soul. I'd bet my bottom dollar there was a shaman somewhere in his family history or my name wasn't Adie Sturm.

He was a thorough enough dive master asking the right questions about the divers before pairing them up. Everyone needed a buddy. That was the rule, no matter how experienced. Only Larry T was the odd man out. An advanced diver, he volunteered to dive solo, sticking close to Usiel.

The sun had hidden itself behind heavy black clouds and now, with a cool breeze whipping across the deck, I zipped up a fleece jacket over my Cressi suit. Though it was a three point five mil, slightly thicker than average, the cold wind chilled to the bone.

The boat shot forward knocking the waves flat, a white cascade crashing over the bow as the crew came around to check rental equipment, distribute weights and adjust the tanks. A drizzle of rain added to the misery. It would be a welcome relief to be below the sea and for once I couldn't wait to get to our first stop.

The sooner this dive was over, the better I'd feel about last night. When Wolf phoned from his meeting and said he was dizzy, I'd told him to go home and get some sleep. It was my stupid foot that had pushed him into the coffee table and caused the concussion. My reaction time is way too fast. For a martial artist that was good thing, for a boyfriend worth keeping, not so good. I had to do my best to salvage the situation.

When the boat stopped abruptly, my stomach lurched with it. I breathed in slowly, steadying my nerves. My private instructor handed me my weight belt. With the inflated vest around me, the belt was crucial in bringing me down.

Cy was my dive instructor. Tall and broad shouldered, he might have been good looking but all I noticed was hair—auburn streaked-black hair to his shoulders, a beard and a moustache.

Carefully checking my equipment, Cy tightened my vest. With eyes as green as the troubled sea, he searched my face. "You know the signals?"

"Some." I ran through what I remembered with my fingers. "Anything else?"

After showing me the signs for lobster, shark and eel he took hold of my shoulders and squeezed. "I'll be near. Don't be afraid."

I smiled slightly. "And you'll take my hand if I am?"

Full lips curled up at the corners.

****

With those long legs it didn't take much effort for Cy to step out and clear the boat. I was next. The last diver to take the plunge. For a second the motion got to me. The bacon and eggs threatened to surface.

Sensing my hesitation, a crew member grabbed my elbow and steered me to the edge of the stern. Besides being a wreck, I was out of my element. Only a so-so swimmer, an unconscious fear of drowning remained in the back of my mind. To clear the boat, I had to stretch my leg out as far as it would go while holding onto my mask and regulator. Along with the lurch of the boat, the tank weight was too much for me to handle. I stood there swaying. One of the crew gave me a push.

After being airborne for a few seconds, I smacked into the water, sank ten feet and then surged straight up to bounce in the waves, wildly flipping my fins and treading water. On the surface I got anxious. Massive waves and not a diver in sight. Where was Cy?

Unsealing my mask, I spit into it, rubbing the inside lens to clear the condensation. A head bobbed up. Ten feet away Cy gave me the "going down" signal. After the mask was in place, I reached up and released air from my BCD. The vest had bladders, which allowed me to sink down.

The water was warm and grew clearer in the descent. Every two feet, I remembered to squeeze just below the bridge of my nose to equalize the pressure in my ears while deflating my BCD. It had been two years since I'd completed the course yet every dive challenged my fears. But something in me refused to give up. After all, living wasn't without risk. And a challenge made life worth living.

The steady suction and release of air from my regulator was the only thing I heard, as I consciously slowed my breathing. Cy swam closer and curled his fingers into an "O". My mask felt right, neither leaking nor uncomfortably tight. I gave him one back. To be on the safe side, I gently breathed out my nose to relieve any built up mask pressure and let out more air from my BCD. It took no more than a few minutes to get down but it seemed an eternity.

The bottom sparkled white from the finely ground coral. With the motion of the current, I pressed air out of my vest ever so slightly, equalizing, until I steadily floated horizontally. Turning my head, I looked up. The water's surface was a shiny mirror. It was hard to believe I was sixty feet under, breathing and alive.

In the crystal clear water, bright yellow striped grunts swam by on their way to the giant hollowed sponges ahead. In the distance I spotted divers from my boat. With everyone in a black wet suit, it was difficult to tell them apart. Then I recognized Larry T in a shorty suit, chunky white legs exposed to the thighs. An underwater camera in his hands, he steadied himself for a photo of Mary Battrock before she was swept away by the current.

Irmgard was supposedly Mary's buddy but she was still there next to Larry. The boss had landed her fish last night or I assumed she did from the wide grin on her face this morning. But Irmgard was not Brock's dive buddy. Larissa had that privilege. I almost felt sorry for the blonde. The Latina took every opportunity to toss her abundant tresses, stick her pert nose in the air, and brag about how Brock admired her skills. She could have been talking about diving but maybe not with those eyelashes batting.

Swimming up close, Cy signaled if I was okay. With my thumb and pointer finger, I formed an "O". So far it was going well. When he motioned for me to follow, I straightened my legs and kicked out to keep up.

As we neared the coral wall, he swung around and looked back, his eyes unreadable green pools behind the black mask. He pointed to a crevice. I swam in to see. A brown fish puffed its body defensively before slipping behind knobby coral. A puffer fish may not be good for dinner but seeing one is amazing. Cy motioned for me to follow.

The beauty of the sea world caught me off guard. Purple fingers of fan coral waved in the current. Anti-social sea turtles with heavy spotted flippers flapped in a slow steady rhythm, propelling themselves away. Gold and turquoise fairy dust sparkled from a queen angelfish. With her pouty lips puckered she floated by eyeing my orange trim black wet suit with one round golden peeper.

We headed after a spotted leopard grouper, long with a substantial girth. The overhang closed in on our space, making it too narrow for more than one diver at a time. Dark shadows blocked out the light. As we neared a depth of eighty feet, I tensed, longing for that hand from the special man who had captured my heart. I was up for some passion but there would be no sea god now. I had ruined everything. Somehow, I had to fix things at Diego's party.

But this was no time to be distracted. It was a dark journey. Long spidery shadows wove webs between patches of pale light, along with glimpses of orange coral and flitting fish. Whatever was hidden deeper in the black cavern was better left alone.

The current swept me dangerously close to sharp prongs of ribbon coral. I realized my mistake. Too much air in my BCD. Pressing the valve once was not quite enough. Cy grabbed hold of me and emptied more, preventing me from hitting the coral. He signaled if I was okay. My ears were a little clogged but otherwise I was feeling alright. I gave him the "O" sign, glad I'd hired him.

I fixed my eyes on the divers ahead. From a distance, they all looked alike in their full length wet suits. Long and lean, outfitted in black neoprene. Daniel, or was it Brockt? Who could tell? Both were about the same build and height.

There was something to be said for wearing color in the depths of the ocean. Easy identification and less chance of getting stranded when the boat takes off. I hadn't heard it happen here but they'd made a movie of an Australian couple stranded, never to be found again. Big whites.

Through a hole in the overhang, light filtered through. Just behind the others, a lone diver hung back to look at a silvery barracuda passing by. He wore a blue wet suit, hot pink edging along the legs and arms. No black or gray fins for him either. Like a brilliant bird, he flapped ahead in a pair of fuchsia fins, matching Mares mask and electric pink BCD. Ronny would not be left behind. Usiel could find him no problem, unless the color police got hold of him first. I forced myself to keep a straight face or lose mask suction and get an eyeful of saltwater.

In the open water ahead, divers gathered. Usiel pointed to a long gray tail peeping out from the coral. The rest of the fish was covered by the overhang. Larry T pushed in with his camera. The whirled up coral crystals from the bottom blurred the water, obscuring the divers.

Cy motioned for me to have a look. I swam in. Someone

above kicked close to my mask. Too close. Forming a fist, I struck out a forearm, forcing the fin back. She felt it. Larissa looked down, eyes hard. I wasn't playing nice but I didn't have a choice unless I wanted my mask torn from my face.

I felt Cy grip my forearm. He pointed. Just as I glanced down, a fourteen foot long shark shot clear, leaving the divers behind to gaze at a cloud of sand in its wake. It was a bottom dweller, mouth on the underside. My guess was a nurse shark.

While the others moved forward into the cave, we stayed behind to look at tentacles peeping out of a coral crevice. Cy gave me a signal. I swam in closer. An unusual lobster, more broad than long, whizzed over the coral before hiding in a hole.

With a hand stop and a touch to his gauge, Cy told me to check my air supply. We'd been under for about thirty minutes, most of it eighty feet. I signaled one thousand. It wasn't good to be too close to seven hundred psi. Not safe. When that happened, I'd have to head to the surface immediately. The way back up needs time and things can always go wrong.

There was also a decompression stop at fifteen feet. It takes three minutes of treading to regulate the body or risk something potentially fatal, like the "bends".

With a wave, Cy motioned to the coral island ahead. The other divers had left a while ago and we were alone. It was dim but I could make out something moving. The current forced us closer. Flashing like a neon sign in the seedy end of town, a moray eel radiated an eerie green light. A black sea creature struggled from its humongous jaws. Religiously, the eel guarded its prey but the ocean current fought back. It was too strong. The pale fleshy section of the victim parted from the black casing. Freed, it shot straight out.

5

Detective Hernandez waited on the pier—a few uniforms milling about. It wasn't easy getting off the *Sagitario*. Like monkeys swinging from treetops, the crew hopped around, fastening ropes before bringing divers to the stern. This was our second attempt. With high waves pounding into the boat, mooring at the La Vida Hotel had been impossible. Fifteen minutes south, we did the drill again.

Tiny drops had turned into globs of rain blown out like a giant spitting sporadically. Even big Larry T had a greenish tinge to his ruddy complexion. Usiel and his crew did a balancing act helping everyone jump to the pier. It was a relief to be on land but no one was too excited about the police reception.

Next to the pier, casual dive hangouts and two-star hotels dotted the road going south. The police had taken over a salsa club for their interrogation office. Corralled into the Grendeza Bar, the crew and divers had been separated for questioning.

I knew Hernandez. He was an okay type and honest as they come but my stomach was still churning. Trying to rid myself of the ugly vision of the dismembered arm wasn't easy. I just wanted to go back to the hotel and take a hot shower. Shivering and wet, I was getting more miserable by the minute.

When he spotted me, Hernandez charged over to my table. The detective had lost weight he couldn't afford to lose. His gray suit hung loosely from a skeletal frame. Deep set eyes as watchful as a crow's peered suspiciously at me. "*Buenos dias,* Señorita Sturm. I see you brought the El Norte with you."

"*Hola,* detective."

Hernandez pursed his lips. "Strange, isn't it? Another fatality and again it involves you. Such a coincidence," he said, sitting down at the square wooden table to face me. "Why do you think that is?"

"I have no idea."

From the breast pocket of his suit, he took out a pad and

flipped it open. "You were alone when you discovered the remains?"

"No, my dive master was with me."

Close as he could, the detective leaned forward, as if by doing so he could suction the truth out of me. "You have an idea who the victim is?"

"I'm pretty sure it's Brock Laval."

"And what leads you to that conclusion, Señorita Sturm?"

"Brock was a member of my tour group and the only one missing. I assume it's him."

Hernandez held up a pen. "How do you spell it, please. L-a-v-a-l?"

I nodded.

He scribbled something further on his notepad.

"Have you found the body yet?"

"No." He paused, and lifted an eyebrow. "It will wash ashore soon enough. Was he a sickly man?"

"About as healthy as they come but only his doctor would have known for sure."

A quick nod and Hernandez asked, "What do you presume happened?"

"I saw a moray chewing up his arm."

Hernandez barked a laugh.

"You're saying it wasn't an accident?"

The detective's eyes narrowed. "Possibly he ran out of air and—"

"The sea creatures did the rest?"

He shook his head. "For a diver with experience and a buddy nearby?"

My tongue curled under my upper teeth. As far as I knew, Brock had been diving for at least twelve years and from what Larissa had said last night, she knew her reefs better than I did. But something had cut his air supply, or should I say *someone*?

He leaned back, knotting his arms behind his head. "What do you think, Señorita Sturm?"

It didn't jive. Too much was going on. Brock might have discovered something about Diego's company that put him in danger. I decided it was best to keep my lips sealed and suspicions to myself. "Your guess is as good as mine, detective."

"You were with a dive master. Where is he now?"

I pointed to the bearded six footer seated at the bar with Usiel having a beer. Both of them had changed to jeans and t-shirts. "That's him. The one with the beard."

A chin jerk brought a police officer over. Hernandez waved his pen and Cy was promptly escorted to our table. On the wooden stool beside Hernandez, the dive master sat a head taller, shoulders twice as broad. Absentmindedly, he stroked his beard.

"You were with Señorita Sturm?" Hernandez flipped the pen between his index and middle fingers. "Your name?"

"Cy Nemesis."

"Identification?"

From his pocket, Cy took out his wallet and flashed a driver's license."

"You knew Laval?"

Cy shook his head.

"Did you speak on the boat?"

"No." Cy smiled thinly. "He was busy talking with the ladies."

"In your opinion, is it possible the eel killed the man?"

"Anything is possible," Cy murmured, "but not likely."

The detective sighed wearily. "All right. I may want to speak to you further but for now, don't leave Cozumel." He turned to me. "Is there something you know about Laval that would have a bearing on this? Did he have any enemies?'

I shook my head. "We just met on this trip. I hardly knew him."

Hernandez made a notation. "Do you know what kind of work he did?"

"He told me he was an accountant for Bolivar Imports and Exports."

Color left the detective's face. His pen dug a hole into the paper. "*Mierda*." He swore softly under his breath.

Cy stared at us intently. "I thought he was Canadian?"

"He worked in the Toronto branch."

Shifting restlessly, Hernandez, forced out his words in a whisper. "Laval was acquainted with Señor Alvarez?"

"They met last night."

"Where?"

"Moray's Eel. I brought the tour group over there." With the mention of an eel, the horrible visual reappeared before my eyes. I shuddered.

Cy sprang to his feet. "If that's all, detective? You can see Señorita Sturm is distressed by this occurrence," he said testily. He picked up our bags. "We have your permission to go?"

"Make sure none of you leave the island." Hernandez peered at me. "Your hotel?"

"La Vida."

Reluctantly, the detective nodded and waved to the uniform. As the man guided Irmgard to our table, she managed to shoot me a look, as if this was somehow my fault.

When we stepped out the door, a weight fell off my shoulders.

"Let's go there," Cy said, jerking his chin to a cantina about twenty yards down the street.

"Okay." Anywhere away from Hernandez would be good.

The wooden sign hanging over the sidewalk pictured a blue whale blowing bubbles with the word *Wally's* in white lettering. Inside, red-checkered plastic covered round resin tables and white lawn chairs housed a scattering of Mexicans and tourists who sat eating and drinking. Off to the left, a steel band was setting up next to the bar. On the ceiling, a fan circulated warm humid air, heavy with the odor of fried garlic and fish.

After putting the bags down on the dirt floor next to an empty table, Cy pulled a seat out for me. I hesitated. Black wet suit sticking to my clammy skin, white flip flops on my feet and hair like a sea witch, I would have happily hid in a hole in the ground and never come out.

Cy eyed my outfit. "You should change."

"I was thinking that." I reached for the blue waterproof duffle bag, then pulled on the zipper but it was stuck.

Helpfully, Cy leaned over and tugged the zipper open.

"Thanks." From inside, I pulled out a sealed semi-transparent plastic bag and looked around for the washroom.

Cy pointed an index finger to a wooden door. "Next to the bar. What can I get you to drink?"

"Anything—doesn't matter." Tote in hand, I shuffled over to the hallway feeling about as energetic as a slug. Tired, hungry and numb. It could simply have been a tragic accident, couldn't it? Or had Brock's investigation of Bolivar Imports and Exports earned him a watery grave?

A mermaid plaque was screwed on the center of the cracked wood panel of the bathroom door. I wasn't surprised to enter a room that had seen better days. The toilet was missing a lid, and the taps and handles of the turquoise ceramic sink were rusted. Water dripped into a stained yellow drain.

Peeling off the wet suit was a struggle. Thank God for the zippers at the ankles. Finally, with a soggy mess heaped on the broken white tiles, I took out my underwear and pulled it on. Damp skin fought my efforts but I forced the red tank and tan shorts over top. Done, I gazed into the tiny mirror screwed into the tiled wall.

My face was pale. The scuba mask had left indentations in my cheek and forehead. After massaging the lines and seeing no improvement, I gave up. From the zipped pocket I found some lip gloss. The mirror told me to put some on my cheeks, too. Finally, after forcing a brush through my salt-matted hair and fluffing it up, I felt human again.

With the wet articles under my arm, I made my way back to the table. After I sat down, I opened the tote on the floor and threw the soggy things in.

The table was equipped with beer, refried beans and a bowl of corn chips. Cy handed me a Dos Equis. It was like finding an oasis in a desert. "Thanks. I'm so thirsty." Beer is not my thing but my throat was desert dry.

"It's from the dive. Breathing with a reg does that." His eyes flitted from the drummer to me. "Ever been to this cantina?"

A young server in a short black skirt and tight low cut tank came by and set down a dish of pale meat and a small container of red sauce.

"No, never. Not this one or any cantina. You ordered food?"

"Comes with the drinks."

I waited for the girl to leave before I probed the appetizer with my fork. "What's this?"

"Shark," he said, watching me dip a piece into the sauce.

Wouldn't be my choice, but then the whole day hadn't been anything I'd have asked for. Slipping a morsel cautiously into my mouth, I let it slide down my throat.

I washed the blah taste down with a sip of beer and glanced at Cy. "Your name is Nemesis?" I eyed his auburn curls and emerald eyes. "You don't look Greek."

"Long story. Actually, I'm Basque."

"That area between France and Spain?"

Cy dipped a corn chip into the refried beans.

"A Spanish French mixture?"

He grinned. "Probably, but the more amusing version is more fascinating."

"Oh?"

"You've heard of Ixchel?"

"The fertility goddess."

"Also known as the white goddess. Her husband Itzamna was the white god. The theory is that those two weren't Mayans at all. They were Basque. When Atlantis was destroyed, the people set off in boats to different areas of the world to impart their superior knowledge supposedly gleaned from a visit from aliens." He laughed dryly. "My father firmly believed he was a god."

"Fathers often do."

"He wasn't the only one."

I laughed. "You?"

"If I am, I don't have the luck of the gods."

"Then who?"

"My brother. He thinks he's blessed and maybe he is."

"Interesting. Is your family still there?"

"Spain?" He shook his head. "Papa met Mama and they moved to Mexico." A frown set on his generous lips. Cy searched my face. "Enough about me. How are you feeling?"

"Better." I was, but plenty worried. It was too much of a coincidence that Brock was dead. Then I remembered how startled Cy had looked when he'd found out Laval worked for Diego's company. "What do you know about Bolivar Import Exports?"

Glancing around the room, Cy placed his hand on mine "Please, speak quietly, Adie. You don't know who could overhear."

I nodded and whispered, "Tell me what you know about Bolivar Import Exports."

He shrugged. "I think everyone knows it's run by Diego Alvarez."

"And what do you know about him?"

"Rich and powerful."

"But you looked surprised at Brock's connection. I get the feeling you've had personal dealings with the company."

"I did."

"What happened?"

Cy stared back.

"Do you know anything about the recent activities of Bolivar Imports and Exports?"

"Why does this concern you?"

A memory of Brock in the hallway of the Moray Eel entered my mind. Handsome and self-assured, yet he had been nervous.

"Adie, what is it?"

"A man died."

His dark green eyes soothing, Cy leaned in. "I understand that." He handed me another beer. "Relax, there's nothing we can do about it now."

"Yes, I know but..."

Cy sucked back on his beer and set it down. "Bad things can happen under the sea."

I shook my head. "It's not that simple. I think Brock was murdered."

6

The door slammed shut. I dropped the tote on the floor and spotted a long lean hottie sprawled on the couch. Hands locked behind his head, eyes closed, legs propped up, he was a touch large for the furniture but somehow Wolf had managed to make himself comfortable.

"You texted and I came," he drawled, opening his eyes. "So, what's up, babe?"

"Something happened."

Wolf sat up, his bright blues immediately alert. "I can see it's not good. Come sit." He patted the couch.

I slumped down.

"Need a drink?"

"Already had a couple."

He tilted my chin up. "If those turquoise eyes are any indication, those drinks were all duds. Hm-mm, I think I need to get them back to that Caribbean blue I see in my dreams. Will this help?" The touch of his lips steamed my core.

"Mm-mm."

"It's helping but," he said, steering me around ninety degrees, "a massage might be needed as well."

If Wolf ever needed another job, this would be it. From my back to my neck, he knew exactly what he was doing. I let out a sigh. "Thanks."

"Not done yet. Lean forward." Fingertips circled on my scalp. He laughed. "Poor princess. I think you need a shower."

"Yes, that would be nice but I should tell you what happened."

He got up and pulled me to my feet. "Wolf Du Lac at your service! My job is to make those eyes sparkle and *then* we will discuss your issues."

My Logical Voice tried to stop me. "You know what this will

*lead to. Don't get caught up in his magic. Yes, he says he misses
you but does he love you? Have you ever heard him say that?"*

"Get off it, Logical," my Hormone Voice wedged in. "Don't
you see how lucky she is that he's so into her? Adie needs
whatever this man gives. You know how badly her dates have gone.
The girl always ends up paying except when she's with Wolf."*

"Diego is just as generous if not more," Logical argued. "All
those gifts, the condo and who knows what."*

Hormone snickered. "I know what. So do you. He just wants
what she's been giving Wolf. Well this guy is upfront and ready to
play."*

"Maybe," Logical conceded, "but you don't know that for a
fact. Wolf has had secrets before. If she encouraged Diego, she'd
never have to give in to Irmgard's demands again. He'd take her
anywhere she wanted. Treat her like a queen."*

I'd had enough. Way too mentally and physically dragged out
to protest, I shut out Logical, especially after I was swept up in
Wolf's arms, carried to the bathroom and set gently on my feet.
With a quick motion, the shower was on and ready.

Wolf pulled off his T-shirt and flung it on the floor. Perfect
abs. The jeans dropped next. The sight of black boxer briefs
encasing a noticeably large bulge perked my spirits considerably.

"Yes!" Hormone screamed.

"I can only help my princess if she allows her slave to assist."

"Alright," I said calmly, lifting my arms.

The tank was flung on the floor.

"Undo my bra," I whispered after wiggling out of the shorts.

That item landed on the tiles along with my shorts.

Wolf gazed up and down. "Gorgeous woman."

Clothes on the floor, we entered a warm gentle spray. Wolf
didn't waste any time stroking a creamy liquid over every curve of
my body. Shivers raced down my spine. Chocolate wafted in the
air.

"Has it done its job yet?" Wolf said in a husky voice.

Did he mean the cocoa body wash or did he mean his magic
hands that sent me into dream mode? "What?"

"The body wash."

I lifted an inquiring brow.

"Has it released endorphins in the Adie Sturm brain. Started the cycle of pleasure?"

"Ah-hh, so that's why you bought it for me."

Wolf shrugged his shoulders and grinned. "I brought something else."

I glanced down. "You sure did."

"Wicked woman." Wolf reached behind him. On the ledge was a small cloth bag. From this, he popped a dark object between his lips and pressed it to my mouth. The scent was pure heaven. My lips parted to allow the chocolate truffle to enter. Momentarily, I held it to the roof of my mouth, savoring the flavor before I swallowed.

Wolf gazed into my eyes. "I want to taste you." He squeezed the tip of his tongue into my mouth, licking the inside of my lip.

I ran my fingers through the wet blond hair. Just touching him made me feel good. "Now let me have a taste." I pulled his head down to mine and kissed that sexy mouth again. "Mm-mm." I sucked his lower lip before giving it a tender nibble. "I'm greedy. One more."

This time, Wolf used his fingers to slide the truffle over my lips before he pushed it into my mouth. Rich, creamy and sinfully delicious. By now, I was thinking about the man more than the chocolate. He was definitely edible.

Wet on wet. Yet the heat I felt was like oil set off with dynamite. From a muscular chest, my fingers slid down his abs and hips, stopping to cup his buns. "Hard and tight."

Wolf's hand guided mine forward. "This part is hard, too."

And it was. But I was not entirely focused. "Wolf, something awful happened out there. I'm not sure I can do this," I said slowly.

"This will wipe your memory." Eyes shimmering with passion, he pulled me out of the shower. The towel did its job and fell to the floor. From the counter he grabbed a bottle and filled his hand with a silky liquid. Lightly skimming over my breasts, he awakened each peak, while a flood of delicious kisses lit on the curve of my neck and shoulder. Dropping down onto a chair, he pulled me on top and cupped a breast. His tongue torched a nipple, and I melted like ice cream under the hot summer sun.

The lotion on his hands slid from one curve to another until it smoothed the inside of my thighs. A teasing finger brought a moan to my lips. I clenched my muscles as he stroked, slowly at first and then quickly. A fire flamed. Passion hurled me high. Feverishly, I cried out.

Gazing up into those mysterious sapphire eyes, I knew it was more than sex—something indescribable. I wanted him more than I had ever wanted anyone. Positioning myself, I pushed him in. Wolf groaned and gripped my hips before filling me with his heat. Each shove was countered. But the nightmare under the sea suddenly reappeared before my eyes. I stopped.

"Adie? What's wrong?"

"Wolf, it was awful. I keep seeing it."

"I'll make you forget."

Feeling stronger as if gaining energy from him, I met his eyes. "Yes, that's what I need." Why did women have such complex brains, always thinking? "Knock it out of my mind."

Wolf backed me against the tile wall. Hands under my butt, he held me up. I lifted a leg to his shoulder while the other fell in a ballet position. Urgently connecting, my fingernails dug into his biceps and I held on. A hand tightly gripped my leg and we rocked in passion until the horror of seeing Brock's dismembered arm faded. Intense impact sparked shudders that consumed my body. Screams and groans magnified hollowly in the tile bathroom until my juices released and I sank into his chest. When I heard his sigh, I grinned. It was good. No doubt about it.

We showered off and headed back to the couch. Wolf handed me a shot of tequila.

I hesitated.

"If you're worried about drinking on an empty stomach, some *pollo de mole* is on its way."

"Thanks, I was, but there was something else. I just remembered my tour group needed to be ready for Diego's party. I sent for costumes but I don't know if they arrived. I should go and see."

"No worries, princess. All is taken care of. I made sure Luis informed your group, and," he grinned, "wrote it on the white board. You are looking at Wolf Du Lac tour group leader assistant."

I smiled weakly. "That's sweet of you. I'm afraid I'm not thinking too straight right now."

"Drink. It'll help."

Taking his advice, I tipped back the glass and felt the fiery liquid burn my throat. I started to relax when we heard the knock on the door. Just as I'd hoped, the Mayan chicken in a chocolate sauce had arrived.

Back on the couch, Wolf handed me a covered plate. "Eat."

It was great being taken care of. Being independent is good but a protective man is truly a find. As I sampled a succulent morsel of chicken, I watched Wolf, thinking he was always my dependable backup man. Someone I trusted. Wolf had hired Brock for a job and knew him as a buddy. It wouldn't be easy breaking the news. When I set my fork down, Wolf tossed back a beer.

"Alright, Adie, I'm all ears," he said.

I bit my lip. "Something awful happened on the dive."

His forehead furrowed.

"We saw a huge moray eel. There was something in its mouth."

"We?"

"I hired a dive instructor to be my buddy."

"I'm sorry I wasn't there. You know I wanted to go but—"

"I shouldn't have been so vicious."

"Forget about all that. I'm okay now. It's not important." Wolf took my hand and gazed into my eyes. "Princess, tell me what happened."

"At first it looked like this black creature, maybe a squid but, Wolf," I squeezed his hand, "it was an arm minus the person."

Wolf arched a brow.

I looked into his eyes. "It was Brock."

"What! How do you know?"

I nodded. "Makes sense. When we surfaced, he was the only one missing."

Wolf shoved his plate away and got up. He walked over to the balcony and stared at the street. "Shit. This is my fault."

"You didn't know this would happen."

He gazed at me, his jaw clenched. "The investigation. Brock must have found something."

"That's what I was thinking."

Thoughtfully, Wolf ran his fingers through his hair. "Did he tell you anything?"

"We spoke a little at the bar last night. Possibly someone overheard."

"How so?"

"Noises. They were coming from the back near the storeroom. I heard them. So did Brock."

Wolf's forehead furrowed. "What did Brock have to say?"

"Diego is importing skulls. Apparently, they're doing really well."

"Did Brock think something was wrong?"

"He was suspicious." I slipped my feet into a pair of flip flops. It occurred to me we had to do something right away. There wouldn't be much time before the police would search Brock's room. "He downloaded information from Bolivar Imports." I jumped up. "Wolf, we've got to get into his computer."

Wolf looked at me in amusement. "Now?"

"If we don't, Hernandez will."

Wolf stood and tightened his towel. "I owe Brock that much. He was a friend."

"I know. I'm so sorry."

A chin nod. "Thanks." He exhaled as if trying to let of go of the pain. "Any ideas how?"

"I think you can get us in there."

Wolf grinned. "I am a man of many skills."

Heat rose to my cheeks. "You sure are." The towel slung low at his waist looked seriously sexy. "How about you use some of that charm on the maid?"

"Where's his room?"

I motioned with my hand. "That part's easy. Right next door."

"Okay. Come on then." Wolf took my hand and pulled me up. His eyes sparkled as blue as the French River at dawn.

"But, shouldn't we get dressed?" I protested, thinking nothing had changed since that day. A vision of deep water edged by junipers. The heavy humidity of summer. A lanky boy with blond surfer hair. Impulsive and sensual, a guy who made my pulse beat at breakneck speed with the touch of his hand. Back then, I was like a rose on the point of blooming. Now, ten years later, I was a woman with a second chance.

"This is crazy, Wolf. What are you thinking? We're wearing towels!" But Wolf wasn't listening. Quickly, I grabbed my key card before he pushed me out into the hall and shut the door behind us.

We didn't have far to go. Just around the corner, a young Latina in a blue uniform, brown hair fastened in a neat bun, brought the cart to a stop. The pin above her breast pocket read Rosita. Her mouth dropped open at the sight of the sea god.

Wolf jumped into his routine. "*Hola. Por favor,* Señorita. *He perdido mi clave.*" He pointed to the room just past mine and motioned for her to follow.

At the entrance to Brock's room, I waited nervously as she opened the door. When she swiveled about, Wolf gave her a *gracias* and a seductive smile. Round cheeks flushed like roses, eyes shyly cast down, the girl was clearly embarrassed, or was she? If she thought she'd get a look when the towel fell, I couldn't blame her. Wolf's package would make any woman weak in the knees.

His hand on my lower back, Wolf steered me inside. I stepped forward with a sense of dread. It wasn't as if I'd find the rest of the body in here, I reassured myself. Looking around, I spotted a pair of tan trousers hung over a chair. The closet doors had been left open to shirts and jackets on hotel hangers while stylish leather dress shoes were lined up like soldiers on the floor.

The room layout was the same as mine. A lone white towel swan had been placed in the middle of a double bed covered with a Navajo-design blanket. Next to it, a wicker couch and coffee table grouping with a bathroom off to the left where we came in. The dark wood TV cabinet was shut. With the drapes drawn, we switched on the light and the entrance light flickered reluctantly. Remembering my room had a switch near the bed, I crept over and clicked it on.

Goosebumps formed on my arms from the cool air blowing from the vents and a shiver raced down my spine. I reminded myself that Brock would want his killer found and arrested. There was nothing in here that would hurt us. Whoever had murdered

Brock had been part of the dive. The laptop could have the answer. If the police had been here already, there would have been crime tape at the door. My eyes searched and came up blank. The room hummed quietly as if in answer. On the shelf below the bedside table I spotted it. The small black notebook blended into the dark surface of the wood.

"There." I took Wolf's hand and pulled him over to the bed.

"Again? Good idea but I'm not sure I'm ready yet, princess."

"That's not what I meant," I hissed before I noticed the twinkle in his eyes. With my finger, I jabbed his side.

"Ouch, be nice." Wolf checked around the table and picked up a black computer case. "There should be a memory stick in here." He stuck his fingers into a pocket. "Yes! Let's take it and leave."

I nodded. "Hernandez is on the case. It wouldn't surprise me if he's already on his way here."

"It's not officially a murder, or is it?"

I shook my head. "No, but he doesn't think it's an accident either. It's my guess he'll follow it up unless—"

"What?"

"Well, when we talked he wasn't happy to find out that Brock was connected to Bolivar Imports and Exports and Diego."

Wolf grinned. "I'll bet he was shaking in his boots. A guy like Hernandez knows what side his bread is buttered on. If Alvarez says jump he'll say *how high*."

"He was jittery but Hernandez is like a dog with a bone. You can be sure he's after the murderer."

"We'd better get a move on."

I stalled, thinking there was something else. "Wait." He wouldn't have taken it with him on a dive. On that chance, I reached over and opened the drawer at the bedside table. Under a notepad and a box of condoms, I found a Blackberry. Snatching up the cell, I dug further and came up with a charger.

"Way to go, babe. Take it." Wolf opened the door to check the hallway. "Coast's clear."

It was but until we were both in my room with the door shut tight, I was wound up tighter than a kite.

"Listen, babe, I'd better go," Wolf said, wrapping an arm around my shoulders. "I'll take the laptop to my house and meet you at the party later."

"Omigod! I forgot about the costume. I'll have to go down to the lobby and find one."

"No, you won't. It's already here."

"What do you mean?" Something about the mischief in his eyes made me suspicious.

Wolf jerked his head to a box lying on the floor of my closet. "All arranged, beautiful. Yours is in that box and mine is back at the house."

"Thank you. You're a life saver."

"If you wear it, I'll be a happy man." Wolf grinned. "Can't wait to see you in it."

"Now, I am curious."

Wolf planted a soft kiss on my lips. "Curiosity killed the cat." He placed a finger on my lips. "I don't want anything happening to my beautiful puss. Be careful not to say too much to Alvarez. Promise?"

I nodded. "I will. How about you? You're going over the document before the party?"

"I'll give it the old college try." He tossed his towel into my bathroom and strode into the room *au naturel*. From the couch, he grabbed his clothes and slipped them on.

It was a bit of a letdown watching him get dressed but the overall effect was sizzling when he leaned on the doorframe in a black T-shirt and jeans giving me a lop-sided smile. Rising on tip toes, I gave him one last slow kiss before he disappeared down the hall. In my hand Brock's Blackberry flashed red.

7

Lights dazzled my eyes. From the Emperor palms surrounding the serpentine-shaped pool, lanterns as colorful as a rainbow reflected patterns on the marble floor. On the center stage curtained with gold, flashy costumed dancers choreographed an intricate tango for the seated guests. In the opposite direction, through the palms, were glimpses of the beach. Moonlight caressed the crests of the Caribbean as it swept onto the deserted sandy shore.

The rhythm of the sea was drowned out by the band. I stood at the bar closest to Diego's villa. The heady fragrance of exotic plants from the gardens bordering the house drifted in with the warm evening breeze. Worth millions, the three storey building was spectacular. White stucco walls and a red tiled roof, only one of several structures situated on acres of prime oceanfront land.

From where I was standing, I could see bedroom windows and balconies on the upper floor, rooms on the second storey where the bodyguards lived, and the offices on the ground level. The kitchen and maid's quarters were somewhere in the back. An elaborate formal dining room and entertainment rooms faced the front entrance where a six car garage was located off of the circular driveway.

A tap on my shoulder brought me about face to a willowy woman. A flimsy white toga clung to her like a second skin. She had the bone structure of a runway model but without the disdainful attitude. Saucy green eyes rimmed with black liner glittered with *joie de vivre*. Her shapely mouth gleamed with red lipstick. Carmelita was every inch a Bolivar Alvarez.

"*Amiga*, you came!" Diego's sister stood back. "Your costume is surprisingly risqué." She stared at my breasts covered by a semi-transparent material jeweled with gold sequins and then at the flashy skirt tightly draped to the floor where it ended in a tail. On my head, I had a glittery tiara. "Where ever did you find that outfit? I have a feeling you didn't select that one, did you?"

I laughed. "Right you are, Carmelita. It was a gift from Wolf."

"Your man has unique sense of style. You make a marvelous mermaid princess. Poor me, I'm only a Mayan goddess." Taking hold of my shoulders, she stooped down and brushed my cheeks with kisses.

"Oh, Carmelita," I protested, "you know you are gorgeous." I admired the up do fastened with a pearl ornament. "I'm so sorry about your father. Tell me, how are you making out? It must have been rough."

A tear appeared at the corner of one eye. Quickly, she wiped it away. "Yes, it was a terrible time though we half expected repercussions after the first heart attack. Luckily, Diego was a rock."

"That's good. And you had your husband with you. He must have been of some comfort?"

Signaling the bartender, she held up two fingers. "Juan, strawberry daiquiris, *por favor*." She grimaced. "I think Fede was more concerned about whether to wear his gray striped Armani suit or the charcoal tailored from London. I was surprised he even came."

"Seriously? But last time I was here you two seemed so happy."

With her hand, Carmelita formed a gun and pointed a finger to her temple. "That was then. I have come to my senses. I could shoot myself for my stupidity. Call it temporary insanity," she smirked, "or an overdose of sex. Fede knows his way around the bedroom but no, that drama is all over. The slime has another mistress who apparently interests him way more than I. Can you think of one reason I should put up with that piece of filth?"

I grinned. "You like unpredictable men?"

A tinkle of laughter. "You are so funny." She flipped her

hand. "Perhaps. But what about you?"

"Same."

That brought about another giggle. "Unpredictable men. Hm-mm. They are bad boys, aren't they, yet men that excite." When the bartender placed the drinks down and she handed me one. "*Salud!* To bad boys."

"Mouthwatering, sinfully delicious, like chocolate!" I added.

Smiling, we clicked glasses. The strawberry daiquiri was fruity without being sugary sweet and the rum hit me like a brick. With the size of the goblet, I would have to practice some self-control. Apparently, I wasn't the only one. Carmelita was getting right into the party spirit. Tilting her head back, she swallowed a good portion before placing her drink back on the counter. "So what is happening with you, Adelina?"

I shrugged. "Who knows? I think I need a psychic."

With fingertips on her temples, Carmelita pretended to enter a trancelike state. "I see a cloud in the form of a heart. It is coming clearer. There is a mysterious blond palomino biting at the bit. Hm-mm. Although he is blond and well hung, I think he is not a horse. No, he has the name and spirit of an animal. It is coming clearer. He howls your name. Yes! It is Wolf, but wait, there is also another man. This one carries a torch for you like a lovestruck teenage boy. At work he doodles hearts and arrows. Yes, he, too, is tall and attractive. His name...hm-mm. It is coming through. Don, Dan—of course, now I know! It's Diego." She laughed at the expression on my face. "Do you still have them following you around like puppy dogs?"

That was funny. Puppies? They were way too alpha for that. Not doglike at all but upon consideration, I recalled how fond they seemed of using their tongues on the tender areas of my body. Housebroken but not trainable. Bad boys for sure. That's what attracted me to them. But I couldn't help smiling, thinking of Wolf and Diego seated at my knees, adoring me with their eyes. Once in a while, I would stroke their heads and run my fingers through their fur.

"Wake up, *amiga!*" Carmelita snipped impatiently. "What's happening with your *novios*?"

"Ask me in a few days. Now what about you?"

"The gardener was young and firm but I think," she made a face, "I need more."

I sighed. "Intellectual and emotional connection? Yes, and let's not forget that elusive thing called love."

"*Caramba*!" Carmelita pinched my cheek. "You are way too serious, my friend. Love has a way of finding us no matter what roadblocks we put up. Enjoy the men and spit on the scum. Thank you, Juan," she said to the bartender as he refilled the glasses from the blender. "Let's take these with us."

Leading the way, Carmelita swerved in and out amongst the guests on the pathway. As I followed I wondered if Wolf had arrived. And where was Diego? My eyes searched the tall well-built men in the crowd and didn't see either of them, but one man seemed vaguely familiar. "Wait! That matador, who is he?"

Squinting her eyes, Carmelita scanned the crowd. "Where?"

I pointed. "That tall dark-haired man talking to the queen of hearts, I think I know him."

Carmelita frowned. "You do."

From the look on her face, I figured it out. It had been a while but it had to be the two-timing husband. "Of course, it's Fede."

"Pond scum! What worries me is who he's talking to. That woman is trouble. She'd better not be his new mistress." Carmelita gazed at me and squeezed my hand. "Did you know she was still here in Cozumel?"

"Who are you talking about?"

Leaning down, she whispered in my ear. "Take a good look. You know her, Adelina. She's a redhead now."

With partiers traipsing in front of us, it wasn't easy to check out the mysterious queen. Even with four inch platforms, I had to peak around a man costumed as a lumpy Humpty Dumpty—a face like a donut and a body that took up an inconsiderate amount of space. When I finally caught another glimpse of the queen, it clicked. She'd been a brunette the last I saw her. The sight of that snake put me in fighting mode.

"Samantha," I said through gritted teeth. "I thought she was back in Canada."

"The story is that she quit the company without notice and scurried back to Cozumel to squander her inheritance. Purchased an extremely large villa a week ago not far from here and hasn't been seen much until tonight." Carmelita swatted a mosquito buzzing around her head. "That snake better not be after my Fede." Taking my hand, she led me towards the house. "We'll talk inside,"she shouted above the trumpets.

The red strobe lights flashed in sync with the headache that was pounding in my temples. Samantha lived in Toronto and had no business being here anymore. It could only mean she wanted Wolf. Their short marriage had ended a few years back. After a string of liaisons, all of which profited her bank account, she had tried to hook up with him again and failed. But I was still worried.

At the side entrance, Carmelita urged me inside. "Adelina, go straight ahead. The door on the right."

It was quiet. The thick walls of the villa shut out the party noises. On the oak table in the marbled hallway, an immense oriental vase had been filled with crimson long stemmed roses. Modern oil paintings of gardens and countryside hung in wide ridged wooden frames lining the white stucco walls. Everything spoke of money yet it was all understated.

The den was filled with plush cream leather chairs and heavy oak tables. Carmelita seated herself on one and motioned for me to take the chair. "Diego was anxious I convey apologies to you as something unforeseen called him to Playa. He has returned and is getting into costume as we speak. Before he comes down I wanted to tell you I heard. How horrible for you to find a body."

"Not really a body. It was an arm." Finding a limb was a death sentence in anyone's book. "Fortunately, I wasn't alone. I'd hired a dive master. If this hadn't happened you might have met him tonight." I thought of the athletic body and the investigator's good looks. "He was quite the charmer. Poor Brock."

"Brock? That was his name?" Carmelita's forehead furrowed. "What was his family name?"

"Laval."

"*¡Dios mio!*" Diego's sister was white as a sheet. "Adelina, I know him."

I stared at Carmelita. "Really?"

"We met several months ago. Fede brought me to a place called Moray's Eel. The slime was busy flirting with the lady bartender. When a handsome man came and sat beside me, of course I noticed. We talked and joked around. He was quite taken by me. And what a sexy smile. When he told me he was single I was interested but Fede and I were at a good place in our marriage so I didn't follow up."

"That is a strange coincidence."

"Not really. San Miguel is a small town. Some live here a few months and go home when the heat comes." She smiled slightly, her eyes taking on a dreamy look.

From that smile, I knew something was up. "I take it you saw him again. From the look on your face I'd guess you two were involved."

The soft smile lingered on her lips. "He smelled so good. I couldn't resist."

I crossed my arms, lost in thought.

Carmelita stroked her lip. "I found him terribly attractive. By that time, Fede had a new mistress."

I nodded. "I understand. Your marriage had a downturn and you needed—"

"An escape. It's hard to be a devout Catholic. I am still committed to him and to our marriage. But, Adelina, tell me what happened? How could the dive end up with Brock dead?"

"I don't know. If I didn't have this tour group with me I'd cancel the rest of the dives."

"I understand completely." Carmelita pursed her lips. "The idea of diving fills me with dread. My brother lost his life in a dive, you know, and now this happens to Brock."

"Diego didn't tell me the whole story."

"That's men. They don't share much." Carmelita picked up her daiquiri and stared at it a moment before she tipped it back. "Amancio was the oldest, Adelina. A wonderful brother, so sensitive and kind. Too honest maybe for his own good. Our family business was difficult for him."

I supposed that would be true with the Bolivar dealings, which always ended up somewhere in the gray area. Where there was money, there was corruption. Wolf called Diego a fox for a variety of reasons, one of which was the way he dealt with business obstacles. If there was a motto for him it would be, "the end justifies the means".

"He was certified for advanced diving. One October he went on a dive with his friend and disappeared. They searched but never found his body." Carmelita's jaw tightened. "The sea consumes what it's given. There was no funeral, only a memorial service." Restlessly, she got up and wandered over to the fireplace. From the mantle, she picked up a couple of framed pictures. She handed me a black and white five by seven. Three smiling children, the boys on the outside with their arms around the girl. "He's on the left. Eight years old. Diego was six and I was only four. Mama believed in spacing her children."

"So cute," I said, staring at the trio. "Diego with his wavy brown hair and you with those blonde curls and Amancio," I stared and asked, "What color was his?"

"Back then it was auburn but it turned darker as an adult, almost black." She placed the picture on the table and handed me a color photograph of the grown-up siblings.

In the middle between her brothers, Carmelita glowed with happiness. Tawny tresses tumbled over creamy shoulders left bare by a strapless yellow dress. Beside her, Diego was film star handsome with charismatic hazel eyes, an aristocratic nose and shapely lips. It was hard to believe someone as drop dead delicious as Diego could find me interesting. He was a definite ten on any woman's scale. Yet the other brother exuded a different masculine energy that was just as compelling. A strong chin and nose, the same lips, and stormy green eyes. Both the brothers looked corporate, hair slicked back, clean shaven, and stylish, in well-cut suits.

"He was CEO of our exports company but after his death, Fede took his position. He had a relatively free hand running the operation. Diego had enough to do with the real estate corporation but when papa died, my brother took over. My husband tried to hide it, but he was upset. Fede had counted on running Bolivar

Imports and Exports alone, but, now, once again, he's lost his power."

"Was he good at it?"

"Yes, I think so, at least he says so." She shrugged. "Papa trained him after all. Fede's family is wealthy but nothing compared to us. He likes—"

"The glory of being a Bolivar Alvarez if only through marriage," Diego pronounced, leaning casually against the jamb. He glanced at the photo on the table. "Amancio should be here running the company with me."

My jaw dropped. The ornate feathered headdress he wore was so huge it brushed the top of the high arched door frame. The long feathered skirt allowed glimpses of his muscular legs. Naked to the waist, his sculpted chest was covered in black hennaed swirls, from head to toe. Diego had gone all out.

"Like it?"

I wasn't sure. His body was perfect, but the warrior body paint that extended to his face lent an evil glow to his smile. "You're a Mayan God. Aren't you?"

"Very perceptive, Adelinita." He strode into the room, perched himself on the armrest of my chair and presented me with a red rose. "For you, *mi amor*. Your beauty is as radiant as this rose."

I could feel the heat in my cheeks. "Thank you."

Diego's eyes swept down my figure. "You make a lovely mermaid. The costume becomes you. I am a lucky man to know a woman so independent, confident, and yet so enchanting." He picked up my hand and kissed my wrist. "When are you moving in with me?"

Startled, I croaked, "Moving in?"

Diego laughed. "Joking, but, seriously, anytime you want, let me know."

"But give him an hour's notice so he can kick out his whore before you arrive," Carmelita remarked dryly. "Is she still there waiting patiently between the sheets?"

"That is a low blow, sweet sister. There is no one in my bed. You know there isn't a lady that excites me like Adelina."

"Hah, who was talking about ladies? If you want Adelina, I

think you'd better say goodbye to those harlots and give her some commitment."

Diego smiled thinly. "My sister is insane. Don't pay attention to her, *cariño*. That sad excuse of a husband has left her high and dry again and her mood is miserable. Where is the bastard anyway?"

"Last we saw, he was talking to the Queen of Hearts, or is that Tarts? Samantha Jurgens."

"Du Lac's ex? But don't worry, sis. She is much too wily to go for a small fish in the sea like him." Diego leaned over and pressed a kiss to my hand. I couldn't help but feel an answering tingle. "My bet is she's after a meatier prize."

"Yes, but it would not be unheard of that Samantha would waste her time on a random man before her trap is set."

"And that trap would be for?" I asked tentatively.

Brother and sister eyed me silently.

"You both think that man is Wolf, don't you?"

"She's been wanting for him for a while. So far she hasn't succeeded." Diego shrugged.

"Wolf has made money here in Cozumel," Carmelita added, "and that's what she likes."

I wouldn't let myself be caught up in this. "There are other men on this island, many of them wealthy. That woman could be after anyone." I checked out Diego. "Tell me about your costume, Diego. Which god are you?"

"I decided to be the Cozumel Island god this year."

"Oh?"

Diego's hand teasingly trailed along my arm. "You know your goddess?"

"Yes, of course, Ixchel." I handled the smooth jade Ixchel pendant on my neck. It had been a gift from Wolf and I treasured it.

"Well, I am her husband, the Mayan god Itzamna."

The sound of heavy footsteps on the marble echoed down the hall. At the doorway, a massive man appeared. Chiseled granite had more animation than that face.

"Yes, Luis?"

Wow, I was impressed. How Diego could tell the twins apart was beyond me.

"There is a matter of some importance, Señor Alvarez."

"What is it?"

"The police are here. I have taken them into the office."

Diego frowned. "*Mierda!* What do those fools want now? Carmelita, please, could you?"

"No problem, I will stay with Adelina. We will return to the party. Look for us." She winked. "There are many fish in the sea, some just waiting to be hooked."

"Before you find a grouper for yourself, Adelina, remember I have everything you need and way more than most." Diego's brandy eyes sparkled. "Save me a dance?"

I felt my cheeks flush. "Of course."

"See you soon, *mi vida*." With a kiss to my cheek and a showstopper smile, Diego strode out into the hall.

"Wasn't that funny?" Carmelita picked up her glass and sipped it as contentedly as a cat with a bowl of milk.

"What?"

"My brother with the Itzamna costume? He's really gone over the top this time." She brushed her bangs back and looked amused.

I smiled. Diego was a born showman. It was no problem for him to carry off the Mayan God look. "Suits him somehow."

Carmelita tipped back her drink. "Such a massive ego, but, *amiga*, it's not all his fault. Since we were children our papa told us the tale of the Bolivars. We are Basque by heritage, the people that inhabit that area between Spain and France, and thus are descendants of Atlantis. In fact, the latest theory is that the white goddess and god were also Basque, can you believe? Apparently, centuries ago, the aliens taught certain groups of people advanced mathematics and astronomy. You have heard about the power of priests?"

"Yes, I've been to several pyramids. The priests were very advanced, on par with the Egyptians." I couldn't forget the tomblike silence in the temple at Coba and the eerie feeling I'd had. Spirits of the past imparting their knowledge. But karate had taught me something valuable about knowledge. Wisdom should be the ultimate goal. Through my own journey, I realized that focus was the key element to success. And right now it was on finding the killer.

Carmelita gazed thoughtfully at the ceiling. "They were wise. The Atlanteans taught them well." She picked up the color photograph again and stared. "It is said that the Basques have prominent noses and light eyes." She turned the picture towards me. "Look carefully. See how we all have those noses and eyes? Amancio even had red highlights just like the Atlanteans."

"Interesting. Someone else just told me about the Basques and Atlantis."

"Oh, who?" She arched a brow. "I suppose Diego told you we were destined to rule the world?"

"No, it wasn't Diego. When Wolf couldn't go on the dive, I hired an instructor for myself. After we found Brock, I went to pieces." I thought back to the cantina. It had taken two beer to ease the trembling in my hands. "He saw how upset I was and took me to a cantina. While we were there, he told me about how he was Basque."

"Really? That is odd. I think I know everyone on this island and have never heard of another Basque family."

"He's a dive instructor, Carmelita. They're practically nomadic, diving the Red Sea, the Great Barrier, the Philippines, you name it. Cozumel is a temporary stop."

"Divers are all hippies. Probably he smoked too much of the funny cigarettes."

"Maybe, but he seems really level-headed to me."

"Oh? What's this man's name?"

"Cy Nemesis."

Carmelita grinned. "You can't be serious! That diver is not only a Greek, but a liar. Although one could give him credit for a unique pick up technique. The man tells women he's an Atlantean. For some women, that would be a turn on."

I emptied my glass and set it down on the table. "He seems nice."

My friend's ears perked right up. "I detect an interest. Is he sexy?"

"I'm not sure."

"What? Why not?"

"He's all beard and hair. Who can tell what he looks like underneath?"

"Nice buns?"

I felt color rise to my cheeks.

"*Dios mio*. Poor Adelina. Two lovesick men are not enough?" Carmelita twisted a tendril of silky brown hair. "But, perhaps you are on to something."

"What?"

Carmelita grinned mischievously. "A harem. Every woman needs one. That way when one man goes off, there are always others, correct?"

****

Salsa. The heavy downbeats found only in Cuban clubs. Knowing Diego, this band was authentic. He probably had them flown in solely for this performance. A kaleidoscope switched into a whirling collage like an expressionist painting. Under the lanterns, dancers shimmied around the sparkling blue water of the freeform pool, arms swinging and bodies twirling to the cadence of drums and sax.

As I searched for a costumed man resembling Wolf, Carmelita whispered in my ear. "Look over there. It's Fede."

The matador was dancing with a slender brunette. Garbed in a metallic body suit and feathered tail, she lunged forward into his arms before he spun her around. They danced with elaborate gestures, like serious contenders for *Dancing with the Stars*.

"Who is she?"

"I'm not sure, especially with that mask. By the way, you should put yours on now," Carmelita said, pulling a feathered mask over her face.

Tiny sequins resembling fish scales adorned the elaborate mask perched on my head. Careful not to ruin the delicate item, I eased it over my eyes and rearranged my hair. The lights had dimmed and our figures cast shadows on the marble. Everyone around us was in costume. The tour group should have been in that area, all of them masked. There was something creepy about a costume party and not recognizing anyone in the mass of bodies.

Near the deep end of the pool, a tall blonde in a tight pink dress stood talking to a man. My gut told me I knew her. "There's someone I need to see."

"Good. I didn't want to leave you but if you have to speak with someone, go ahead. I'll catch up with you later." She shoved the mask off her eyes and let it perch on her crown. "I have to find out who that woman dancing with Fede is," she said tersely.

From the set of her jaw, I could see that Carmelita was not so cool about this situation. The Bolivar Alvarez temperament unleashed could be hurricane destructive. She might need a buffer. "You want me to come?"

"No," Carmelita said abruptly. "Don't worry about it. I'll deal with this. You have fun."

Marching through the throngs of dancers didn't seem to be any problem for Carmelita. The look in her eyes was enough for them to give way. From where I was standing, I followed her approach. A break in the crowd gave me a view of a slim brunette in Fede's arms. The merengue was a dance opportunity for full body contact and they had it nailed from every possible angle.

As the song ended, the woman sank dramatically to the floor, but at the last beat the matador jerked her up into his arms again. Fede might be a sleaze but he sure knew his moves. Watching the woman, I was admittedly a little jealous. From my standpoint I was no slouch when it came to heels, having done everything from running on ice, plowing through flooded streets and some sound on-the-mark karate kicks in them when I needed to, but this woman was a scientific wonder. How she steadily completed double spins and twists balanced on five inch stilettos defied the laws of psychics.

Maybe I shouldn't have left Carmelita up to her own devices but I had to check out the flashy blonde. They say the first twenty-four hours are prime when it comes to a murder investigation. After that, the trail becomes stale. Since the tour group members were all here, it was my big chance to dig up clues.

With some maneuvering I closed in on the blonde. She had the height advantage over her partner, even without the platform shoes. Decked out in a gladiator costume, I didn't recognize Larry T, at first, yet there was no mistaking that square head with the military buzz cut. Had he decided Mary Battrock was a lost cause and gone for the statuesque blonde? The man might be obnoxious but he had street smarts. Someone like him could have made sure Brock never surfaced.

8

"Whaddya know!" the firefighter boomed. "It's Adie under that li'l mask."

"Hi, Larry T." I smiled brightly. "Who's your friend?"

"Wahs urname, sweet cheeks?" The bulldozer patted the blonde's behind. "Wowee! That's one solid caboose. Gotta feelin' your train could chugga chugga all night long."

The prom queen-wannabe firmly pushed the fleshy hand away. "It's been fun, hun, but this choo-choo is leaving the station." With one heavily fringed eye loaded with shimmering blue shadow, she winked at me. "See, over there?" Long fuchsia-tipped fingers indicated the bar. "Isn't that your girlfriend with the devil dude?"

Larry squinted.

With her arm, the blonde forced him back, blocking his view. "She's sure having a good time."

Straining away from the blonde, he pushed her aside and tore off in the direction of the bar.

From this distance, I wasn't too sure if the woman in the witch costume really was Mary. Wide hips and a solid body. Could be. And what about the guy? Next to her, the slinky red devil rubbing her back leaned in for a kiss. Might be Daniel. "Is that Mary?"

The blonde glanced at the stocky witch. "Looks a lot like her."

"You lied?"

"It was time to set the dude free. Besides, he could do with a good time, something I'm neither willing nor able to give."

"Mary hates Larry."

"We don't know that for a fact, do we?"

'No, we don't, but you really think she would go for a guy like that?"

"Well-ll."

"The man is smelly, crude and loud."

"Some women like them raunchy," he said, with a toss of his mane. "Who knows, Mary might." Ronny leaned in. "Listen up, Adie. The pursuit is everything. A girl makes it too easy and the dude won't get a thrill when he hits third base." Tipping back his daiquiri, he added, "Your game plan is *perfecto*. Your guy is super loaded. Keep it up and you'll be the queen of Cozumel."

I'd been holding off Diego from the get-go. Not because he didn't turn me on. Any sane woman would feel a rush just looking at the man. It was purely my fascination for the sea god that held me back, but if Ronny was right, I'd already lost Wolf. Darn those hormones! But I couldn't help it. When he flashed those sexy blues, my brain waves straight-lined.

Ronny had given me something to consider. Maybe it wasn't too late to join the rest of the female population and play games. It was either that or lose Wolf Du Lac. "Thanks for the advice." Unconsciously, I tightened the silver and jade bracelet on my arm. Diego had told me jade was for the nobility before presenting me with the unusual jewelry. "I enjoy being with him."

"I sense a *but*."

"Let's just say the jury's out on that one. Now in the case of Larry T and Mary, I think she can't stand him and isn't playing hard to get." Anxiously, my eyes shot over to the bar. If the dust buster was hooking up with another man, she wouldn't like Larry charging in. "I hope she won't go crazy."

"This party is kind of a snooze anyway. A little drama is just what we need." He rubbed his hands together and grinned. "Maybe we'll get to see some action." Ronny peered down at my face. "Say, by the way, how are you doing?"

"I'm good, why?'

"Duh? You found Brock's body today, remember?"

I hesitated. There wasn't any reason to believe Ronny was involved in the murder but he had been on the boat and someone on that dive had killed Brock. I was just assuming it had to do with Bolivar Imports and Exports. What if there was some other reason someone wanted him dead?

"Adie? You okay? What happened with the police?"

"They wanted the whole story about what we'd found. Didn't

they question you?"

"Naw. I didn't see anything anyway." Ronny scratched his head. "It's hard to believe any of this. Especially as there's no body."

"The police believe it'll wash up on shore any day."

Ronny's lips twisted. "Adie, what do you think caused Brock's death?"

"I'm not an expert but my guess was his air supply was cut off."

"You mean someone slashed his reg?" Ronny's face froze. 'Who would do that?"

"It could have been coral."

"I suppose," he scratched his head reflectively before he shot me a look. "But you don't really believe that, do you?"

The band started up. If we were to speak, we had to go over to the ocean side. "Come," I said, taking his hand. "It's too loud over here."

By the time we reached the terrace, Ronny looked anxious. "Well? Do you believe it was coral?"

The ocean between the palm fronds glittered with silvery moonlight.

"It depends."

"On what?"

Did he know more than he was letting on? Adjusting my tiara, I searched Ronny's face. "You were sitting with them, right?"

"Yup. Brock, Larissa and Irmgard. Lucky son of a gun had a pretty lady at each side." He frowned. "Not so lucky, I guess. That was a stupid thing to say. I didn't mean to make light of Brock's death."

"I know." I patted his arm.

"Poor sweet thing was pretty upset."

"Who?"

"Irm."

Irmgard was a sweet thing? It was like calling a barracuda a cute little fish. "When? After the dive?"

He twisted his lips considering. "Before and later."

"How so?"

"Larissa was provoking her. I gathered they both wanted the Brockster and Irm had lucked out."

"So the women were angry with each other?"

"Yah, and Brock wasn't in such a great mood either."

I stared. "Why?"

"Apparently, he'd just found out Larissa had another guy."

"Really. Who?"

Ronny shook his head. "That's as much as I heard. The rest of that conversation," he shrugged, "your guess is as good as mine."

"What do you mean?"

"Larissa got mad and I guess she didn't want anyone knowing her business so she started in on him in Spanish."

"Interesting. Tell me, Ronny, did you see them during the dive?"

"Irm not so much. Larissa, well, she was staying behind taking pictures a lot. I'm not the greatest diver, Adie. I got panicky, afraid of losing Daniel again."

"He wasn't with you?"

"Most of the time he was booting around looking at things. I hung close to Usiel just in case. Say, how did your dive instructor take Brock's death?"

"Okay, I guess. Why do you ask?"

"I got the impression they knew each other. When we were gathering on the dock I heard them talking about your friend."

"What friend?"

"The Armani model."

I must have looked confused.

"Does Diego Bolivar Alvarez ring a bell?" Ronny's eyes narrowed. "Why are you asking these questions anyway? What are you after, Adie?"

Before I had a chance to say more, a shriek broke out over the salsa rhythm.

I almost jumped out of my skin when a husky voice said, "It's about time someone livened up the party. Swinging around, I was surprised to see Diego with a bemused expression on his face. He beckoned a waiter with a wave. "Get the ladies some strawberry daiquiris, *por favor*. Is that agreeable?"

Ronny grinned widely and slightly inclined his head.

"A Don Julio for me and bring us some shrimp. So sorry it took so long, Adelinita. Damn police could have waited until tomorrow." Although our host was a six footer and then some, Ronny in his six inch platforms towered above. Diego tilted his head up. "You must be one of Carmelita's models?"

"No," I said quickly, and added, "but Ronnette is a model in Toronto."

"You don't say." Diego's eyes roamed down Ronny's curves. "I'm Diego Bolivar Alvarez, your host." He took Ronny's hand and dropped a light kiss on his wrist "*Encantado.* Charmed. You look familiar. Have you done any magazine covers?"

A Marilyn Monroe whisper. "No-oo."

"Oh, well, perhaps I'm just imagining that we've met before. Are you having a good time?"

"Very much. Thank you for the invitation."

"You're with Adie's tour group?"

Ronny batted his lashes. "I sure am."

Diego took a step back. "You must meet my sister. Carmelita is a talented designer. In a short while she's made quite the name for herself. Possibly she might have some work for you."

"Oh, wouldn't that be exciting. Imagine living here in Cozumel! I so love the ocean. Adie, could you introduce me to Señor Alvarez's sister?"

"I'm sure she could but it will have to be later," Diego said briskly. "If you don't mind, I need to steal this lovely lady away. But do ask the staff. One of them should know where she is." With the return of the waiter, he smiled. "Quick work, Carlos. You will find your gratuity generous tonight. "Please," he waved his hand to the glasses and took a snifter of tequila from the tray, "set the shrimp here." He indicated a table. Spearing one, he brought it to my lips. "I know how you like chilies. The Mayans say they are aphrodisiacs."

One look into his passionate eyes and I was in no need of any help in that direction. The man was a sex bomb.

"Good?"

"Pleasingly spicy. Delicious."

"Have another one. I don't want you fainting from hunger." He turned to Ron. "Please do try one." Diego eyed Ron's broad shoulders. "You need to keep up your strength too."

The daiquiris were in huge goblets. After the last powerful blast, I hesitated.

"Adelinita, what's wrong?"

"This drink."

"You didn't like the last one?"

I shook my head. "It was fabulous, Diego, but rather strong."

"This coming from the lady that can down a cognac with the best of men? You surprise me. Leon, our bartender prides himself in the creation of outstanding cocktails. At least try it, otherwise he will surely be offended."

"I can do that but as far as finishing it—" I examined the goblet doubtfully, "no, I don't think so." The frozen liquid shot straight to the roof of my mouth.

Diego read my pain. "Are you alright, *mi amor*? You've forgotten how cold they were, hadn't you? Tiny sips remember." He turned to Ronny. "Please enjoy yourself. If you will excuse us?"

"No problem." A finger stroked the heavily coated fuchsia lips. "Time for a trip to the powder room, dearies."

"You'll find one next to the bar," Diego said helpfully. For a second, he watched Ronny sashay through the crowd.

My insecurity surprised me. A drop dead gorgeous man can do that. The body paint couldn't take away from the perfect face. I was a woman who loved hair on a man and he didn't disappoint in that way either. Wavy dark hair fell on a high forehead and over his ears, curling onto his neck.

"Shall we?"

Before I could reply, Diego took my elbow and steered me away. Into my ear, he said in an undertone, "Why are models always so ugly? Gawky young boys in drag look sexier. This one has passable legs but," he grinned, "a face like a horse. Much too tall for a woman." He snickered. "And what a godawful chin."

I giggled. "Not your type, Diego?"

He set his empty glass on a passing waiter's tray. "How's your drink?"

"Wonderful. Not too sweet. Just right."

Diego stroked my cheek. "Like you, *cariño*. Have I told you how stunning you are tonight? More radiant," he gazed up at the sky, "than the brightest star." He bent his head to my shoulder. "Your perfume, ah-hh. Fiery and intoxicating. It must be Eau de Goddess."

I laughed.

Brandy eyes glimmered green in the evening light. "You make me melt." He stooped down and kissed my lips before I could protest. Once I felt them I was caught up in their heat. When he suddenly withdrew, I gazed up to see him smiling. "You feel it too. I think we should rid ourselves of Du Lac and you shall live with me." He pointed. "There. In that house. Forget the condo I gave you. You deserve a palace."

A shout was followed by a splash.

"I'd better see what's happening. Let's have a look." Diego took my hand and we pushed through a crowd which parted for him like the Red Sea. By the time we reached the pool, two dripping wet costumed partiers had climbed up the ladder and were back on firm marble.

"They look like the drowned rats that they are," Carmelita slurred as she came up beside me. "She's not so sexy now, is she?"

Diego smirked. "It might be advisable to cut down on the daiquiris, sweet sister. You are quite dangerous tonight."

By the wide berth the guests gave Carmelita, I gathered he wasn't the only one who thought so.

"That slime and his *puta* got what they deserve. A soaking to cool their jets. You wouldn't want them to have sex on your marble tiles, would you?" Carmelita grinned. "We'd have to bring in the janitorial staff to clean up and that would surely ruin your party."

"Are you alright, Larissa?" Diego inquired solicitously. The organza gown clung to the shapely fairy climbing the pool ladder. He snapped his fingers at a passing server and said, "Bring towels, *por favor*."

"She's drunk," Larissa snapped.

"True," Diego agreed, "but you, *cariño*, do need to keep better company." His eyes flicked to the soaking wet matador behind her. "With so many single men to choose from, why bother with this *cabrón?*"

"You Bolivars are crazy," Carmelita's husband said tersely. "Francisco was the only sane one."

Diego smiled thinly. "You might be right but we're the ones you need to deal with now. If you don't like your rather insignificant job as an executive assistant, you can go back to doing whatever an imbecile like you does best."

"Everything was being handled beautifully and you know it. We were making a profit and now you have me pushing paper clips. Your father would be furious if he knew how his wishes have been ignored." Federico's eyes shot daggers. "I deserve the title of CEO."

"That was then and this is now." Diego yawned. "I'm his son. It's my legacy. Be thankful I pay you a salary." He took my elbow. "Shall we? It is so rare I have an opportunity to be with you."

So Bolivar Imports and Exports was making a profit. Wolf shouldn't be afraid of a loss unless Diego was steering the company in a new direction.

The band had decided to change the pace with a soft romantic ballad. Diego took up my hand and spun me around and back bringing me up close, my hands clasped to his chest. We rocked to the rhythm. It was a love song I'd heard before. An Enrique Iglesias song about a lover's promise to return. The band's lead singer picked up on the passion of two people reuniting. We danced slowly until the last note poignantly ended.

"It is how I feel for you, *mi amor*. Our timing has always been wrong but I am the eternal optimist." Gently, Diego threaded fingers through a lock of my hair. "If you gave me a chance, I would make you the center of my world." His eyes dropped to the jade bracelet on my arm. "You are wearing the gift I gave you. Does that mean you think of me?"

"Every time I see you I enjoy our time together." Those hazel eyes fascinated me the way they changed from green to brown.

Diego sighed. "I know it's still Du Lac. He's the one in your heart?"

"Yes, he is."

"And yet, do you consider the lack of commitment on his part? Don't you want stability?"

"Recently," I said wistfully, "I started to think about it."

Diego kissed me gently on the nape of my neck. "I have to tell you this. I want to be your man. Every day I wake up thinking of your lovely voice, beautiful eyes and the taste of you. I was so happy we could see each other in Toronto. "

A whiff of citron. His cologne sent my pulse fluttering like a finch in a cage. Diego could be sincere. He said all the right things. Carmelita could have pegged him all wrong.

"Listen to me, *mi amor*. I admit there are women but I could give them all up," he snapped his fingers, "for you." Suddenly, Diego straightened, his attention on the dancers.

I swiveled around to see what had distracted him.

Decked out in a stiff taffeta dress splattered with tiny red hearts, the Queen waving a scepter commanded our attention. My stomach somersaulted. It was Wolf's ex.

Samantha schmoozed up to Diego. "Hello, handsome. How are you? Nice costume. Shows off some of your exceptional assets. You do know how to make the other men seem so insignificant."

"Thank you. A compliment indeed coming from such a fetching Queen."

The tip of a pink tongue skimmed her lips. "So sweet of you to say so, Diego." Ignoring my presence, she stroked his biceps. "I've looked but I haven't seen Wolf. I understood him to say to meet him here."

"If he said he was coming I'm sure you shall see him. Du Lac must be delayed."

She was so smug. As if their marriage hadn't ended years ago. I could bet my bottom dollar she had something up her sleeve.

"*Amigos!*" a lilting voice called out. "Guess who I found at the beach? Just as I was about to dive in, this man grabbed me. He insisted I put my clothes on." Carmelita pulled up a very familiar blond man. "Can you believe this guy? He wanted me to get dressed!"

Wolf's simple costume was an eyeful. Bare broad shoulders and chest. A solid six pack ended with a pair of shorts covered with a makeshift scales and tail.

"Neptune?"

"Yeah, like it, princess? Thought it would go with that gauzy thing I got for you."

Carmelita sighed. "How clever of you. A sexy sea god! But, *mi amor*, perhaps you should have worn nothing and then there would be no doubt you were a god. In fact, if there is a judging tonight you could win on your package alone."

Diego frowned. "Carmelita, perhaps it would be best if you went into the house and lay down."

"That would be a treat if Neptune joined me." She giggled. "Oh, sorry, Adelina, I did not mean anything by that."

Wolf's mouth twitched at the corners.

"Thank you, Du Lac. It was kind of you to help," Diego said stiffly. "I doubt if my sister is sober enough to survive a swim in that current." He rolled his eyes. "No doubt there'd be another funeral to attend."

"How can you joke about a funeral, Diego? It was a horrible thing. I miss Papa so much." Carmelita stared at me. "Did you know he was in fine health until the day he died? I can't believe he had a heart attack especially when his last check-up was so excellent." She squeezed her brother's arm. "Isn't that right? No one understood why it happened."

"True." Pain clouded Diego's eyes. "His doctor was puzzled."

"Cheer up, darling," Samantha chirped. "After all, the whole empire is now yours." The queen adjusted her necklace thoughtfully. "Isn't it time for you to seriously consider marriage and make yourself an heir?"

"Somewhat of an enjoyable experience with the right woman," Diego mused, a smile on his lips.

"And who shall you choose to be your consort, my dear brother?"

"So many flowers in the garden," Diego said, his eyes wandering in my direction.

"How about you consider that while Adie and I dance?"

Without waiting for an answer, Wolf took my hand and led me to the dance floor beside the pool.

"That was rather rude."

"If you'd stayed any longer he'd have offered you his bed."

Meeting my eyes, Wolf stopped in midstride. "He already did, didn't he?"

"No, only his house. But more importantly, why does Samantha want to speak with you? What's going on?"

Wolf waved his hand vaguely. "Who knows. She's a whack job. Something about when we were at that shareholders' meeting in Tulum."

"Diego's nudist hotel?"

With my hands in his, Wolf swayed to the salsa beat. If a man could move his hips like that, there was no doubt his skills were extensive. This man was too magnetic for his own good. We had history. That sultry summer at the river. We'd driven off in the boat and stopped at an isolated inlet in the middle of nowhere. I never forgot how his lips tasted. He was always in the back of my mind even when I'd said *yes* to marrying Jay.

When the music switched to a slow rhythm, Wolf held me closer. He was tall but I wore stilettos, which brought his mouth close to mine. Those full sensuous lips were so tempting I almost forgot what I wanted to say.

Wolf didn't. He leaned into my ear. "I got into Brock's computer. There are two offshore bank accounts for Bolivar Exports and Imports. One is Swiss and the other is in the Turks and Caicos. You know what that means."

"Someone is hiding something."

"Most likely." Wolf frowned. "What puzzles me is the Swiss account. The Caymans and Turks could be legitimate offshore accounts. On the other hand, the Swiss have secretive number codes. Finding out who has the accounts will be difficult."

"No names on the Caribbean accounts?"

"No. If Brock found out, it could be there somewhere in a file. There was something else."

"What?"

"The shipment of skulls seems to be very profitable."

"Did Brock mention where the warehouse is?"

"Diego would tell me."

His jaw clenched. "Not a good idea. He would be suspicious," Wolf said tersely. He frowned. "If Alvarez arranged Brock's death, he needs to be behind bars. Two can play this game. I want justice for my buddy."

I clutched his arm in alarm. "What are you saying? I don't want you doing anything to Diego. He's not a killer."

"No?" Wolf raised an eyebrow. "Not personally, maybe, but don't forget he has his henchmen."

"The murderer was on the boat," I said pointedly.

"And could have been hired by Alvarez."

Gritting my teeth, I glared at Wolf. "You're always trying to pin something on him."

"You need to open your blinders. If Brock found something subversive going on, it would point to Alvarez."

"I can't believe that." Pulling away, I said over my shoulder as I stalked off. "I need to talk to someone from the dive,"

Two strides and Wolf caught up to me. "Don't be angry, princess. Be reasonable."

I swung around. "And you think I'm not?" I poked him in the chest. "Maybe I'm hormonal?" Women have PMS if they get emotional. That's how a man saw it. Women were overpowered by their emotions and men were always terribly logical.

"No, of course not," Wolf said steadily. "I'm sorry. I didn't mean that. Go ahead. Talk to some people. But don't drink any more, eh?"

"Why is that? You think I'm drunk?"

Wolf's lips twitched. "Maybe a little."

"So-oo? It's a party."

"Booze can make you careless. It would be better if no one knew why you were asking."

"I can be subtle."

Wolf grinned widely.

Near the bar, I spotted a slender blonde in a gypsy outfit. Beside her, the skinny red devil was looking friendly. With another last glance at the man who could have made the cover of Men's

Health, I said, "Bye, Neptune. Thanks for the dance."

"Babe, wait. Did you bring your cell?"

I gave him a suspicious glance. "Why?"

"When you're finished, let's do something."

Wolf's eyes sparkled. "I'll text in about half an hour?"

It was downright evil the way he made my body respond. A man shouldn't have that kind of power over a woman. "Sure," I muttered.

9

In the midst of a throng of partiers, Irmgard sat slumped on a bar stool staring at her hands.

"Hey."

Haunted blue eyes flicked up. "Why, Adie? Why?" she muttered.

I shook my head.

"Honestly, I can't understand this. Brock was an angel." Tears welled up in her eyes.

"I know." I patted her arm. "He was a really nice guy. But at least you two had a night together."

"We did." A trace of a smile appeared. "Larissa thought Brock was hers, but she was wrong."

"They argued, didn't they?"

"He didn't want Larissa anymore," she said tightly. "I was his girlfriend, not her."

"She was seeing another man?"

Irmgard nodded. "The woman was a slut. She had no loyalty. Brock told her off."

"He was into you."

"Yup." Her eyes narrowed. "You don't believe that, do you? Well, let me tell you something, Adie Sturm. I have morals and Brock admired that. After the dive we were planning to go out for dinner at the Casa. It's a romantic place just for lovers." She wiped a tear from her cheek.

Elbowing Humpty Dumpty aside, a red devil planted himself firmly between us. In the light, his eyes gleamed yellow. "Take it easy, Irm. Don't upset yourself," the devil interjected gruffly. "We were just getting past that, remember? The man's gone and ain't comin' back no more."

Irmgard straightened up and glared. "What's wrong with you, Daniel? You think I'd forget someone like Brock," she snapped her fingers, "just like that? He made me feel like the only woman in the world. No man has ever done that." She tossed back a shot of tequila. "And now he's dead."

"Come on, hun, you're taking this way too hard. Things go wrong on a dive. We don't have control over everything. Listen, why don't we go back to the hotel and I'll help you relax."

Lost in a cloud of grief, Irmgard didn't answer.

"Look what you've done, Adie," Daniel growled. "Can't you see you're makin' it worse? I had her all calm and accepting an hour ago." As I opened my mouth to protest, he made a stop gesture. "No, let me handle this. Darlin'." Helping Irmgard up, he kept her steady as she swayed on the five inch heels. "You've had enough to drink." Grabbing the shot glass, he set it firmly on the counter. "Come on, Irm, we're goin' back to the hotel. Night, Adie." Daniel steered the woman away before I could say, *Hasta la vista.*

I had my own share of guilt. Brock wasn't the saint Irmgard made him out to be but he didn't deserve a horrible death either. I had to find the murderer and time was a-ticking.

With the daiquiris starting to run through me, I glanced at the mansion and came up with a plan. The cobblestone walkway beside the bar led to the side door of the villa. Guests were meant to use the pool house washroom but I was a personal friend so if anyone could take the liberty of entering the house, it would be me.

At the entrance, I tried to remember where the bathroom was but nothing came to mind. The dimly lit hallway was clear. If I moved fast, I could sneak into the den. On tiptoes, I edged into the room where we had sat earlier.

The photo of the Bolivars was still on the table. From the gold mini purse I had clipped on my waistband I dug out my cell and snapped a picture of the photo.

"*Por favor,* Señorita Sturm. You are looking for something?" a hoarse voice murmured from behind as I straightened up.

I nearly jumped out of my skin. Swiveling about, I saw a

massive giant of a man with an impassive face blocking the doorway. Up close, the bodyguard was downright scary. *"Baño?"* I squeaked.

"It is the next door on the right. Let me take you there." Gripping my elbow, he steered me firmly out of the den directly to the washroom.

As he opened the door for me, he informed me stiffly, "I will tell Señor Alvarez you are here in the house. He has been anxious to speak with you."

When I finished, hoping to avoid Diego, I rushed out into the hall, but from behind warm hands pulled me into a strong hard body. The faint scent of citron perked my senses. A husky voice whispered in my ear. "No, you must not go. Not just yet."

When I saw the muscular arms covered in black paint I knew exactly which hottie this was. The soft press of a kiss on my neck made me momentarily forget the growing suspicion that Diego had something to do with Brock's death. As I turned to the alluring Mayan god, I prayed I was wrong.

Those lips knew how to melt a mountain of chocolate with their heat. They moved over mine and even though I tried to resist, I couldn't help but wonder if I was waiting for a man who took me for granted. Wolf would never say he loved me.

After all, he had been in that situation once before. Maybe that had been enough for him. On the other hand, I had yet to be with a man who could commit to me.

Diego laughed. "Holding back still, aren't you, *cariño*, but you are more interested than you admit." He reached over to the vase on the hallway table. "A rose for my beautiful friend."

Twice in one night? Maybe he did have a thing for me. "Thank you," I said, taking a whiff of the spicy scent.

"Give me some time tomorrow, Adelinita. I'll drive you around and show you some of my holdings on Cozumel. We can have lunch at one of the east coast restaurants. What do you say?"

"I have to work tomorrow evening."

"You will be back in plenty of time."

My cell bleeped. It had to be Wolf. "I have to go."

Diego took my hand and gently kissed my wrist. "Say you

will."

I don't know if it was the daiquiris or the touch of his lips, but I convinced myself this was the right move, a chance to investigate I couldn't very well refuse. "Alright. Will you pick me up?"

"Ten thirty on the dot. I shall wait for you in the driveway of your hotel. La Vida?"

I nodded. "Thank you for the party invitations. The tour group really needed something fun after what happened."

"Anything that pleases you, *mi amor*."

"All of us were upset about Brock."

Diego nodded. "The police have found the body."

"Really? Where?"

"It washed up on the south end of the island a couple of hours ago."

"And it's him, for sure?"

"I think they wanted you to identify him but I told them Larissa would. They'll contact any relatives."

"Why did they come to you, Diego?"

"Laval worked for Exports in the Toronto office. Last night, he told me he was interested in seeing our Cozumel operation but in reality he was an investigator according to Hernandez."

"Did you tell him anything?"

Diego smiled thinly. "No, nothing. Shall I drive you back or will you stay for a bit yet?"

"I'll take over from here, Alvarez." Wolf had entered the hallway as silently as a ninja.

I experienced a twinge of guilt. From the thin line of his mouth, I knew he was not pleased. "We were just…"

"Sure." He caught up the hand that had so recently been the recipient of Diego's kiss. "Let's go."

But the skirmish wasn't over quite yet. Diego had to get a dig in. "Did you get a chance to speak to your lovely ex?"

"I'm sure it will keep."

"I had the impression it was serious, Du Lac."

Wolf grinned. "She would make it seem so. The woman is a drama queen." He shrugged. "Samantha can wait. The night is yet young and I am taking Adie for a special treat. So thanks for the invite, Alvarez. Have a great night." That was said with a smile but I think it was Wolf's jab.

Diego was Mr. Cool. "I shall, but there is good reason to believe my tomorrow will be even more sensational. *Buenas noches, amigos.*"

****

The coastal road was relatively clear of traffic. We drove past the Playa Azul and headed south. Near the museum, we made a left, passed the shops and slowed down. The wrought iron gates beside a large house had been left open. From somewhere nearby a dog barked as we got out.

"What is this place?"

"A buddy's house. He lets me park here. It's a short walk. You okay in those shoes?"

The metallic stilettos might be a challenge on cobblestone. "If you hold on to me, I'll be fine but Wolf—"

"What?"

"If we walk into town won't they think we look a little strange?"

"Nope. It's *Carnaval*. The costume judging is starting tonight in the square. I doubt if anyone would think we look odd."

"We're going to the square?"

"No. Not that far."

With the night steamy and unusually warm for February, it was a perfect evening for a stroll with a handsome sea god. Linking arms, we started a slow trek towards the city center.

They'd renovated the narrow sidewalk since my last trip. Those random iron loops sticking out of the cement were gone and smooth brown cobblestone had replaced the pedestrian hazard. A store keeper nodded as we approached.

"Where *are* we going?"

"My little cat is very curious tonight."

It was true he had piqued my curiosity with the mention of a treat. I had visions of chocolate cake or would it be something equally delicious more to do with that vivid imagination of his? I nudged him. "So-oo, what's the treat?"

"You'll love this place."

"Spill the beans, Du Lac."

Suddenly, Wolf bent down and kissed me.

That impulsive, passionate touch of his mouth left me breathless, buzzing with anticipation.

A smile warmed his lips. "You think I want to ruin your surprise?"

"No, you love keeping secrets."

Wolf shot me a look. "You really think that?"

I nodded.

"You think I'm holding something back? I've told you about Bolivar Exports or as much as I could find out. As far as the company is concerned, I'm not worried about losing my investment. The books show a profit. Skulls might be an odd export but the demand for occult paraphernalia has increased."

"And the bank accounts?"

"They can be legit. A lot of companies have offshore accounts."

As we passed a gift shop, I caught our reflections, Wolf frowning. "There probably is something illegal going on but with Brock dead it might be wise to let it go, Adie. If you continue to investigate Brock's murder, it would be a mistake."

"Really, why would you say that?"

Wolf shrugged. "Alvarez is involved. It's like looking under a log. Don't be surprised at what's there. Remember, Eduardo, Alvarez's hit man?"

"Okay, but why murder Brock?"

"Alvarez doesn't want anyone snooping into his business." Wolf brought his arm around my shoulders and squeezed me lightly. "Let's not talk about it anymore. I want us to be happy tonight."

Ahead we saw the bright lights of a restaurant. As we came closer, I saw the name *Wet Wendy's* above a circular bar.

"I think you'll like it. Great drinks and food."

"Cool place," I said, taking in the laughter, music, and busy tables piled with food.

With the tables occupied, we took a spot at the bar. The high stools were a climb but the sea god helped me up. The band was playing a bluesy tune loud enough to keep me from hearing Wolf's order.

When the vivacious brunette carried over a greenish-blue goblet filled with a brown crushed ice mixture topped with a heaping dose of whipped cream and a cherry, I was blown away. Her grin widened as she set the drink down. "A chocolate margarita."

"It's huge, Wolf. I'm not sure I can drink all this."

"They are delicious." The petite bartender smiled encouragingly. "This one is specially prepared."

Wolf tipped back a Dos Equis, his eyes crinkling at the corners.

"Would you mind splitting it up?" I asked the bartender. "Maybe someone here might want to try it. Don't worry," I added to Wolf, whose brow was furrowed. "There's plenty here."

The bartender loaded up another goblet and set it in front of lady, carefully leaving me the cherry and plenty of whipped cream.

My glass held high, I raised a questioning eyebrow. "What are we drinking to?"

"*Una tostada para amar.*" With an enigmatic smile, Wolf clicked his bottle to my glass.

"What's that? Hm-mm. Let me guess. A toast to love?"

Wolf smiled. "And to Adie, the fairest princess in Cozumel!"

I met his eyes. "And you're my prince?"

"I am. Definitely."

One look at the sea god and I felt an unbelievable heat that didn't cool off with a sip of frozen chocolate margarita. Rich, sinfully delicious nectar swept my taste buds, activating that feel-good force in my brain. "Mm-mm, I'm getting a chocolate buzz."

"Ah-hh, those crazy endorphins. Maybe I need a sip, too. I don't want you to be alone in this."

"Here." As I shoved the goblet over, the tequila hit my stomach like a bullet on impact, exploding to my extremities. If Diego hadn't enticed me to try those jumbo shrimp earlier, I would really be in trouble.

After he tipped the drink back downing a good third, Wolf sat back his lips tilting upwards at the corners. He was up to something.

"I like your treat," I said. "You can never go wrong with chocolate. It has the ability to arouse the pleasure principle."

Wolf stroked my cheek. "My favorite principle."

I stirred the frozen chocolate. "The ancient Mayans believed chocolate gave us wisdom."

"And they're right. Adie Sturm is the wisest woman I know. Imagine what ideas you'll come up with when you've finished."

I glanced down at the little bit left in the glass. "Maybe we should get working on those. How about going to your place?"

"Leave now? What about all that chocolate tequila? You want to waste it?"

"You're sounding suspiciously like Diego. What is it with you guys? Are you trying to get me drunk?"

Wolf threw me a sidelong glance. "You are a bit stressed," he noted.

"With good reason."

"Let it go, princess. Relax." He tilted his head and narrowed his eyes. "Hey! What's that?"

"Where?"

"In your glass."

A dead bug? "Yuk!" I stabbed at the bottom with my straw.

"Take it easy, babe. It's not alive."

I peered in the goblet and saw a glimmer of gold. Now I was really puzzled. "There's something in there."

"That's what I said."

With a spoon, I dipped into the liquid and picked up the object. It was a ring.

10

I was numb. Every step I took made me wonder if I had imagined finding a ring covered with brown slush.

"We're almost there, babe. You have to answer me sometime." Wolf stopped and drew me close. The sparkle in his eyes was like the sunlight skimming a deep fresh water stream. The warmth of his body heat ignited a flame deep inside.

At the corner, after looking both ways and seeing we were alone, he took my face in his hands. "Will you marry me?" he asked in a husky voice.

Words stuck in my throat. "Er-rr."

"Is that a yes or a maybe?" Wolf laughed. "Give me your hand, princess." When I gave him my left hand, he slipped the cleaned up ring on my finger.

I gave it a tug over my knuckle.

Wolf looked worried. "A little tight."

"It's the heat. Swells my fingers."

Under the lamplight, the square-cut emerald surrounded by diamonds caught the lights from the patio of a nearby residence and shimmered magically. "It's lovely."

"Like you, princess."

"I'm sorry if I'm acting strange, Wolf, but this is a little sudden. I didn't know you were even thinking of marriage."

"I wasn't, but hear me out?"

I nodded.

"We've known each other since we were teens. Our parents were friends and you would've thought they wanted us to be together but…"

"Your mother and my father hated the idea."

"But there was an undeniable chemistry even then, right?'

Gazing up at him, I thought how true that was.

"Two years ago Sam and I split up. She was never right for me. When you came back into my life a year ago it was like fate.

No matter what obstacles came between us, we overcame them. No games."

"True. We survived a lot of dangerous situations," I said seriously. "You always had my back."

"And now I want you in my life." Wolf stroked my cheek. "If you can't answer me tonight, think about it. Keep the ring on and remember how good we are together."

"Alright." I met his eyes. "But I have questions. You've always had women. How do you know I'm 'the one'?"

"We're like magnets. It's impossible to pull us apart."

I grinned. "That's sex."

He shook his head. "We make love, babe. I understand what makes you tick and you know me like no one else. It's never been just sex with us."

"So you're saying you love me?"

Wolf flashed a smile. "You're in my heart. Every morning I wake up and picture your face."

"With or without mascara?"

"Mascara is the only thing you're wearing."

"Oh-hh." There was no denying he was a man of passion. I liked that. But there was more. Besides the fact that he made me laugh, he was genuine. Nothing fake about this guy. Yet this was the first time he'd told me about his feelings. This proposal would take some time getting used to.

"When you're in Canada I go on with my life but a little piece is always missing." He squeezed my hands. "You told me once you wanted children." He grinned. "You might need a partner."

A while ago I had seriously considered marriage in my future. I was closing in on thirty and my life centered around travel. It was an exciting but lonely life. Not that I wanted to give up my job but it would be nice to have a permanent man in my life. A couple of years back I was sure Jay was "the one" but I'd been dead wrong about him. The question was, did I know who was right for me? Was I wise enough now to make that decision?

"How could we manage a marriage with you living in Cozumel and me living in Canada?"

"We don't have to know all the answers now." Wolf took my

hand and we headed down Calle 4."

At the corner was a cantina, the latest addition to Wolf's complex. *Cerrado,* it said on the sign. No noise if it was closed.

With cottages accommodating families, he had meant the resort to be a home away from home. A stone wall about six feet high started at the edge of the cantina and continued for forty feet before a wrought iron gate came in sight.

Wolf pulled out a large key and unfastened the lock. He held the gate open for me to enter. Down a stone path and around an in-ground pool, he guided me to his house. On the other side of the property, a distance away, a few buildings had lights on.

"Renters?"

"A family from Mexico City, grandparents, their four sons and grandchildren. But don't worry. They keep to themselves."

"And that's it?"

"A dive couple is in the cottage facing Calle 6."

Past a lime tree, I spotted the front door of Wolf's cottage. It was an unpretentious yellow building with a red tile roof. Inside it had been renovated but the exterior was the original Spanish style.

The night was humid and still yet, from above, the trees rustled.

"What's that?"

Wolf gazed at the lime tree without answering. A shadowy beast larger than a squirrel leaped over a branch. Dark eyes glowered in the night. It hissed a warning.

I froze. "A coati?" They were similar to raccoons. Cute faces but the razor sharp fangs and unpredictable behavior had me looking for a branch for protection.

Wolf put an arm around me. "The little guy's harmless, Adie. He's almost tame. The housekeeper feeds him."

"But not you?"

"Seriously, don't worry. He won't do anything."

"And if he does?"

"I'll do the princely thing."

"Like?"

Looking around, he spotted a garden tool leaning against the wall by the door. "Crush the beast."

I pulled back. "Oo-oo, that's awful."

"Alright how would you deal with it, karate woman?"

"A quick tap on the snout."

"With the hoe or a finger?"

A jab into his chest. "Stop teasing me."

Wolf retracted grinning. "But you are so much fun to tease."

"You're lucky I—"

Full lips lowered to mine, moving slowly. A burning heat set me on fire. Like an alien invasion, my hormones took over my brain. Every part of me tingled.

"You love me?"

Wolf's question caught me off guard. I didn't have an answer.

"Never mind." Wolf took my hand and led me to his cottage. At the door, the sea god swung it open and pulled me into the darkness. Moonlight filtered through the shutters into the living room. Shadowy shapes of furniture. From the back, a light illuminated the hallway.

Shutting the door gently, Wolf pressed me against it. His body was warm. I let my hand wander up, threading thick soft clean hair. I grasped a handful before I pushed his head lower. Like in a dream, everything around us went hazy with the kisses that started at my neck and lingered at the valley between my breasts.

Just as my body went wild, he brought my hand down and whispered, "Look what you've done."

"The poor thing is hard as a rock! Oh-hh, how awful for you."

"Cruel woman," he murmured as his hand slid over a breast, fingertips circling the nipple jutting through the fabric. On my shoulder, his kisses worked an undeniable magic. Electricity shot through me.

I unfastened the button on his shorts and yanked them over his hips. Sliding my hands over the smooth skin, I caressed the hard curve of his cheeks before pushing them down.

In the dim light, Wolf's eyes sparked with fire. He gripped the zipper at the back of my costume and forcefully tugged it until the flimsy material fell to the floor. I stood before him in lacy undergarments. In one sweep, he lifted me up and carried me down the hallway like a fairytale princess.

The bedroom was dark aside from the flickering candles on the bedside table. Crisp cotton pillow cases doubled up on the head of the king-sized oak bed and the plain white sheets were turned back.

Gently, he set me on the covers and joined me. "This is how every day will end, babe," he murmured softly.

"Come here, big guy." I drew him near. Relaxing against the pillows, eyes closed, the warmth of his body made me want him like a kid in a candy store. "I could get used to this."

"I wouldn't if I were you," a sulky voice said from the armchair.

Bed bugs creep out under the cover of night. Samantha was no exception.

"Don't look so surprised. Who do you think lit the candles, folks?" She stared at Wolf. "The idea was you and me and lots of lovin', Mr. Big Guy. You should have left Aggie back at the party."

"What the hell are you doing here, Sam?" Wolf sprang up, grabbed a terry robe from the rattan chair and threw it on.

"No need to cover up." She yawned. "I've seen it all before."

I switched on the light. The viper was wearing a red corset and matching panties, fish net stockings and sky high heels.

"Got a light, handsome?" Samantha waved a cigarette.

Wolf frowned. "Put your clothes on, Sam. I'll call you a cab." He headed to the hallway.

"I'm not leaving until you've heard the good news."

Wolf stopped in his tracks and swung around. "Alright. I'll bite. Tell me and get out."

Crossing long legs, she smirked. "Are you sure you want your girlfriend to hear?"

I stood. "If it's personal I can leave you two alone. You stay," I said, touching Wolf's arm. "We can talk tomorrow."

"No, Adie, don't go."

Samantha laughed. "Let her, daddy. My baby news might be upsetting."

This time I froze.

"Surprised? Yup, you guessed it, Aggie dear." She patted her stomach. "Wolf is finally a father and guess who the mama is?"

****

In a cab heading down Avenida Raphael Melgar, I sunk back trying to make sense of it. The shareholders' meeting in Tulum. Both Wolf and his ex had been there according to Samantha and had apparently done more than discuss equities.

Her words kept ringing in my ears. DNA. They had slept together and Sam had proof. Nothing could change that. There was no way we would ever be together now. It was over.

I was in too much shock to cry. I stared listlessly out the window as we neared an orange building. On the ground floor facing the street, the light inside Moray's Eel was still on.

"Wait. Stop here." I couldn't go back to an empty hotel room. Not just yet. There might be a friendly face in there and if not, a drink to kill the pain. After handing the driver a couple of bills, I stepped inside.

The bar was quiet. The leather couches at the entrance were unoccupied. I walked further. Near the back, the billiard tables were set up for a game. A half empty glass of beer had been left on the counter of the bar yet there were no patrons or bartender. Puzzled, I perched myself on a stool.

This was when I saw a slender brunette with long wavy tresses kneeling, hunched over the fridge. It looked like Larissa but I couldn't see her face. "*Hola,*" I called out.

When the bartender didn't answer, I grew concerned. I slipped back off the seat, and edged around the bar. "Larissa?" With no response from the woman, I touched her arm. "Are you alright?"

She slumped forward. Grabbing her by the shoulders, I swung her towards me. From under long curly lashes, the chestnut-brown eyes stared blindly. A chalky white had replaced the tan glow of her once radiant complexion. From the corner of perfectly glossed lips, blood had trickled down her cheek and dried.

I was having trouble realizing what I was seeing. My gaze swept to the spandex top, no longer a fresh ivory white. Blood as dark as a rich cab merlot permeated the thin material clinging to her breasts. Even the jeans were blotched. Blood had run off and pooled in a puddle under her body. A knife was firmly lodged in her chest.

I covered my mouth and gulped. Released from my grasp, Larissa slumped to the floor. In a panic I looked around. No one in sight.

If the murderer was inside, he could be hiding in the store room. I unclipped the glittery clutch from my waist and jerked out my cell.

Scrolling through the text messages, I found the contact and clicked the icon.

"*Bueno*," a man's voice drawled.

"Diego. It's me, Adie," I whispered. "I need your help. Something has happened."

"What is it, Adelina?"

I forced the words out. "Larissa is dead."

Diego's voice was composed. "How?"

"She's been stabbed." My eyes shot down to the blood on my wrist where it had brushed Larissa's tank top.

"Are you alright?"

I stared at the bright red spot. "Yes."

"Where are you?"

"Moray's Eel.

"Have you touched anything?"

I glanced at the counter. "Maybe."

"It would be best if you weren't there when the police arrive." Diego paused before he continued. "Listen to me, *mi amor*. Take the side door out. Walk to the Chedraui and catch a taxi there. Can you do that?"

I gazed down at my feet, swollen from the humidity. The gold straps squeezed my toes uncomfortably. A dark red smeared the sandals.

"Adelina? Do what I say." His voice had an edge. "It's important no one sees you leave Moray's Eel. Understand? And don't worry. I shall take care of the situation."

"Okay, thank you, Diego. Could you call me? I'll be up."

A pause. "I'll try. Remember our plan for tomorrow. Get a

good night's sleep. One more thing—"

"Yes?" I said, staring at Larissa's flowing hair brushing the ceramic floor. She had been so beautiful.

"Did you kill her?"

The cell slipped in my hand. I gripped it before it fell and brought it back up to my mouth. "What? Why would you think that?"

"I had to know. Now go quickly, my love. Everything will be taken care of."

When the phone went silent, I tossed it back into my purse and took out a tissue to wipe the back of the bar stool before I headed past the billiard tables to the corridor. This hallway connected to another area of the bar with an outside door. It was latched. With the tissue, I opened the door to cautiously peek out. A car passed on the street and then a scooter. I waited for an empty street and seeing nothing, ventured out.

Creeping close against the wall, I slowly made my way to the road. It was dark and deserted. Without incident, I crossed over to the Mega parking lot where a few cars were parked.

Sweat coated my brow. I took a deep breath, slowly letting the air out of my body in an attempt to relieve the terror of seeing yet another body. But it didn't work.

A nightmare in the dark. Every building blurred as bloody images of Larissa surfaced before my eyes. On the uneven sidewalk, I stumbled on my high heels. As the rain lightly sprinkled, I scurried faster, wanting the safety of my hotel room more than ever. When the Chedraui Center came in sight, I raised my hand and flagged down a cab.

A short silent ride and I was back at the La Vida lobby. Avoiding the elevator, I trekked up the stairs and to my room. After I'd slipped off the gauzy costume, a tissue wet with soap took care of the blood stains on the metallic sandals.

Every muscle relaxed under the hot spray of the shower. But my brain wouldn't let up. Images of Larissa flashed before my eyes. I had just placed the hair dryer back into the wall slot when I heard the vibration of the cell. The text icon flashed a message.

It's not true. U need to believe me. Sam is lying. I'll take her to a doctor tomorrow. W

There was nothing I wanted to believe more but Samantha wasn't stupid. She wouldn't play the pregnancy card unless she could prove it. I glanced down at my ring. The overhead light reflected brilliant green sparkles from the emerald. Diamonds surrounded it like a halo. It was beautiful. But tonight, death's song was louder than love.

Before I could decide whether to wear the ring, my cell rang. I glanced at the caller ID, climbed into bed and settled in. "Hello?"

"It's all taken care of, Adelina. I had Luis call the police."

"From Moray's Eel?"

"Yes, he discovered the body. I thought that would work."

Diego's words caught me unawares. Larissa was really dead…a lifeless body. Not many hours earlier, Larissa had danced, her movements exquisite. "Ten thirty, I'll pick you up. Wear your bathing suit, okay?"

"Mm-mm. I don't know, Diego."

"You'd rather stress?"

"No, it's not that. So much happened today."

"Adelina, go to bed. Have a good night's sleep and tomorrow I shall help you forget everything."

"Alright, Diego. I really appreciate it."

"Kisses," he said softly.

I ended the call, set the cell down on the end table and opened a pill box. With water to wash it down, I swallowed a tiny blue tablet. It would take a few minutes for the sleeping pill to work. A dreamless night was all I wanted but as I closed my eyes, the memories wouldn't quit. Irmgard furious with Larissa, Carmelita pushing through the crowd, Diego's words to Fede.

From the drawer of the bedside table, I dug out Brock's cell. Luckily, I had charged it. When I pressed on the text icon, three messages appeared.

Tonight xoxo Irmgard

What have you found out? L

Meet me in the square. We have something to discuss. This one had been sent to a number. I copied the number on the hotel notepad and stuck it into my wallet. The last one from Brock to

Carmelita.

Come back to Toronto with me, darling. You don't need him.

B

Blood or money. Sure, it was old school, but it worked. Passion, love, hate. Brock played the ladies. Out of jealousy one of them gets angry and kills him. Or did I have it all wrong? Was Larissa working with Brock and the murderer caught on? In that case, the motive was money. Bolivar Imports and Exports. Oh, yes, money drives people to do inconceivable evil.

11

Bright and early. Two words that didn't belong together. It was a warm sunny morning in Cozumel and I was leaning against the hotel wall waiting for my ride—asleep, eyes wide open. Too dozy to get myself in gear in time for the hotel's buffet breakfast, my stomach rumbled a complaint. I had managed to haphazardly pack a beach bag and as a fashion forward tour agent, had donned a white romper, metallic sandals and aviator sunglasses. I was outwardly ready for an island expedition. Inwardly, I felt like digging a hole and climbing in. But there was no use running.

Chutzpah. Granny said I had lots. Saucy, cheeky or downright presumptuous. I could be any of those but today it took all of them for me to make it. As in Tai Chi, I inhaled, lifting my arms. When I exhaled, I brought them down, letting go of the negative energy. I was ready. Waves to my shoulders and a face glowing with a hint of blush, there was no sign of the broken heart inside. If I was barely hanging on, no one would ever guess.

In front of me, Volkswagen Beetles dotted the parking lot like bright flowers amongst the black Jeeps. Neither of these would have been a Bolivar Alvarez choice. Last I'd heard, Diego had four cars—a Porsche Boxster, a Ferrari, a Mercedes, and of course the Rolls. The story was he enjoyed a spin in a sports car but seldom got around to it. Usually, Churo or the little chauffeur drove the Rolls while Diego relaxed in the back seat.

I heard the roar first. A Ferrari convertible shot around the bend and screeched to a halt a couple of meters away. In jeans and a white cotton shirt, Diego jumped out of the car and flung open the passenger door.

"Wow." I stared at the fire engine red roadster.

"Ferrari 458 Spider. Like it?"

Built for speed. A prince amongst cars. "Amazing!" I was

referring to more than the car. I'd caught a glimpse of a firmly rounded tush before I slipped down into a plush leather seat.

"We'll a have fine day, Adelina."

If anything would make me forget the horror of last night, a day with Diego would. I placed the beach bag at my feet and couldn't help but stare at the high tech steering wheel with road condition options and launch button. As an owner of a VW, none of this was familiar. I was a touch envious. Money had its advantages. Seat belt pulled taut, I buckled in. If I knew anything about Diego, this ride would be fast and furious.

The break released and the clutch engaged. Diego hit the gas. The motor snarled like an angry MGM lion and the Ferrari zoomed out into the street. It was an adrenaline rush. The wind tossed my hair every which way as the sports car picked up speed heading out towards the cruise ship dock. Hotels and bars were a blur. In no time, we tore past the entrance of the Hotel Presidente.

"Where are we going, Diego?" I shouted over the growl of the engine.

"Beach!" he yelled back.

"Luis and Churo?"

"Day off!" He took a hand from the wheel, drew his fingers through a tendril of my hair and flashed me a Hollywood smile. His happiness perked me up. I would try my best to forget Wolf's betrayal.

Down the highway, I half expected to see cloned giants in an armored Jeep appear out of a dust cloud but there was only a rickety truck that rapidly became a speck in the distance.

The police car parked at the road side was smart enough not to interfere with the Ferrari that blitzed by. There was no doubt in my mind every resident of San Miguel knew whose sports car it was.

Around the point, the rear end of the car dug in, zigzagging until it finally gripped the pavement and veered to the left. We were heading up the other side of the island.

On this very same coastline, Wolf had leased us a home on the cliff. My heart pounded as wildly as the surf breaking the shore, remembering our fiery union. But I had to block that out. Hopefully, Diego had no intention of taking me anywhere near that romantic spot.

Thankfully, Diego had his own idea. The Ferrari screeched to a halt into a leveled area alongside the highway. From a compartment, he pulled out a bottle of wine.

"You approve?"

I glanced at the unfamiliar label. "I trust your judgement."

The dark sunglasses hid his expression but his shapely lips curled into a smile. He held out his arm and we trekked up a flight of stairs to the veranda of a restaurant. A wooden sign hung from a beam, dancers etched in blue and the letters *Playa Linda.*

"I think you'll find this place agreeable. It's never very busy." Diego glanced around. "Shall we eat up here or take a table on the beach?"

Though it was nearly noon, only one table was occupied. Sun filtered in through fluffy cottonball clouds and a warm breeze kept the flies at bay. The deck was perched on a rocky cliff. About thirty feet below, the coconut palms swayed with the wind. Three striped blue and white unoccupied umbrella tables sat on the sandy shore. Just beyond those white caps frothed onto the sand. From here it looked like paradise. "Let's sit down there, Diego."

"*Bueno.*" He motioned to the waiter. "Bring the prearranged meal to the beach table. We will need the glasses immediately for the wine."

"Very good, Señor Alvarez." The server inclined his head politely and disappeared into the kitchen.

My cell vibrated. I thought I'd turned it off last night after I returned to the hotel. If it was Wolf I didn't want to read it but it could be something else. "Excuse me, Diego, but I think I should check my cell in case it's someone from my tour group." Not that I really believed any of that. Curiosity was definitely my downfall yet it didn't stop me from doing something self-destructive. I took out the cell.

"Go ahead, *mi amor.* I shall check mine as well."

One of his girlfriends? Not my business. I wasn't the jealous type. Well, not when it came to Diego. Wolf was a different story. I checked the text.

Babe. Sam is pregnant but I swear it's not mine. I L U! W

That hollow feeling in the pit of my stomach came back. If only Samantha wasn't pregnant. But, wait, there was still that little matter of conception and what had led up to them having sex. Sooner or later I'd have to talk to him, but at this point I preferred later.

"Done. Some inane business matter." Diego wrapped an arm around my shoulders. "It feels good to be out here," his eyes spanned the turquoise waters of the Caribbean before he whispered in my ear, "with you."

My glance swept over the mouthwatering man beside me. I wasn't salivating but any moment I could be. No doubt that would be a mistake. I held myself in check and vowed to be logical. Wolf could be right. Diego had so much power he could get away with anything in Cozumel. Even murder.

"Let's sit over there." With one hand around the bottleneck and the other pulling me along to a canopied table, Diego propelled me into a cushioned resin chair. "I know it's a little simplistic..."

I shook my head. "No, don't say that. This is a lovely place," I broke in. "Thank you for bringing me."

"Shall I pour the wine, Señor Alvarez?" the server said from behind us.

"*Si*." He turned to me. "Australian shiraz from the Barossa Valley. I think you'll like the flavors."

I watched as the waiter poured the ink-dark red liquid into two crystal glasses. Probably vintage—more than two hundred dollars a bottle.

"To you, Adelina." Diego lifted his glass. "And many more lunches like this." He chuckled. "Maybe even dinner?"

I grinned. "Anything is possible. *Salud*."

Diego watched intently as I tipped back my wine and let it swirl over my tongue before swallowing. "Well?"

It was his habit to test my palate, which he deemed as exceptionally accurate. "Very smooth. Cherries, blackberries and maybe, is it coffee?" I laughed. "And if you brought it for me, it must have..." I took a tiny sip and perked. "Yes, I detect a touch of chocolate. Mm-mm." I met his eyes. "You've outdone yourself."

Waving his hand in a spiral, Diego bowed his head. "Elixir for a goddess. You deserve the best."

I grinned.

Diego leaned in. "Adelina, every god needs a goddess. I would like," he paused, "to have you in my life."

"What are you saying?"

"When you are near, I feel like I'm under a spell. You have this hypnotic effect on me. Have you considered ending it with Du Lac?"

I glanced at the square cut emerald ring. Green lights sparkled. In the sunlight the gold sprinkled with clear white diamonds glowed a pale pink.

Diego frowned and picked up my hand. "What's this? A gift from Du Lac?"

"An engagement ring."

Abruptly, he dropped my hand. "You are marrying him?"

"No, not exactly."

"Then, why wear it?"

"He asked me last night. It was a complete surprise. I said I needed time," I bit my lip, "to decide."

At this point, the waiter arrived with a tray full of covered plates. With a flourish, he uncovered two enormous dishes piled high with mussels and lobster, as well as rice and beans. A butter pot heated by a tea light was placed in front of me.

"Spanish lobster. There's a hot pepper sauce you might like to try for dipping." Diego's tone was subdued. I think he was taking the engagement news hard. He wasn't the only one. I wasn't at all sure about it either. "The flesh has been removed." He smiled slightly. "Who wants to work to eat?"

With a fork I speared a piece of lobster, submerged it in sizzling butter, and brought it to my lips. After the juicy morsel caressed my tongue, it slid down like a dream. Seafood heaven. "Delicious." I sighed.

"Try it with the sauce. It's got a bite. Did you know chilies are an aphrodisiac?" Diego lapsed into silence as if realizing his mistake. "Pardon me for that remark, Adelina. It will take some getting used to that you are considering an engagement. I don't want to interfere but do you think he really is "the one"?"

For a moment I didn't answer. Last night's surprise visitor haunted me—Samantha on the chair in her flaming-red hooker outfit. Seduction I could handle but I couldn't do anything about the pregnancy. And now it was a reality. If he had slept with her and he was the father, could I deal with that and did I want to? "There are complications." That was putting it mildly. I squirmed uncomfortably with Diego's piercing gaze.

"I am a good listener, *mi amor*."

"After we left your party, he proposed."

"And you said what?"

"I told him I needed to think."

"But?"

Suddenly the hurt whelmed up inside. That phase of Wolf's life should have been history. But it wasn't. Now my glass house was shattered in a million pieces. Tears trickled over my cheeks. Distraught, I picked up a paper napkin and dabbed my eyes.

"What happened, Adelina?"

"Samantha. She was waiting when we arrived. Neither of us knew. It was a nightmare."

Diego brushed a stray strand away from my cheek. "She was there for sex?"

"More. Samantha came to tell Wolf she was pregnant."

"So-oo," Diego said harshly, "the bastard screwed around on you."

"I'm not sure. He said he didn't."

"You believe him?"

I shrugged my shoulders.

"And now what?"

"Another DNA test."

Diego picked up his glass and drank deeply. "Why another?"

"According to the test she had, Wolf is the father but he denies it. He says she's lying."

Leaning back in his chair, hands crossed behind his head, Diego gazed at the ocean.

I sighed.

"Well, let the proof tell the story." He grinned. "But I admit I am a trifle taken aback. Du Lac is a man of experience yet he doesn't use protection?"

"That's why it seems off somehow. Wolf isn't a fool."

"True but remember," Diego lifted my hand to his lips, "Samantha isn't the type any man would throw out of bed. It could have been an act of impulse."

"I get that but how could he go from me to her?"

"Bad taste?" With a small fork he dug out a mussel, dipped it and brought it to my mouth. "Try this. You need to forget about all this turmoil. Let the tension leave you. Look at the sea and breathe in the air. If anything can make you relax, it is this."

Shimmering sunlight flecked the aqua waters of the Caribbean. The Emperor palms on the cliff swayed majestically with the sea breeze. "I suppose you're right."

"I most certainly am. Let's enjoy the meal and the wine and to hell with Du Lac and the drama."

My glass tipped back. I could taste the chocolate finish. Bittersweet, yet intriguing, just like Wolf. "Alright, I won't let it ruin our day."

The surf rushed in and bubbled on the white sand, dark with salty brine. Diego gazed out at the ocean again, lost in thought. "I'm sorry you were hurt. I would like to help you heal your heart."

"Time will give me direction. I can't go back...only forward," I whispered, squeezing his arm.

A powerful breaker crashing against the coral wall jutting out from the far edge of the restaurant's wharf almost drowned out his husky voice. "With me?"

I shook my head. "I can't answer that. But, Diego, we have to talk. There is something else that needs to be discussed."

Diego shoved his plate away. "What?"

"Last night. Did you go over to Moray's Eel?"

Our eyes met before Diego's glance averted. "Why don't we go for a walk? I had them set up a blanket somewhere private," he pointed, "near the bend. It'll be pleasant, don't you think?"

"Okay." My eyes shot to the other side of the bay shaded with palms. "But I need to hear the whole story."

"Of course. And I will tell you in due time." He took my hand.

"Wait." I pulled away. "It's hot. I want to take these things off and just wear my bikini."

Diego grinned. "Mm-mm, I like your thinking. If you don't mind, I'll join you." He unfastened the top button of his shirt. "I think your bag is large enough."

By the time he had zipped open my tote, I had slipped off my things and was eager to watch the show. I perched myself on the stone wall and feasted my eyes on Diego undressing. With his shirt open and jeans unbuckled, the strip tease stopped mid action. Diego regarded me with heavy-lidded eyes.

"What?"

"Your body is lovely."

Suddenly self-conscious, I blushed and looked away. "You flatter me."

"No. A beautiful woman should be adored."

My jaw dropped. Whether I was looking at a pair of Speedos or a designer gitch, I wasn't sure. They were black, that's all I could say, and stretched firmly over a significant package with the words Dolce & Gabbana printed on the waistband. The shirt was next. He peeled it off his shoulders like a stripper on ladies' night. If Cosmopolitan needed a male centerfold with a six pack, Diego would be a perfect choice. In fact, he earned bonus heat for the athletic shoulders and legs.

"Let me carry that." Diego scooped up the beach bag.

"Sure, thanks," I said, impressed. Out of the corner of my eye, I saw the waiters watching us as we walked off. The ferret-faced guy disguised a snort with a cough. I didn't care what he thought; in fact, my respect for Diego had gone up a notch. Here was this macho guy, confident enough to carry a purple tie-dyed tote.

"See over there?" Diego pointed to a red speck on a stretch of beach jetting out into the bay. "That's our blanket."

"Mm-mm. I can't wait." Tugging off my sandals, I tossed them into the bag and took Diego's offered hand. With the salty breeze playing in my hair and heating my skin, it was like a lover's caress. I was feeling much better. It didn't hurt that Diego was a gorgeous man and all mine for the day.

We walked at a leisurely pace, occasionally pausing to examine sea treasures. I picked up a piece of coral washed in with the tide. "Pretty the way it curls." I held it up for Diego.

"Brain coral?"

"It looks more like star coral. See the grooves. I think I'll keep it," I said, tossing it in the bag.

"To remember us together?"

I felt the heat in my cheeks. "Yes, and to remember today. Did I tell you how grateful I was for last night?"

"You did." Diego grinned. "But showing me would be better." He pulled me close, stooping down for a kiss. The soft touch of his mouth left me breathless.

I broke away.

"I'm sorry, *cariño*. No pressure. I want you to enjoy our time."

It was a therapeutic trek on a pristine shore with the sun's heat on our shoulders. The turquoise waves rhythmically rushed in our path. Sinking into the soft sand, the soles of my feet were massaged into happiness.

I suppose I should have felt guilty. Two-timing my fiancé. Had everything gone as planned, I would have been in the cottage right now making love with Wolf. But he had made a mess of that. Or had I?

Guilt weighed me down. My thoughts bounced back and forth like a ping pong ball. Had I been too unavailable, pushing him to her?

This trip was so confusing. Murder and love bubbled like a pot full of spicy gumbo coming to a boil. That was another problem. My overactive hormones. As a wave splashed my calf I visualized Wolf, the magnificent sea god.

Physically strong but also spiritual, a man true to his own beliefs. Intelligence sparkled in eyes as bright as a fresh water stream. And his passion was untamed. I dreamt of those full lips playing over my body, tuning every fiber until I sang out surrendering.

Diego's pressure on my palm broke through my reverie. "Look back, Adelina. We have an entire beach reserved for us."

Playa Linda appeared tiny in the distance. Aside from the isolated restaurant, the shore was deserted.

"So tell me, how did the blanket get there?"

Diego laughed. "Magic, my darling Adelina. My genie was told I had a goddess to please today. She winked and said, *I will make sure she is happy."*

"If only happiness was so easy to find." I sighed. "And why does murder follow me? I think the Mayans may be right."

"About?"

"According to their calendar, my birthday is the day of death. Sometimes I think I am cursed."

"If death follows you, I must be cursed as well. First my brother, then my father. Maybe I'm next."

"Don't say that."

Diego arm encircled my waist. "If anyone is to die it should be Carmelita's worthless husband." He laughed. "And I'll make sure I live if only to claim you from Du Lac."

"I wish I could be so light-hearted about it. This whole thing has been upsetting."

Swinging me around, he stared into to my eyes. "It is hardest to see what is right in front of you. Perhaps it's the intensity. Our perception becomes blurred. When you're confused, it pays to step back and all will become clear. Trust me."

My mind raced over Larissa's murder. A knife in the chest. What was the trail? Blood or money?

I made a mental list of the suspects.

First, there was Irmgard. Jealousy would be her motive but something puzzled me. Even if she was capable of murder, what would be the reasoning behind it if Brock was already dead? Next on my list. Carmelita. She didn't want Larissa near her husband. It was hard to believe my friend could murder anyone but, playing the devil's advocate, I could argue she had the Bolivar Alvarez temper.

Another thing I couldn't ignore were the wounds. A vicious stabbing meant a crime of passion. As far as I could figure, there was only one other person who could have done this.

12

"Relax, Adelina. Stretch out. I'll slather you with lotion. We wouldn't want a painful burn to mar that lovely skin, would we?"

Beneath a row of towering high emperor palms, Diego's minions had set a cooler on top of a fuzzy red blanket where the sun filtered through the fronds dancing in the Caribbean breeze.

"No," I said, drowsy from the wine. "Sunscreen, please."

The creamy liquid gently coated my skin as he lightly stroked my back. "That bikini is very sexy, by the way."

"Thanks." The gentle pressure took the knots out of my shoulders. "And that massage feels heavenly. Do continue."

"Certainly. Anything for you, darling. But I have one question."

"Yes?"

"Wouldn't you feel better without it?"

"Without what?"

Diego leaned over. "Without this binding top." He undid the bow but the Selena's Secret pushup top didn't move, holding each breast up high.

I grabbed the strings and retied it. "Diego," I said, a warning in my voice.

"Yes, Adelina?"

Astonished, I turned my head to see those incredible hazel eyes. "You're joking."

"Yes, but seriously, imagine the touch of the sun on your skin."

I love the sun. "Mm-mm."

"It's legal enough." He shrugged. "Who would care? Surely you went nude in Tulum?"

I grinned over my shoulder. "Not this Canuck."

"It's not a regional thing, Adelina. Everyone does it. The Germans, the French, the Italians go topless or nude."

"Right. Europeans."

"Come on. You're not a provincial narrow-minded peasant. I know you're a worldly uninhibited woman."

I swiveled about. "And how would you know that? Our relationship has never been an intimate one."

"But it should be."

"Hm-mm. Sex," I said dryly, laying down on my stomach.

"No need to be bitter about love, *cariño.* Anyone can make a mistake." Diego spread the lotion on my legs.

Back on the fuzzy blanket, I relaxed, letting those long fingers slide over my skin. "You mean Wolf or do you mean Samantha?" I wondered what his take was.

"Neither. Those two belong together. You, on the other hand, need a man who values your attributes. What I mean to say is you have intelligence, a sense of humor and a rather unpredictable personality. All enticing qualities. I don't think I need to tell you that my pulse races faster whenever you're near."

I knew where this was going. Beside me, Diego's husky voice whispered in my ear. "My house, my heart and my body are all yours." Sweeping my hair away, he softy kissed the nape of my neck. Tingles from top to bottom. I sighed. A man as delicious as chocolate—like my sea god.

There was no denying how Wolf and I connected, even beyond the sexual. He was a mental challenge and had the additional bonus of a quirky sense of humor. A prize. But I wasn't ready. If I could move on it might be with Diego. Reality check. I had to remember why I was here. Brock and Larissa. I had to find the killer.

A warm hand followed the curve of my hip while tender caresses nuzzled my shoulder. Being with this man was like walking on the edge of an active volcano. I had to tread carefully. "Stop, Diego. We need to talk."

Leaning on his elbow, Diego met my gaze. "I drove over with Luis." He frowned. "We found her on the floor."

Blood on her face, ivory tank top and jeans. And a red puddle on the creamy tiles. Was it a crime of passion or had someone wanted it to look that way? If only I hadn't stopped at the bar. What should have been the happiest night of my life had turned out to be a nightmare.

"I think she knew her assailant."

"Why do you say that?"

In profile, staring out to the sea, his face was arrestingly attractive. He spoke deliberately. "There were no signs of a struggle."

Thinking back, I recalled Larissa's hair and perfect makeup. There were no noticeable scratches or bruises. "You're right. She knew him. How else could the killer get that near so easily? There should have been self-defence wounds on her arms."

"Cuts."

I nodded. "The murderer must have said something in order to come so close. Hopefully, the police will find prints and evidence."

Diego took my hand. "I understand what you're feeling. Larissa murdered—brutally. But I'm afraid the police will have their work cut out for them. To protect you, Luis wiped all the countertops and furniture clean. We made sure the knife handle didn't carry any prints either."

"Omigod, Diego. There won't be any evidence!" I shook my head ruefully. "What have I done? I should never have gotten you involved."

Diego gripped my shoulders. "I'm glad you did. Surely you don't want Hernandez on your doorstep? You've been down that road before, remember?"

"Believe me, I'm grateful." When Hernandez questioned me about Brock, he'd been a pit bull. My guess was he'd hang on until I was dead meat. If I reported Larissa's murder, I might as well go directly to jail. That's the way the system worked here. Guilty until proven innocent. "But, Diego, won't the police be suspicious when they can't find prints anywhere?"

"They might but remember, if Luis contacted them, they will think twice before making trouble."

"They're afraid of you."

Diego grinned. "Hernandez knows better than to put his nose where it doesn't belong."

It didn't seem right that by some fluke, a killer got away with murder. First Brock and now Larissa. "I suppose the police will contact the people she is closest to."

"Her family is in Acapulco."

"Parents or children?"

"I think she was divorced but I'm not sure about children. It's possible. I really don't know."

I stared at Diego. "She had a lover."

"Fede?" Diego laughed. "He may have been, but do you really think that peacock is capable of murder?"

"I don't know him like you do." The breeze blew a strand of hair into my eyes. I brushed it away. "Did you see Larissa leave your party?"

"No. Why?"

"That fairy costume. I guess she changed at the bar. "But why was she back there?"

"Simple explanation. Perhaps the bartender had to leave and she had to fill in."

"Someone else knew Larissa would be there and took that opportunity to kill her."

Diego brought his hand to my shoulder and wiped away the sand that had stuck to the sunscreen. "And who would want to do that, Adelina?"

My tone challenged. "A jealous woman."

His eyes narrowed. "You don't mean my sister?"

Tension filled my shoulders. I sat up. "Carmelita is my friend but you along with everyone at your party saw how she reacted when Larissa danced with Fede."

"He's filth," Diego said dismissively, reaching over to the beach bag. He dug out a glass and filled it with red wine before passing it to me. "I don't blame her for shoving them into the pool."

I watched him fill a glass for himself.

"Federico has no sense of honor." He tipped back the wine. "The bastard displays his affairs in public." He frowned. "I wonder why Carmelita keeps him."

"Love?"

Diego shook his head. "Infatuation. My poor impetuous sister needs to be protected from her own impulses."

"And you would do that."

"Of course." He brought the glass to his lips and tipped it back, shutting his eyes a moment as if letting the flavors of the wine ease through his body. He sighed. "With my father deceased it's up to me. Carmelita is confused. Her world is falling apart bit by bit."

"So you sent someone over to make sure her husband is no longer distracted." The dark plum shiraz as red as blood, shimmered in the sunlight. Reflectively, I gazed into the wine, wishing for answers. "With Larissa dead, Fede would have a warning to behave more respectfully towards the family."

Diego picked up his glass and drank deeply. "Hadn't thought of it that way. You are brilliant. I am impressed. You sound like my father way back in the day." Even white teeth flashed through a wide grin. "Just one problem with that plan."

What was it with men? Sure, he was intelligent, but did he think he was the only one with any smarts? Far be it for a woman to figure out what Diego was up to.

"I wouldn't have to kill her."

From the beach bag, I tugged out lip balm and applied it on my dry lips. As I stuck it back into the makeup case, I retorted, "No, there are others that would do it for you. People you pay."

Diego raised his hands in a stop gesture. "Be reasonable, sweetheart. Think this through. In this case, violence is hardly necessary."

"Why not?'

"I think you are a bit bloodthirsty," he remarked with a snicker. Running his fingers in my hair, he pushed it back. "An endearing quality in a woman." A kiss landed on my shoulder and an answering spark surprised me. Diego gave me a soulful look. "There are other ways to solve problems."

"Such as?"

Diego leaned back, a dreamy look in his eyes. "Did I tell you why I find you intriguing, Adelina? Money isn't that important to you, is it?" He rubbed the back of his neck. "But the others aren't like you. Most women like security. Larissa wanted a bit of a nest egg for her old age." From the blanket, Diego handed me a bottle of sunscreen and indicated his shoulders. "Please?"

I set my wine glass down. Squeezing out some lotion into my hand, I smoothed it over the hard tennis shoulders.

"A payoff."

"Perhaps."

"And what if she wanted more?"

"Blackmail?" Diego indicated his neck. "Would you mind?"

With my fingertips I spread the lotion, giving him a massage at the same time. "Not money...a bigger prize."

"You think she wanted to marry Federico? Alright. I suppose she might have been thinking along those lines. He wasn't poor and a divorce from Carmelita would be profitable."

"But then he'd lose the power of being part of the Bolivar Alvarez family."

"True."

"So she came to you knowing you wouldn't want Carmelita hurt. Possibly she threatened to go public with the affair?"

"And you think I silenced her permanently?" Diego laughed. "A little drastic, Adelina. You forget I have other means. A warning from my man would squelch that plan."

"Your hit man?"

"Tsk, tsk, Adelina. Enforcer is a better term." He sighed. "Eduardo was too big for his britches. I had to terminate his employment. Stefano is my new right hand. Much more civilized."

"I don't think we'll agree on this."

"Perhaps not, but we can agree on other things, right? Like food, wine...pleasure." Diego leaned in for a kiss.

I thrust up my hand to stop him. "I just became engaged."

"To a man that makes a baby with another woman. Not a wise choice, don't you think?"

"Maybe not." I gave my wine glass to Diego. "But sometimes the heart decides."

He picked up the bottle and poured. "You are confused, trying to be strong. I know. I can help."

"How?"

"A diversion from your situation." He poured himself some wine. "Let's toast your freedom."

An optimistic approach if ever I heard one. "To almost single." I clicked his glass and settled back on the blanket. This situation had to be dealt with but for now I wanted to forget about Wolf and his snake. "I've been rather insensitive, Diego. I'm sorry."

"How so?"

"You've had to deal with the loss of your father."

"It was a little unexpected."

"But the Import Export business is going well?"

Diego snuggled up to me, wrapping his free arm around my shoulders. His lips made contact with the curve of my neck. Toe-curling heat. I pulled away. "Is it?"

"It's not a yes or no, *mi amor*." He brushed his wavy lock away from his forehead. "I'm rather overloaded, what with Royal Investments and now the complete operation."

I took a sip of shiraz before asking, "Why not let Fede deal with the Mexico City angle?"

Diego rolled his eyes. "The man can't be trusted. My father must have been in the first stages of senility, at least I suspect as much, when he started training that rat. I can't imagine why Francisco wanted to play golf every day."

"He was getting older."

"And tolerant. Stupidly so." On the blanket Diego stretched out his arms like a lazy lion. "It was his downfall. That bastard husband of Carmelita's took advantage. If I had liked Brock Duval I might have given him a job to look into Fede's deals."

"What's that music?" It sounded like the opening bars of *Miss You* by the Stones. Diego ignored my question and dug into my tote for his cell. He spoke to someone in Spanish, his tone impatient. When he clicked off, his smile had lost some of its radiance.

"What's wrong?"

"A mix-up in an order. Would you mind if we stopped at the warehouse on the way back?"

Wow, this was better than I'd hoped for. I didn't care if Wolf wanted me to stop the investigation. Brock's murderer was free and I had to find him. "Yes, no problem."

"Drink, *cariño*. Hate to waste a great shiraz, don't you?" Seeing my expression, he added, "Still lots of time before I need to drive. Don't worry." He stroked my cheek. "I will keep you safe. I did last night, didn't I?"

"Yes, I appreciate that. Who knows what would have happened if you hadn't fixed things."

Shifting, I stretched out my legs. Diego set down his glass and picked up my foot. "You have dainty feet. *Muy linda*." He dropped some lotion on his palm. Rubbing his hands together, he smoothed the sunscreen in a circular motion over my foot.

"That feels good." I propped both my feet on Diego's leg. "Seriously, it's not like I had a motive but Hernandez is suspicious because I was the one who found Brock's body. I'm sure he'd be happy to interrogate me again."

Diego laughed. "Well, the man is normal. Of course, he'd want to escape dreary police life and sit with a lovely woman, like you. I imagine he's already making follow ups from the party."

"And he'll see a connection with Larissa dead. They were dive buddies."

"Oh? I didn't know that." Diego gently ran his fingers over my toes.

"What do you know about Larissa?"

"Besides the fact that she was an exceedingly attractive woman?" His thumbs rubbed the sole of my foot. "There have been numerous renovations at the hotel, mostly the bar."

"Was she the sole owner of Moray's Eel?"

"I believe so."

"Then your theory doesn't make sense, does it?"

"How so?"

"You said she needed money."

Diego ran a finger over my toes. "I did, didn't I? Well, call it a hunch. I didn't get the impression she came from wealth."

"Yet..."

Easing himself onto the blanket beside me, Diego placed a finger on my lips. "No one will come after you. And it's too late for Larissa. Let it go, Adelina."

I pushed away his hand. "I can't forget."

Grinning devilishly, he pulled me down and brought me close. Tasting like wine, his tongue lightly traced my lips. A sensuous deliberate caress willed me to respond while Diego's hands gently stoked a fire inside me.

Starting at his face, I explored down the length of his long lean body lingering at the curve of a rounded butt. Lost in the journey, I vaguely noticed the straps of my bikini loosen and the material replaced with Diego's hand. Fingertips teased my nipple a moment before his mouth claimed ownership. I pushed him away.

"What's wrong, Adelina? This will be good. I know it."

"No, Diego. I can't. I need time."

"I understand." The *Miss You* ringtone started up. Diego reached for the bag. "I'd completely forgotten the warehouse problem." He took out the phone. "I'll need to get this." After a quick response he threw the cell into the bag.

In the meantime, I pulled up the bikini top and tied it on.

"Now I am really sorry," Diego said, his eyes dancing.

"Because?"

He checked the deserted beach. "We were so close, weren't we? I might have changed your mind?"

This time I placed a finger on his lips. "Maybe...maybe not."

****

The warehouse was a few blocks from the airport road. A truck was parked in the entrance. Ropes hoisted huge crates up a ramp. If they were labeled I couldn't tell from the car.

When Diego disappeared into the building, I jumped out and edged over to the truck. I didn't know if I would find anything but after I was told to stay in the car, curiosity got the better of me.

"Adelina? What are you doing out here?" Diego called out from the other side of the truck and trekked over.

Hastily removing a stud earring, I curled my fingers. "I had a cramp so I thought I'd get out and walk."

His eyes narrowed. "It's dangerous. They're loading. I'll bring you back to the car."

"In a minute. My earring just fell off," I said, tilting my head so he could see the hole in my ear."

"Oh?" he said suspiciously.

"I must have flicked it out when I pushed my hair away. I think it dropped near the wheels."

"I'll look." Diego stooped down.

I took that moment to peek into the truck. The lettering on a box read *Crañeos.* My Spanish is rather limited. If it doesn't have anything to do with shoes or food, it was hit or miss—mostly miss. Luckily, the small skull etched in black ink on the label gave it away. Satisfied, I dropped on my knees near one of the tires.

"Adelina," Diego snapped, "that's dangerous. You need to get out of there."

"I found it," I said, scrambling back onto my feet. I held up a shiny object before sticking it back in. "Luckily, the end stuck to the back of my ear when it fell out. I am so relieved. They're a favorite pair."

"Diamonds?" Diego peered closely at my ear.

"Yes," I lied, "a gift."

"I suppose I shouldn't ask from whom." He couldn't have looked any more peeved.

"No, maybe you shouldn't." I headed back to the car. Before I could open the door, Diego was Johnny on the spot. Ever the gentleman, he swept his hand in a wave. "My lady," he said, swinging the door ajar. "Thank you." I felt a little bad for pulling fast one but I had to be discreet. Who knows what he would do if he caught on?

Diego was no fool. If he thought I was interested in his warehouse, he would be more guarded than ever.

With the wind whipping my hair, we zoomed out of the lot and roared down a side street. A few more twists and turns and we were back on Rafael Melgar. Traffic was thick near the ferry dock. Police were directing the three way stop while hordes of tourists jay-walked every which way.

But it didn't take long once we were noticed. In San Miguel, it was an unwritten rule that a Bolivar Alvarez was not to be kept waiting. Still, Diego had not regained his previous good mood. With a rather sullen expression on his handsome face, he drove, speaking only monosyllabically the rest of the route.

Soon the Ferrari veered into the driveway of the La Vida.

When I turned to say goodbye, Diego suddenly took my face in his hands and planted a kiss on my lips.

He gazed into my eyes. "I hope you know how much you mean to me," he said very seriously. "You're special. Du Lac is a screwup if he doesn't see that." He pushed a strand of my hair back over my ear. "You don't need him. I hope you realize that. I'll always be there for you. You believe that, don't you?" I nodded and picked up my bag, trying for a quick exit but Diego jumped out to open my door.

"I want you to feel comfortable dropping in to see me anytime."

"Thank you, Diego. I appreciate you bringing me over to the other side of the island for lunch." At this point, his face was so close it would have been rude to not kiss him. His lips were soft and warm—delicious like chocolate. "Good bye. I'll see you?"

Diego grinned, the sparkle back in his eyes. "Soon."

13

The verticals in my room were shut. Cool air blasted out of the vents. I shivered from the chill, which was intense after coming back from the beach. A towel twisted into the shape of a flower had been placed in the center of my bed. The tile floor was shiny, wet in spots from a recent mopping. At the bedside table, the coins left for a tip were gone. Everything was neat and clean.

It was like one of those "what's wrong with this picture". Something was out of whack.

I'm a shoeaholic. When I'm happy, I buy shoes. When I'm sad, I buy shoes. When I'm excited, I buy shoes. It's not quite as bad as my chocolate addiction but still, plenty serious. Every one of my babies is special. It was a ritual with me taking care of them, spraying and shining them before I meticulously put them back into the closet, sorted by color and style. But not yesterday. That was the night from hell and even the metallic shoes didn't change my mood.

First, Samantha was ruining my future with the man of my dreams. Then, thinking I could chill at Moray's Eel and forget my broken heart, I discovered Larissa's body. By the time I returned to my hotel, I was a wreck. I'd kicked off those painful toe-biters, not caring where they flew. But if I recalled correctly, the gold platforms had landed near the bed. Later, when I got up in the night, I had stumbled on them.

Throwing the beach bag on the bed, I got down on my knees

and lifted the bedspread to search. A few popped rusty springs and dust bunnies. And then I saw them. The shoes—straight and tall like soldiers. Odd. Someone had entered my room, searched, and played "Tidy Heidi". It wouldn't be the first time that the maid tried on my shoes but even conscientious types don't go crawling under the bed. Omigod! A thief must have broken into my safe!

I ran over to my closet to check the contents of the wall safe. My passport, money, and jewelry were all there just as I had left them. The intruder had wanted something else. Rushing to the bedside table, I opened the drawer. Under the tissues and lotions I found my cell phone and charger.

But Brock's cell was gone.

****

The Diva was as elegant as its name. On the tenth floor of a high-rise overlooking the ocean, this upscale Italian restaurant did it up fancy. Chandeliers glittered high on a cathedral ceiling, above tables covered with crisp white linen and fancy white dishes.

From here, the view was spectacular. Cruise ships lit up like Christmas trees anchored in the harbor. In the distance the north island hotels twinkled brightly along the coast.

Our table at the window was overflowing with wine and food. A full-bodied Amarone tasting of herbs, cherries, and lingering chocolate brought a smile of pleasure to my lips. And no, I hadn't forgotten the intruder in my room or the killer on the loose but negative energy gives off a deadly atmosphere. Bad for the Chi.

I was apparently the only one at our table trying to turn things around. A funeral reception would have been livelier than this group.

Daniel's arm was slung over Irmgard's chair. Wearing sunglasses and a frown, his mood matched the black blazer and shirt. From what I'd seen last night, I guessed one too many margaritas.

For all her strict religious principles, the boss lady hadn't hesitated to jack up the heat a notch with a mind-blowing metallic mini dress slashed to the waist. It was the clone of the black designer number she'd worn last night. If it was attention she wanted, the film editor wasn't shy to show his interest. In between tossing back wine, he made a point of ogling Irmgard's twins.

Mary Battrock didn't look any happier. But something told me it wasn't because of Brock. In between hostile glares across the table, the dust buster chowed down on a plateful of ribs coated in pepper sauce.

Tonight she looked bigger than the eighties. Teased and sprayed for volume, her thick red locks billowed onto broad bare shoulders. A shiny burgundy gown suspended by fragile satin straps plunged dangerously low, barely supporting the overflowing double D's.

"Watcha lookin' at, mister?" she snapped at Larry T.

When I made myself comfortable beside her, Mary turned her disgust to me and growled, "Brock bit the dust and now that skank Larissa cashed in her chips. What's happenin' here, girl? Our dive boat's gonna be empty soon."

"I believe the police are seeing these as separate crimes, Mary. Nothing to do with our tour group. No reason to get upset. Our next dive will be just fine." Of course, I didn't know that but the last thing I needed was Mary's thoughtless remarks breaking Irmgard's bubble. She'd been on the edge last night and apparently spending it with Daniel hadn't helped one iota.

Larry slurped his wine and burped. "Everybody's gonna deep six sooner or later. What I saw from the Brockster, he was burning both ends." He leered at the eighties mama. "Ya know what I mean?" His eyes flicked to the door. "Whoa! Git a load of that!" Flushed with excitement.

Ronny pranced into the restaurant, as flamboyant as a flamingo. Pink shirt, fuchsia tie, white jeans and candy-striped slip-ons.

"*Hola*, everyone," he sang out, waving a bright plastic bag with a ribbon tied on the string handle.

"Whatsa matter? Ya lost yer boyfriend?" Larry T drawled.

Ronny grinned at the gender stab. "Gee whiz. Should I be worried, Larry?"

I wasn't sure if the firefighter knew Ronny was the blonde

from Diego's party. He was about as sharp as a bowling ball but he might figure this out and if that happened, all hell would break loose.

Ronny flipped his hand up and down, surveying the group. "Don't you just love pink?"

"Red's my color," Mary muttered, in between shoveling in mouthfuls of potatoes.

Irmgard watched Ronny sit. "Why are you so late?"

"Been shopping. Punta Langosta has great designer shops. Irm, you'd love their Prada." He stage whispered, "I didn't want to spend so much but when I get upset, shopping is the only thing that helps."

"Upset?" Daniel lifted an eyebrow. "About what?"

Larry T snickered. "His boyfriend left 'im."

A glass of wine at his mouth, Ronny cackled. "Maybe he did." He stared at Mary's bouffant do. "Dumped me for a certain babelicious redhead."

Finally, the light switched on in Larry T's brain. He shifted around nervously.

I took affirmative action. "Have some salad, Ronny." Before he could speak, I pushed a plateful in front of him. "You'll love the dressing."

Curiously, Ronny forked some up. "Excellent raspberry vinaigrette." He gazed out the window at the harbor. "This is some place, Adie. Such a splendid view!" He waved his fork significantly. "So-oo, anyway, as I was saying. It's such a tragedy. Poor Larissa. I was so upset. All ready to pack. That's two down, you know. Makes me wonder if someone is targeting our group." Ronny fluttered his lashes. "Maybe you're next, Larry T."

Larry T glared. "It was you, weren't it?" He'd figured out the blonde thing for sure.

"What?" Ronny asked innocently.

A red flush crept up his neck. Larry T was about to combust.

Irmgard's lips twisted. "Put a lid on it, you two. Have some respect! They found Brock's body, remember?" She shuddered. "God Almighty! A killer is out there waiting to pick us off one by one."

"Calm down, sweetheart. Nobody's after you." Daniel stared at the group. "It's a sad thing when some lunatic stabs pretty girls. Larissa was a babe. She didn't deserve to die. Some whacky bitch killed Larissa." He yawned. "Now Laval's a different story. That dude was a big phony."

Ronny perked right up. "Do tell."

Irmgard dug her long red talons into Daniel's arm.

He squirmed uncomfortably. "Just saying," he muttered.

Irmgard sprang up. "You're out of your friggin' mind! Nobody liked Larissa! Who cares about trash like her? I should know. Brock was a real man." With that, she burst into tears. Before anyone could stop her, she flew past the tables and into the hall, leaving me wondering if there could have been genuine feelings locked up in that paper doll figure.

Out of the corner of my eye, I could see the maitre d' waltzing to our table, his jaw clenched. This was my cue to stop a feeding frenzy. Always the tour group leader, I knew the routine. I stood, clapping for attention. "Listen up, group. Salsa dancing at the Time Tok tonight. Tropical cocktails to die for." *Ooops, did I say that?* "Go party, folks! Taxis are waiting downstairs as we speak."

****

The Snuba-Snork Dive Shop was a basic place with a fish poster on the wall and a few racks of masks and fins. The skinny guy at the desk assured me the tour group was booked on the *Sagitario* but his pinched face sent another message.

"Is there a problem?"

"No, *no problema*." But his eyes darted away as if caught in a lie.

"What's going on?"

The name tag on his lapel said *Fabio*. His hair was short and dark—his shoulders were as wide as a twelve year old boy's. "Looks like an El Norte." He shrugged. "It could be bad but maybe it will be good. Wait until the morning, Señorita."

"Why? Won't the diving be okay no matter what the weather?"

"Sure, but sometimes the boats can't dock."

I flopped down in the rattan chair across from him. "If the waves are high, what then?"

"Divers can take the boat from the marina."

"Oh-hh." Big waves and that horrible up and down motion. My stomach heaved at the thought.

Fabio glanced at the paper in front of him. "You want to hire an individual instructor for yourself?"

"Yes. The same one. Cy Nemesis. Is he available?"

"I'll check." He dug out his cell from his pocket. With his thumbs, Fabio tapped out a text.

A vibrating drone sounded. He picked up his mobile and fired off some Spanish. The Snuba-Snork man turned to me. "He'll meet you at the La Vida dock at eight."

"Say, Fabio, I'd like to speak with Cy. Can you ask him if I could meet him somewhere right now?"

Holding the cell, Fabio smirked. "No can do. We have rules."

I dug in my purse and dropped a few bills on the desk. When I shoved a fiver towards him, he snatched it up and narrowed his eyes.

"Address and cell number, *por favor*, Fabio." The ball was in his court.

He leaned over to grab the rest but I stopped him, a hand on the money. "Write it down," I said, with a chin jerk to the pad on his desk.

Frowning, Fabio scribbled the information and slid the paper across. "He might not like me giving you this."

I shoved the moolah towards him. "He doesn't have to know, does he?"

The loot in his wallet, Fabio went back to texting. I was hoping it wasn't to Cy. The element of surprise was my only weapon.

On Melgar, I hopped into a cab and headed down a narrow street past the Mega. The streets were shadowy with only an occasional street light. Stone walls hid the Spanish style houses, the pastel hues murky in the dim light.

When the taxi stopped, I paid the driver and stepped out into an empty street and into the rain. The light shining from a barred window glimmered on the wet wrought iron fence. Drops drizzled on my face and legs. A cardigan over my flimsy ruffled dress gave me some protection but I wished I was inside my hotel room, warm and comfortable. Why was I here? It was purely a hunch. Hadn't my grandma always said not to ignore my instincts?

From here, nothing but the fence was visible. Assuming the gate was around the corner, I trekked over. A dog barked sharply overhead. Scuffling sounds. I paused and looked up. A huge Doberman stared down from the rooftop. The Hound of the Baskervilles was held in by a low wall. The threatening growls were too near for comfort. Not keen to be a dog treat, I shuffled forward, carefully avoiding a broken bottle. The gate had to be near.

Like a bat out of hell, a heavy black figure flew out of the shadows. A long narrow blade flashed. I screamed. Adrenaline rushed in my veins. With my bag, I pounded the knife. It clattered on the cement. Big hands reached forward.

Balancing on my left foot, I thrust hard, kicking out at his groin. My heel made contact. He hunched over, groaning.

A light flicked on in the house. I turned. It was my mistake. A fist slammed into my chest and I fell backwards. At the last second, I broke my fall, landing arms first. Pain flashed through my body. There was no time to waste. When a foot came for my face, I blocked it with a back hand strike. Bone contact. My arm throbbed but I kept it up protectively.

A door slammed and a male voice yelled, "*¿Hey, que está pasando?*"

My Spanish forgotten I called out, "Help!"

A door slammed. That distraction gave me time to struggle to my feet. Twisting my supporting foot, I kicked my back foot out in a roundhouse, making contact. His curse told me I'd struck gold.

The gate clanged open and a tall man stepped out. "What's going on here?"

The thug scrambled up, pulled down his hood and scooted across the street, disappearing into the night. I rescued my bag from the sidewalk. By this time, it was raining cats and dogs.

"Hello?"

I hobbled into the light. "Cy?" I said hesitantly.

His face registered shock. "Adie, are you alright?" He rushed out the gate and taking my hands in his, he said softly, "Come into the house, *cariño*."

The place was small. Hammocks strung in reds and blues along with dive photographs decorated the white stucco walls of the apartment. Rattan furniture lay scattered randomly in the living area. A sink, stove and fridge was tucked into the corner of the room. The doorway at the end could have been either the bathroom or the bedroom.

"It's a temporary place. But it's mine," Cy said quietly, looking me up and down. "Sit." He gestured to the cushioned couch. "I'll be right back." I sank down, focusing on the peeling paint. It was run down, and a little messy. Clothes were thrown on a chair but nothing I'd call a health hazard. Mentally, I made a list starting with Brock and ending with me. This was a close call. I should have been victim number three. The killer would be a little disappointed tonight.

There was no doubt this game was getting rough.

A glance at the raw skin and bruises on my legs and arms proved that. On the plus side, I was alive. My lips twisted into a grin. It was true, I might not have pulled it off without Cy but I had hurt the thug. Not bad for a petite woman training for a black belt.

A towel and a first aid box in hand, Cy took the seat next to me. He shook his head. "It would be easier if you washed off in the shower."

"What?"

With his finger, Cy traced a trail of dirt and blood on my leg. I flinched at the contact.

Rubbing his chin reflectively, he let his eyes travel to mine. "Get clean. Then I'll fix you up. I'll find you something to wear." He pulled me to my feet and handed me the towel. "Lots of soap."

When I didn't say anything, he steered me to the back of the apartment. He stopped at the door. "Warm water and soap," he repeated.

When I hesitated, he added, "Believe me. You'll feel better."

I nodded and stepped into the tiny bathroom. No one could call me a nature girl. I had to have eyeliner and mascara. My products were ocean-proof. A shower would be lucky to leave a smudge. As for my hair, well, there was no choice but to give it the beach look.

With the bathroom door shut, I examined the condition of my dress. After the scuffle, it was more beige than white, the seam torn open from the hem to mid-point at the hip. The dress was salvageable but my exposed skin was raw, bruised and bleeding.

The shower was as narrow as a broom closet. A pitiful stream of water trickled out. Soap stung on the open wounds. I gritted my teeth to stop myself from crying. The shock of being attacked was beginning to hit me hard. Hurriedly, I rinsed and shut off the water, grabbed a towel and dabbed at my skin.

A bang on the door. "Adie, I have a T-shirt for you. Put it on. If you hand me your dress I'll wash it, okay?"

With the door open a crack, we made a quick exchange. Grateful but not happy. A return to the hotel looking like a barroom brawler was not an alternative.

With my gitch and bra on, I pulled the yellow cotton T over my head. The shirt hung loose, long enough to reach mid-thigh. Picking up my sandals, I padded out into the living room.

"I put your dress in the wash on delicate cold. Is that alright?" Cy called out from the kitchen.

"Sure, thanks."

My host was pouring a golden hued liquid into two snifters as I padded in. "I thought you might…" He turned around holding the glasses.

"Yes?"

His eyes swept my figure. "Er-rr."

"Tequila?"

Cy nodded slowly. "*Don Julio 1942.*"

As I took the glass from his hand, he asked, "Do you know anything about tequilas?"

"It's a premium. Meant for sipping not mixing."

He raised an eyebrow. "You've had *1942* before?"

I lifted the glass to my nose. "The *blanco* and *añejo* but not

42."

"It's the one best suited for a snifter. I think you'll like it." Cy clicked his glass to mine. "To annihilating the wicked."

"I suppose that's what we did tonight."

"Damn right!" Cy smiled and leaned in. His kiss was soft and furry.

I backed off.

"You have nice lips, Adie Sturm."

"I…"

He pressed a fingertip to my mouth. "Don't say anything. Forget that happened." He took my hand and led me to the couch. "Let's sit, have a drink and then I'll fix all those cuts."

"I'm not sure I should sit, Cy. What if I get blood on the cushions?"

"No problem." From the nearby chair, he picked up a towel and arranged it on the couch before he guided me down. "There, see. The landlord won't charge me for damage."

Outside, the wind howled rattling the window panes as it rushed against the cottage. The El Norte had come in with a roar.

Settling myself down, glass in hand, I asked, "Why are you here in Cozumel, Cy?"

"I'm here like everyone else. I came to dive."

Sipping the tequila, I stared at him from over the rim. "You knew Brock."

Cy shrugged in that Latin way.

"Yet you told Hernandez you didn't."

"A cop with too much information is a menace, Adie." He glanced at my glass. "What do you think?"

"Silky. Caramel, vanilla, and cherry?" I took another sip. "Oh-hh."

Cy's eyes sparkled green. "It's chocolate. I'm a fan. You?"

"Um-mm. Very nice."

"You have quite the palate."

I watched him closely. "Diego Alvarez said the exact same thing to me."

His fist tightened but he stared at me impassively. "I don't think you can compare us."

"Why? Do you think you're superior? Perhaps because you're a Basque? A descendent of Atlantis?"

Cy laughed. "It's a great way to pick up women. They can't resist the story." He tipped back his tequila. "You're a funny girl. It's just an old wives tale. Not much different from the Bermuda triangle theory."

"But not many would claim that Basque connection. Do you have relatives on the island?"

Leaning back, Cy rested his head on the couch, eyes half-closed. "None that I know of."

From the glass table top I snatched up my bag. I withdrew a small scrap of paper and my cell phone. When I clicked in a number a vibrating noise went off in Cy's jean pocket. He tugged it out and glanced down.

"What's this all about, Adie? Why are you calling me?"

"It's the number I found on Brock's cell. Someone stole that cell from me today."

"You had Brock's phone? Why?"

"I think you know. That's the reason you were talking to him, isn't it?"

Cy stared. "What are you saying?"

"Brock was an investigator."

"How would that involve me, Adie?" Cy pushed a strand of damp hair away from my face, his lips dangerously near. Dark green eyes pierced through me.

"You had similar interests."

Cy picked up the first aid kit from the table and opened it. "I'll cleanse the wound with this first." He took out a solution and cotton pads.

"You think I haven't guessed, don't you? It all made sense when I saw your cell number on Brock's phone."

"Let me see your arm." With a little solution on a pad, the dive instructor dabbed the cut on the sensitive area of my forearm.

It stung but I gritted my teeth to continue. "I know who you are so don't try to pretend otherwise."

"I'm a diver," he said nonchalantly, "and a traveler."

"And you decided to return to Cozumel to see your family?"

"Why would you think that? I'm a dive instructor." A square stick-on pad applied successfully, Cy dug out another. "Did you know I speak several languages? The reason for that is the dive. People from all over the world are here. If I can communicate and do a good job, I am well rewarded."

The spartan apartment said otherwise. I lifted an eyebrow significantly. "Oh? Surely it doesn't pay that well." I brought my leg up for him to work on the cut on my shin.

"I don't need money."

"But you need your family. Your sister misses you."

"I have no family," he muttered, cleaning the wound.

While Cy situated the pad on my leg, I searched the cell for the photo. After a zoom-in, I flipped the phone around. "Have a look, *amigo*. You with Diego and Carmelita."

"I told you—" he started.

"Don't lie to me. They are your family."

"This whole thing is none of your business."

Jerking my leg away, I grabbed his arm. "It's my business when someone tries to kill me!"

This caught him by surprise. Cy sat up. "You mean the guy outside?"

"He had a knife but it wasn't a robbery." With my finger, I stroked his beard. "Now, tell me what this is all about."

"Alright, you win. I admit it. I am Amancio Edgar Bolivar Alvarez."

"The brother who drowned."

"I had no choice, Adie." He settled himself back in the couch and looked idly around the room. "It's at times like this that I need a cigarette."

"You smoke?"

"No, not anymore. It's not good for a diver." Suddenly, he flashed his pearly whites. "Who would have thought a tiny woman like you would blow my cover?"

"Size doesn't equate with intelligence."

"No, it doesn't. You are quite perceptive." His fingers played with his unruly shoulder length locks. "I wouldn't mind getting rid of some of this but—"

"Do you know how upset your sister was and still is about your death? How can you be so cruel?"

"And my brother," Cy said sarcastically. "Is he missing me, too?"

I took his hand. "He does. I saw it in his eyes. When your father died Diego had to take charge of everything. I think he likes it but he's stressed," I said gently.

"You don't know what my brother is capable of."

"Diego is complex."

"He's a killer. When my father was murdered, I had to return," he said tightly, teeth clenched.

I shook my head. "No, Cy. He wasn't murdered. Your father had a heart attack."

"I don't think so." Back up on his feet, Cy paced the floor before speaking again. "A week ago I made contact with the housekeeper. She and I were close. When I asked what happened,Teresa said my father had a visitor just before his collapse. Two snifters of tequila were on the table in the study. She doesn't know who was with my father but my guess is Diego. I'd guess he was poisoned."

Outside, the wind banged the shutters against the rails. Lost in thought, Cy stared at the window. A chill raced down my spine. I crossed my arms for warmth. The storm was getting fierce. It was as if the spirits had banded together to demand justice.

"Why are you so sure?"

Diego's brother filled our glasses and sat back down. He handed me mine. "Drink that." Warmth returned to my hands as I sipped the golden liquid.

He spoke softly. "The family was there visiting when my father suddenly died. Teresa said his death was out of the blue. The idea of murder didn't occur to anyone, hence, no autopsy."

I nodded. "And why should it be? Just because someone was there in the room with your father doesn't mean it was murder."

Cy rubbed his chin. "I can't prove it but I know Diego tried to kill me."

That shook me awake. "What? I thought you were in a dive accident." I stared. "You mean it was like Brock's murder?

Someone cut your reg?"

He shook his head. "No. I set that up in order to disappear. But only after my brakes were tampered with."

"No one told me that."

"That's because no one knew. Except my brother."

Doubt festered in my mind. *Who else could gain from Cy's death?* He was the heir to Bolivar Imports and Exports. Diego was the spare in case anything happened to Cy. Isn't that how it worked with Cozumel royalty?

Cy answered my unspoken question. "No one stood to gain except my brother. Diego is running the show." It was true. Diego managed Royal Investments and now Bolivar Exports. Whereas Carmelita's life was the same as it had always been. "So why kill Brock and Larissa?"

"Larissa from Moray's Eel? She's dead?"

"Stabbed last night after Diego's Carnaval Party."

Leaning back, he closed his eyes. When he opened them, the green had changed to thundercloud gray. "Was Larissa Diego's mistress?"

"That's absurd. Larissa had a relationship with Brock and probably Fede, but Diego?"

"She was lovely."

I glared at him. "So Diego had to have her? That's the kind of man you think he is?"

"Women love him and," he shrugged, "my brother can't resist."

"But why would he kill Larissa?"

"He wouldn't."

"What?" I rolled my eyes. "You just implied..."

"Stab wounds are so messy." He laughed. "Diego would hate to ruin his Armani duds."

"Get serious." I examined my glass. "When did you start hating him?"

Cy shot me a look. "We were brothers. Sometimes we fought and maybe I was a little jealous, but I didn't hate him."

"Jealous? Why?"

Cy shrugged. "I suppose it was all that charm."

"That couldn't be the whole story. Seems to me you have the Bolivar Alvarez mystique. So the rivalry started in your teens or later when you worked together?"

An elbow on the armrest, chin cupped in the palm of his hand, he said, "He liked the business, I didn't. Money, power and all the trappings. That's Diego."

"So you were different. Why hate him for that?"

"He was just like the old man. Twisted situations to suit himself."

"You didn't like your father either?"

"I loved him but I didn't like the person he was. But what choice did I have? I'm a Bolivar."

"I'm sure it was really rough being rich and working for the company," I said sarcastically.

He looked surprised. "You don't understand, Adie."

"You're not the only one who has ever had domineering parents." My father and Wolf's mother ruined our chances years ago. Parents liked to control their kid's choices. Glancing at my cell, I saw the red light flashing. Was it a text from my guy? It tore my heart how he'd had slept with Sam. It would be doubly difficult to lose him now after he made a commitment to me.

"I suppose you're right. Parents are the same everywhere and believe me, I was trying to be the son they wanted. Maybe Diego did me a favor cutting the brake linings in my Lamborghini. It forced me to disappear."

"Where did you go?"

"Isla de Mujeres for starters and then Costa Rica. I lived a simple life."

"When your father died you came out of hiding."

He nodded.

"How did you meet Brock?"

"There was an advanced dive a couple of months ago. He hired me."

"Did you know your sister was involved with him?"

"Who could blame her?" Cy sighed. "From day one that scumbag of a husband was cheating on her. It made her miserable. I was pleased to hear she has her own design company."

"And she is good at it." I smiled. "Carmelita has talent and a great business sense." I put my hand on his. "Can you think of any reason she might?"

Cy sat up. "Listen, Adie. Carmelita is a Bolivar and revenge and honor are engrained in us but for her to kill Larissa?" He shook his head. "No, even if she thought she was avenging Brock's death."

That hit me like a brick. "Brock wanted to go away with her. I know that. It was on his cell texts. At the party, Carmelita admitted she was miserable about his death. If Larissa cut his reg, Carmelita could have asked one of the hit men to do the job."

"And you claim to be my sister's friend?"

"Of course."

He glared.

I shot him a look. "You didn't see Carmelita push Fede *and* Larissa into the pool last night. Believe me, she was very angry. And now it looks like she had plenty of motivation."

"Carmelita is a gentle soul. She couldn't possibly kill anyone."

"And you think Diego could?"

Placing the glass on the table, he refilled mine and then his.

I took the snifter. "If Diego thought Larissa was a threat to Carmelita, he'd send one of the men. He's protective of her."

"I love my sister but I wouldn't play God. It's not up to us to judge."

I let the smooth liquor trickle between my lips. "Yet you condemn Diego without a trial."

"My brother manipulates situations. Surely you know that?"

"I owe him…big time."

Elbows back and hands entwined behind his neck, Cy yawned. "How?"

"I'm the one who discovered Larissa's body. Diego made sure one of his men reported the murder. Unfortunately, they destroyed the evidence. There's another reason I need to find the killer. You can help me, Cy."

"You're suggesting we combine forces? I need to find out who put a hit on me. It's not quite the same."

"Yet there's a common denominator."

"Bolivar Imports and Exports."

Sharp as a whip. I was getting more curious to find out what was beneath the beard. Who was Armancio Bolivar Alvarez…really?

"You have a plan?" Cy asked carefully.

I nodded "What products were imported and exported?"

Cy stared thoughtfully at the blue hammock hung on the wall. "The usual tourist things, mostly art objects. Replicas of Mayan gods."

"Skulls?"

Cy frowned. "Yes, now that you mention it. Just before my car was tampered with, I was checking into a shipment of skulls. Not real ones. Carved out of stone."

"I have this feeling."

"What, Adie?"

"The skulls are making a huge profit." A thought occurred to me. "Do you know who would have an account in the Turks?"

"A company account?" Cy swung his feet up onto the coffee table and settled himself against the couch.

"Maybe, maybe not."

"There has always been one in the Caymans, possibly another in the Turks. Our family had branches of operation in off-shore accounts. Taxes add up. " Cy smiled. "It helped."

"What about a Swiss account? "Those are coded. I don't think there were any like that." He shook his head. "If there are any, my guess is that they're personal accounts." Cy frowned. "You're not speculating, are you? How did you find this out?"

"From my fiancé, Wolf Du Lac. Brock was his investigator."

"You're engaged?"

"As of last night but—"

"What?"

"I'm not sure about it anymore."

When Cy raised an eyebrow, I added in way of explanation, "It's complicated."

"You don't want to be married or is it this Wolf person who puts you off? Or is there someone else? The way you were going on about my brother, I thought you might be involved with him.

Are you?"

I blushed. "No, Diego and I are just—"

Cy put his hands to his ears. "No details, please," he warned.

I pushed his hands away. "Cy!"

With a smile, Cy turned to me. "Wolf couldn't possibly have the power or position that my little bro has. Or the Bolivar looks. I'd guess your fiancé has money but he's a dog."

Grabbing my tote, I searched for my wallet. Out of the slot, I pulled out a photo and thrust it before his face. "This is not the face of a dog."

Cy gave the photo a once over before he snatched up the wallet. Two more photos fell out. "Ah-hh! Adie and again the fiancé. Snow! Where was this taken?"

"Skiing."

He gave it another look. "A Beckham type. Okay, he's not a dog. But, Latinos are passionate men," he said with a grin.

"I know for a fact you're wrong about Wolf. He's French and German. So he's half Latin." The sea god knew exactly how to excite me. Bedroom, bathroom or living room. Spontaneous was his middle name. "Wolf is not lacking in the passion department."

"And my brother?"

I laughed. "You would have to ask one of his girlfriends."

He snuggled up closer. "He's never tried to?"

"You're getting personal," I warned.

"Oh, sorry." His eyes swept down. "Diego must be losing it."

14

Cell phones are irritating. Right up there with screaming kids and howling dogs. But I had a job to do and there was no time to lose. The tinkling melody was to be obeyed.

I was feeling the effects from last night's nightmare. When I climbed out of bed and checked out the bruises and scratches on my body, there was no doubt the attack had been real.

After a quick shower and a coat of mascara, I jumped into a pair of jeans and T-shirt. The cell flashed six thirty. Racing down the stairs, I was about to step out into the garden area to take the fastest route to the lobby when a blast of wind threw me back. Outside on the stone pathway, palm fronds lay broken on the stone. I wasn't in the mood to play obstacle course. The hallway to the lobby entrance was sheltered and ultimately drier.

To get to the beach and dive shop, the stairs led to an underground passageway that met up with the beach restaurant. Along the way, the terracotta walls were decorated with Mayan stylized drawings of snakes, spiders and lizards.

The storm waged a full force battle through the empty Restaurante Las Iguanas. From the looks of it, tables and chairs had been tossed about in the night. Nothing broken that I noticed, but I stepped carefully, pushing the hair out of my eyes as the wind blew in from the sea.

It was easy to see why the restaurant was a mess. The normally calm turquoise sea was a mass of enormous white caps invasively coating the beach. A smile played on my lips. The foreboding gray sky heavy with black clouds meant a dive today was unlikely. And after that last disastrous dive, I'd lost my enthusiasm. If anyone from my tour group wanted to go out, they needed their head examined. Holding onto the railing, I made my way down the wet cement steps to the Snuba-Snork window.

There were three such shops on the island. The place where I'd booked for my group was close to the Chedraui Shopping Area. I was a little surprised to see Fabio at the open air dive shop here at the La Vida.

He stood at the wooden counter, busy scribbling a notation on a pad of white lined paper. Otherwise, the place was deserted.

"*Hola*," I called out as I approached.

Fabio's coal dark eyes widened. "Señorita Sturm!" He waved his hand in greeting.

Poor guy worked long hours. "You got up early."

"The shrimp that sleeps in the sea wakes up in a cocktail," he said with a grin.

Zen this time of the day? "Is that like fish that sleep are taken by the current?"

Fabio guffawed loudly. "You've heard that one? You are a woman of surprises."

"So what's happening with the dive?"

"So sorry, Señorita Sturm, but we need to cancel today."

"No problem. I just wanted to make sure we had a rain check for that."

"We will try for tomorrow," he shrugged," but when the El Norte comes in it could be two, maybe three days."

I handed him a paper. "This is a list of my tour group. If anyone phones can you let them know we are not diving?"

"Of course," he slyly grinned, "and also your dive instructor. You want him cancelled for today but reserved for tomorrow?"

"He has me in his book," I said with a wink.

Fabio laughed. "Your visit was successful?"

"Very." With a wave, I headed back to the street through the shop. The brunette sitting on the stool behind the counter didn't look up from her book as I shot past.

The storm lulled and taking advantage, I scurried across Rafael Melgar with a brief pause on the boulevard for traffic. At the steps, I slowed down. Suitcases grouped near the entrance crowded the lobby. An elderly couple huddled with the front desk manager but apart from them, the place was deserted. I went to the white board and took a moment to fill in the dive cancellation and the movie details for my tour group, then headed to the dining room.

Activity behind the double doors of the Restaurante Guacamole signaled the start of breakfast. At my approach, the maitre d' in a white shirt and black pants opened the door, greeting me in Spanish. I gave him an *hola* and trekked over to a table as far away from a family of screaming children as possible. To claim it, I set my bag on top.

A buffet breakfast was going strong. It was hardly fine dining but served a decent dose of eggs, waffles, sausages and bacon. My stomach didn't care what it ate. I'd had about two hours sleep and my system needed a top up. Bypassing a red head, I zipped into the buffet, filling a bowl with ham, onions, and mushrooms.

"What's goin' on? There's a line up here. You think you got a corner on the omelet market, Adie Sturm?" a nasal voice griped in my ear.

I swiveled about. Mary Battrock's lips were pursed into twin elongated balloons. As I shrunk back, my mind struggled with the concept of needles systematically injected into a virgin mouth.

Well, maybe those lips weren't quite as innocent as all that. She was hard core, from the raccoon eyes to the leather fringed jacket, black corset and thigh-high boots. Tattoos on both biceps and one on her neck. The dust consultant knew what pain was. I looked at her plate. "I thought you were getting some rolls."

Mary smacked her lips watching a brawny dive instructor strut by, his buff butt rounded in a tight pair of jeans. "Those buns would be worth gettin'." She glanced contemptuously at the bread and bagels piled high on a table. "Those ain't. Now explain what you wrote on that board outside. I understand no diving. Cozumel sucks bad." She rolled her eyes. "What's all this about Chedraui and a mission?

"Mission Impossible is showing at the Chedraui movie theatre in English. If you're interested, meet me there at eleven twenty. I'm buying tickets for our tour group."

"Señorita?" the sturdy brunette asked.

I handed her my bowl. "Omelet, *por favor.*"

"Excuse me," I said to Mary and headed to the fruit table. Here I selected an assortment of pineapples and a banana for later. Back at my table, I sighed with relief, happy to escape the dust consultant from hell.

"Coffee?" a server inquired.

"Tea, *por favor.*" There was no need to be totally awake. Too much awareness creates stress. My system was in overdrive as it was. From somewhere in my purse, my cell bleeped. I tugged it out and clicked the text icon.

We need to get together. Where are you? W

I texted. *Busy. Breakfast then Mission Impossible @ Chedraui.* This was meant to be discouraging to the rat. I knew we had to talk but I was dreading it as much as a root canal.

I brought a hand up to massage my temple, hoping to ease the stress. While waiting for Wolf to return the text, I picked at the pineapples segment by segment. Yet, the cell stared back silently. By the time the server returned with the tea, I'd given up. Remembering the omelet, I sprang up, scooted over and picked up my plate from the warming rack, nabbing the ketchup on the way back.

My server was the kind of man who remembered the tippers. Slices of lemon lined a small dish next to the metal tea pot. Everything was as it should be on the table. The same did not apply to my life. And it got worse.

Larry T shuffled over and pulled out the seat opposite me.

I prayed I was asleep. Soon I'd awake to a lovely sunny day with not a care in the world. But I was wrong.

"Good mornin'." When he set a plateful of bacon and eggs on the table, I knew he was staying.

"Hey," I replied unenthusiastically.

Small brown eyes flicked over my face. "You left kind of early last night. From the looks of you I'd say you must have got sauced somewheres else? Don't blame ya. Comin' face to face with death does that, don't it?"

"Does it?"

"Yup. I should know. Afghanistan. Firefighting is a breeze compared to that BS."

So he *was* a military man. That could account for his ape man manners.

"Lemme tell ya." Larry T stuffed bacon into his mouth. "The heat was bad. Bugs, snakes and dead soldiers. You have no clue, Adie. So you saw a piece of Brock eighty feet under." He guffawed loudly. "There's much worse goin' on out in the real world."

I nodded, thinking of Larissa. "I imagine you had combat training."

He grinned. "Damn straight. All kinds of weapons."

I studied his stocky body. He would be a perfect hit man. "Knives?"

Elbows out, he dug into his breakfast. "Oh-hh, yeah," he mumbled, mouth half open chewing, his fish eyes hooded. "But rifles were more my thing. Tac-50. Loved the army. Twelve years of it."

"Get injured?"

"Took a few bullets. Nothing permanent." He pointed to his chest. "Played it safe. Heroes die."

"So why quit?"

"Turned forty and was still a sergeant." He buttered a piece of toast. "Besides, I have a decent pension. Have a huge house from my divorce."

"And you didn't go into another line of work?"

Larry T sucked the butter off his finger. "Didn't need to. I made a killin'."

Seeing the look on my face, he snickered. "Scare ya?"

I shook my head. "Nope." There'd been more than one encounter with death in my life. None of them had been pleasant. But no one should get away with murder. The victims deserved justice. Finding the killer excited me. The omelet and fruit consumed, I stuck the banana in my bag and stood. "You might like Mission Impossible."

"Huh?"

"The movie we're scheduled to see. Action, killings, that sort of thing. Didn't you see the activity board? Eleven-thirty at the Chedraui theatre."

****

A nap and a hot shower later, I tugged on a body-hugging floral print dress and stepped into my favorite metallic sandals. Before I forgot, I texted my best friend in Cozumel to meet me at the square after the show. Although filthy rich and a successful designer, Carmelita never flaunted her status as a Bolivar Alvarez. She hadn't taken Fede's last name. Why bother with that archaic custom? Carmelita was literally queen of the island and as a

Bolivar Alvarez, she was untouchable. But she was also down to earth. Pretentious was not her way. That tinkling laugh and optimistic attitude of hers always brightened my day. Then, as an afterthought before I stuck my cell in my purse, I sent one more text.

My face in the mirror desperately needed color. Coral lip gloss and a touch of blush did the trick. With raindrops spotting the patio doors, there was no need for sunscreen. Burberry umbrella in hand I slipped out into the corridor.

By the time I hit the street, the drops were the size of poker chips. It was a relief to enter the Chedraui department store. Imagine a Mexican version of Walmutts. I paused to look at furniture. If I married Wolf I would need all kinds of regular practical stuff found in places like this. Fortunately, there were fun places to shop on the island where authentic hand carved furniture was sold.

That is if I committed myself to him. Did I really want the shackles of marriage? But buying new furniture would be fun, not quite as exciting as shoes—still casual rattan suited me. Although I had to admit the Italian leather couches and oak tables at the condo were unbeatably stylish.

On my next trip, I would definitely stay there. The apartment close to the museum was so much nicer than any hotel on the island and it was all mine.

"Really? Logical Voice spoke up. "Nothing in life is free. Diego has an agenda. And you're part of his package."

"And what a package he has!" Hormone enthused. "That man is hotter than a bubbling chocolate fondue. Snatch him up before he gets bored and moves on, sweetie."

"Adie will never get that man to the altar," Logical muttered. "All he wants is a night in the sack."

"So-oo? She'd be an idiot if she gave him the boot."

How crazy was this? The voices in my brain were arguing about me getting it on with a possible murderer. "Shut up!" I snapped angrily. What did they know? Neither of them was thinking of the gap in my heart. At least I knew Wolf didn't kill anyone.

Plenty of boutiques sat on the bottom level. I was so worked up, I almost stepped in to buy a sweater. Luckily, the designer tags were out of my price range. As for my real obsession, shoes, they weren't here on this level. The stores with the great prices and sexy shoes were close to the cinema. Unfortunately, I had an appointment to meet the tour group in a few minutes.

On my way up the escalator, I started to wonder what Wolf wanted to talk about. Had he squeezed the truth out of that snake? She was a clever viper. It would be difficult to force her hand but he could be as smooth as butter when it came to women. And I was sure he wouldn't let her slide back into his life.

Plastic ads about the movies hung on each side of the pillar in front of the cinema, with a visual of the film and details in Spanish or English.

"Adie, hurry!" a female voice screeched from the theatre box office. Back to reality. Time for Adie the tour agent to round up those doggies and steer them into the corral.

"We're all here. What took you so long already?" Irmgard's lips were pursed in a thin line."

"Calm down, Irmgard. It hasn't started." I passed some bills to the cashier and paid for the group. At the snack stand, I bought popcorn and water before herding them into the theatre. With Irmgard on his arm, Daniel traipsed up the stairs ahead of me. The rest scattered. I picked a seat near the center and made myself comfortable. After unscrewing the cap, I set my water bottle in the holder. Buttery popcorn made the movie experience complete. I'd hate myself for the calories tomorrow but as Scarlet said, "Tomorrow is another day".

The movie started with a bang. I hardly noticed when someone took the seat beside me. On the screen, Tom Cruise accepted the mission. As the message blew up I dug into the popcorn bag propped on my lap and munched nervously. With eyes on the action, I reached for another just as the bag was snatched away. "What the—"

"Um-mm, popcorn."

"That's not funny. Hand it over," I said sharply, turning to my neighbor.

Lips softly caressed my mouth before a husky voice whispered, "I would share with you."

In the darkness, the cobalt blue of his eyes shocked me with their intensity. "Wolf," I breathed. "How?"

A kiss on my fingertips sparked a flame. This man wasn't fighting fair. He knew me too well. There was no way on God's green earth this man would suck me back into his trap. "Don't!"

Explosions on screen happened in sync with my rapid pulse. Inhaling the exhilarating scent of soap and balmy ocean breeze, I sank back into my seat.

Wolf nuzzled my neck. "Let's go eat," he growled seductively. "I have to talk to you."

"No!" I protested. But my curiosity was getting the better of me. I was torn between wanting to know what he had to say and giving him the heave-ho.

"Babe, after the movie we'll go to the square, okay?" Wolf whispered in my ear.

That magnetic asymmetrical face was steamier than hot chocolate. My brain felt like jello. Like a puppet on a string, I found myself nodding.

Wolf squeezed my hand reassuringly. As I berated myself for my stupidity, I felt someone take the chair in the row behind me. His knees thudded annoyingly on the back of my seat as he settled in. I picked up my umbrella which was about to fall. It was much too expensive an item to end up on a dirty cement floor. Annoyed, I peered over my shoulder.

From nowhere, a narrow plastic cylinder zoomed in. The target was my neck. A needle point glinted in the dim light. With a reflex action, I swung my umbrella. The object fell to the floor. "What the heck!"

Jumping up on his feet, Wolf grabbed the thug's collar. "Oh no, you don't."

The punk in a hooded fleece jacket and jeans struggled.

"Who sent you?" Wolf jerked him closer.

The theatre chairs were so high-backed I had to stand to see. Facial hair and a swarthy complexion. He was young. Barely a man.

"Quiet down there! Some of us want to see the movie," a man hollered from a few rows above.

"Call security!" I screamed back.

From Wolf's position behind the high backed seats, he couldn't take the guy down but at the same time the punk couldn't make a run for it. Realizing this, the kid bit down on Wolf's hand.

Wolf's jaw tightened and he let go.

On the loose, the kid zoomed down the aisle and down the stairs, disappearing from view.

Our aisle had people seated at the exit. Scaling around them would slow me down considerably and then I'd have to run in heels. Not impossible, but he'd have the advantage.

"Leave it, Adie. There's no way we can catch him."

A uniformed attendant shone a flashlight at us. "Is there some problem, Señor?"

"There was a man bothering us but he left."

"Would you like me to call security?"

"No, it's too late. The man is far gone by now."

I sighed, knowing Wolf was right. Once security heard the story they'd hand it over to the police. Hernandez would only complicate the situation and twist it around to blame me. I needed to keep this under wraps.

The attendant switched off the light. "So sorry, Señor."

"How's your hand?" I asked when he'd sat back down.

"I'll live." Wolf stroked my cheek, "More importantly, are you alright?"

"Yes." I stared at my fiancé. How could I coldheartedly break up with him? He had my back. Whatever made me think there was a man out there better than he was?

The lights flicked on.

"Look by your feet, babe. I think you flipped it down there with your umbrella. Do you see anything?"

My hand went to my mouth realizing what had just happened. "That kid was about to inject me."

"Move your feet. I'll check the floor." The sea god craned his neck up as his hand skimmed the cement. "Nice view," he commented with a grin, his eyes scanning my legs.

"Found it." With a plastic syringe in his hand Wolf pulled himself up and sat down. "Do you have a tissue? I'll have it analyzed at a lab. But for now, I think we can safely assume it's lethal."

From out of my purse, I pulled a couple of paper napkins and handed them to Wolf. "That man bit you. Let me see your hand."

"I'm fine."

"Reality check, Superman. Do you have a doctor or should we

go to the clinic?"

"We?"

"Don't fight me on this. He could be a druggie."

"Alright. Take a look." He lifted his hand for my perusal. Indentations but the skin hadn't broken.

"See? I told you there was nothing to be alarmed about."

"And I'm telling you that you're lucky. This is serious business. You have no idea."

"What are you talking about, Adie?"

"Last night I was attacked in the street. With a knife. Do you realize what this means? Larissa, Brock, and now me."

"My guess is you know too much."

Anxiously, I shook my head. "But, Wolf, I don't. Not any more than you."

"Just a minute." Confusion in his eyes. "What did you say? Larissa is dead?"

I nodded. "Last night. I discovered the body."

"Where?"

"Moray's Eel. I stopped in after I left you," I said slowly. "I needed a friendly face and a stiff drink."

Wolf's eyes were sad. "I didn't know Sam would be there at the cottage. You have to believe me." He took my hand. "What happened at the Eel?"

A visual of Larissa huddled over the fridge, long flowing waves, assailed me. Beautiful and so dead. "It was awful. There was so much blood."

"Why didn't you call me?"

"How could I?" I protested accusingly. "You were with her."

"That's another thing we have to talk about." He looked around at the empty theatre. A teen in a red uniform came in to scoop up garbage. "Let's head out to the square." He shot up on his feet, his face animated. "I know. We'll order some of that *mole* for you. That might cheer you up."

I nodded. The tour group had free time after the show and I had arranged to meet up with Carmelita but not for an hour so I might as well see what the man had to say.

As we trekked carefully down the stairs, Wolf's hand under my elbow, I kept thinking about the assailant. He had a thin build, very much like the teenage employee sweeping the theatre. A perfect plan. He'd inject me and run. A skinny guy like that would have no problem with an escape through the narrow aisle between the seats. It was obvious he was athletic too, the way he'd taken the steep stairs. The incredible hulk from last night would have had a problem with that.

By the time we left the mall and hit the street, the rain was plummeting down. A sturdy Burberry is perfect for a romantic walk in Paris—even better for tropical rain. I gave it to Wolf to hold as he was eager to please and suited the job. Everyone knows the prince is the one in charge of the romantic gestures, not the princess.

This afternoon, San Miguel was rainy and considerably cooler than usual. But life went on whether someone wanted me dead or not. Vendors with carts huddled under awnings selling jewelry and Mexican souvenirs, while pedestrians hoofed it under the cover of umbrellas. A few fearless souls trekked hatless through the puddles that had filled up the potholes and cracks in the uneven sidewalk. In fact, the street was flooded. Cars wickedly splashed muddy showers on those that made the mistake of coming too close.

Once we passed Moray's Eel and the Mega Supermarket, we entered the downtown with its restaurants, jewelry shops and souvenir places. It was as busy as on a sweltering hot day, maybe even more so. Funny how the fresh sea air has a way of energizing. All that was wrong with the world seemed to disappear.

On the way, we window shopped just like any couple in love, almost as if Samantha had never happened. I knew this couldn't last but right now, after narrowly disarming a creep with a syringe, I needed Wolf. As he pushed through the crowd, I was glad he was a capable take-control sort of guy.

Steam rose from the ground as the humid air from outside met the cool air-conditioning from inside the pricy stores. Slick salespeople in dark suits standing in front of jewelry stores accosted us with tanzanite deals. Yet I knew the most spectacular tanzanite ring would be hard pressed to compare to the emerald and diamond job sparkling on my finger. It was ridiculous but in the back of my mind I hadn't given up on Wolf or his proposal.

By the time we entered the square, the rain had turned into a gentle spray. In the park they'd set up a stage for a salsa band. Cobblestone sidewalks bordered restaurants on three sides while the ocean edged the fourth.

"Have you been to Pablo's?" Wolf indicated the orange building straight ahead with the painted macaws in greens and turquoise on the yellow awning. As we approached, he closed up the Burberry.

The narrow restaurant had a bar and tables inside. Under umbrellas, round patio tables were occupied with a group of partying Americans. A hefty balding man in a white shirt and black dress pants stood menus in hand at the entrance. "Señor Du Lac? I have a good table right here. The people just left." He signaled a young man who appeared with a rag to clean the plastic table cloth. "In a short time the band will start and you will have the best view."

"Excellent, Ramon. We'll take it." Wolf pulled out a chair for me right next to the fence. "A Dos Equis for me and a *margarita sin sel* for the lady," he turned to me, "Is that okay? I know you like to switch it up."

I nodded. Daiquiris were getting boring. Drinking hadn't been part of my afternoon plan but neither had I imagined being a human pincushion. I had another big concern sitting right across from me. I crossed my leg, tapping my sandal in the air. "Is it true?"

"What?" Wolf sat back his hands behind his head, jean clad legs stretched into the aisle.

"You slept with Samantha?"

The waiter, a round face and slicked back hair with Miguel on his tag interrupted my interrogation. A goblet of green slush and a bottle of Dos Equis was set on the table alongside a basket of chips and a dish of salsa.

Wolf signaled a glass wasn't necessary and tipped back the beer.

Clasping his hands on top of his rotund belly, the server waited legs astride. "Are you ready to order?"

"No, not yet," I said abruptly, a little put out with the disruption.

"*Un momento.*" Wolf told the server, handing me the menu. He pointed out the entrees. "You'll feel better with some food in your stomach."

I didn't like the implication or the delay tactics. "We need to talk now."

Wolf smiled lazily. "First we order the food and then you'll hear all my secrets, okay?"

"Alright." I nodded reluctantly.

"How about the chicken?"

Wolf knew me so well. When I read the description, my taste buds hopped in anticipation. Mayan chicken in spicy chocolate sauce. "*Pollo de mole, please.*"

"And for you, Señor?"

"*Sopa mariscos, por favor.*"

So he was going for something light, like soup. Most likely he'd eaten a huge breakfast with the snake. I tapped my fingers as Miguel retreated into the kitchen. "You think I'm in a bad mood? Well guess what, mister, you're right on."

Wolf grabbed my hand, stroking it lightly. "Seriously, Adie. You can demolish me and I'd understand completely but I don't remember having sex. I really don't. It's all a big blank."

"You were drunk?" That was hard to believe. Wolf could hold his liquor when lesser men were unconscious on the floor.

"No, not wasted, but something wasn't right." Wolf gazed earnestly at me. "Everything went hazy and didn't make sense. I thought I'd come down with dengue fever."

"You had a temperature?"

He nodded.

"Was Samantha with you?"

"Yeah. Neither of us had been drinking. They didn't allow it at that hotel, remember? It was all natural food and organic drinks."

"Yup." I remembered the place. A nudist hotel with a health-conscious approach.

As the waiter arrived with our lunches, Wolf held off. I filled up a tortilla, rolled it and bit in. It was heaven but my stomach was somersaulting.

Wolf started his soup and then, seeing my expression, said, "Not good?"

"It's delicious." I needed to hear the story no matter how ugly it was. "You were saying?"

"Sam had orange juice and I had a coffee."

"So you had nothing to cause a black out?"

"No."

I speared a slice of tomato. "I'm trying to believe your story. If you didn't have sex, why did she say you were the father?"

"It was all a lie. She made that up to get rid of you. The woman is a whack-job. When I checked with my doctor, he said the test is done between ten and thirteen weeks. It's way too early for a DNA test." He tipped back his beer, then contemplatively searched the amber hue for answers.

"But, she is pregnant?"

Wolf shrugged. "Sam had a urine test."

"And?"

"It came out positive but they're not always accurate. You know that." He gazed at me earnestly. "I told them to do a blood test to make sure. They should have the results by tomorrow."

I processed the situation. "Okay, let's replay this. I want to be sure I understand."

"Sure."

"A few weeks ago there was a stockholders meeting at Tulum del Mar. When I left for San Miguel, you stayed behind with Samantha. You had drinks at the bar and then what?"

"I don't remember much."

"Think."

"I had coffee and talked to Sam."

"About?"

"Our marriage and divorce. Nothing detailed."

"And then?"

"I started feeling dizzy and out of it."

"Are you saying you blacked out after you had coffee?"

"Yeah, but not right away."

"Drugs?"

"I don't know. If it wasn't dengue she might have slipped something in my coffee."

I gave him a look of disbelief. "And then what? She went with you to your room and seduced you?"

"I remember her walking back with me. I told her I needed to lie down. I was sweating and feeling nauseous. After that, I'm not too clear."

"Do you think you had sex with her?"

"Sam's attractive but," Wolf frowned, "if I did it wasn't willingly."

I rolled my eyes. "She raped you?"

"It doesn't take much for a male to get turned on. That's true but—" Wolf's clear blue eyes met mine. "Listen to me, Adie."

That was the problem. I didn't want to. Cheating was cheating. I was ready to shut him out.

"Please listen to me. Will you?"

When he stroked my cheek, I looked back.

"After I returned to Cozumel I had recurring dreams and headaches. I knew something wasn't right." He set his spoon down. "At first I thought this was because of a bout with dengue but now that she claims I slept with her. I'm inclined to think it was GHB or roofies."

"Are those the known after effects?"

Wolf tipped back his beer and gazed at me. "Yeah. I checked on the net today."

"Have you spoken with the hotel personnel?" I twirled my fork thoughtfully. "They might be able to help you reconstruct what happened."

"That was six weeks ago, babe." The wind tossed a wave of thick blond hair over his forehead. He pushed it back. "The hotel was full. I doubt that they'll remember anything about those two days."

A whiff of soap and balmy ocean breeze perked my senses. For a moment, I was lost. His magnetic face drew me in. I wanted to thread my fingers through his hair. What was it about a man with clean soft hair and a body that smelled good? I struggled to collect my thoughts. A sip of margarita and I said, "They'd know if you passed out at the bar. Especially since everyone drinks juice."

"And smokes weed. Don't forget these people have money to buy designer drugs. Sam is no exception."

"If you want to find out the truth, you need to go back to the resort." The sparkling blue of his eyes switched my mode into reverse. Memories of his powerful naked body, skin glistening with droplets of water, making love after the shower. Involuntarily, a shiver surged to my core.

Wolf's hand against my cheek startled me.

"Babe, you're right. I owe it to us. I'll go back." He softly kissed me. "I love you."

"Once you know the truth, we can deal with love. Not before."

"There's no way in hell that baby is mine. No matter how much she wants it to be true." Wolf ran his fingers down my arm. "Sam is lying about all of this, Adie. I wouldn't have sex with her willingly. You believe me, don't you?"

I nodded.

"Thank you for that." He set his beer down. "Now, it's your turn. What's going on? Who sent that thug after you?"

"I've continued my investigation. I can't see letting a killer get away with two murders. My guess is that somehow, the mastermind caught on. I think he wants to take me out."

"Damn! This is my fault! I knowingly dragged you into this mess, Adie. We stirred up a hornet's nest. You've got to stop digging."

The tart taste of the margarita lingered on my lips. "It's too late now. Someone is gunning for me." I leaned in. "And you'd better watch out too, Wolf."

"I'm good. Don't worry." He took up my hand. "Babe, I want you to move in with me. You'll be safe that way."

"That's silly, Wolf. You work. You go places."

"I could hire someone when I'm not with you. Let's face it. You need me. Let me remind you that you're not Wonder Woman."

"Oh?" I laughed. "That's not what you thought in the shower."

"Yeah? You're exceptional alright, princess. But somehow I think I had a little something to do with it."

"More like a big something."

Wolf had the cat that swallowed the canary grin.

"Can you keep a secret?"

He nodded.

"I just found this out. I want you to promise not to tell anyone."

Wolf's brow furrowed. "This has to do with Alvarez, doesn't it?"

"You promise not to tell anyone?"

"Cross my heart and hope to die," he said with a smile.

"Sh-hh! Don't talk like that," I said, alarmed. "That's the last thing I want to deal with."

"Sorry. You just looked so serious."

"And so I should. You know that Diego had a brother?"

"Right. Died in a dive accident, didn't he?"

"Yes and no."

Wolf looked perplexed.

"I met him. He's my dive instructor. Cy arranged his own death after someone tampered with his car."

He lowered his voice. "How do you know this?"

I speared a piece of chicken and savored it. "Cy told me. Last night."

The band came back up to play. As they announced a song entitled *Amor,* a deep voice called out from the restaurant entrance. "*Hola,* Adie!"

I turned to see a broad-shouldered man in a white T-shirt and jeans. His dark curly hair flew wildly around in the breeze. Sunglasses covered his eyes. A beard and moustache took care of the rest.

"Cy! You're early." To Wolf I whispered, "I asked him to meet me but I didn't know you'd be here with me."

"That's okay," Wolf muttered. Standing, he extended his hand. "Wolf Du Lac."

Cy took it. "Cy Nemisis." And then the grin abruptly vanished. He glanced from me to Wolf. "The fiancé?"

"Join us. It's okay. You don't mind, do you, Wolf?"

"No, of course not." He took his seat and scrutinized the dive master. "So-oo, Cy, aka Amancio."

Cy shot him a look. "Adie told you."

"Some of the story. But don't worry I won't say a word to Alvarez. You can count on that." He contemplated the hippy dive master. "One question. Why didn't you take your accident to the police when it happened? You are Amancio Bolivar Alvarez, the older brother. They would listen to you."

"True. I'm not proud of running away but honor was involved." He took off the sunglasses and set them on the table. "If my brother was trying to kill me to inherit the business, my parents, well, it would be too hard on them."

Wolf contemplated the golden hue of his beer before he spoke. "And now that your father died you returned to Cozumel."

Cy shot me a look.

"It's okay. You can trust him," I said, patting Cy's arm. "He hired Brock to investigate Bolivar Imports and Exports. Wolf searched Brock's computer. I told you what we've found out so far."

"The Turks and Swiss accounts?" Signaling the waiter, Cy held up his hand and circled a finger for a round. It was obvious he was a regular when the waiter brought two Dos Equis and a margarita to our table. Interesting. Even though he was covered with facial fur, the Alvarez interior shone through. Power and position is difficult to hide.

Wolf was steely eyed. All testosterone. Fierce like a gladiator in a lion's den. Did he think Cy was a threat? I had to admit, after seeing him, all corporate and handsome in that photo, I wouldn't mind another look. "Cy thinks Diego is responsible for his father's death."

"How?" Wolf's eyes flicked from me to Cy.

"Supposedly my father had a heart attack. But apart from a minor scare years ago he was healthy. He should have lived for another twenty years, yet after a mysterious visitor, he is suddenly found dead."

"Was there an autopsy?"

Cy knocked back his beer. After he set it back on the table he leaned forward, elbows on the table. "No. They thought it was a heart attack. Broken blood vessels in his eyes, but I know that can be induced. I took first year med school. An injection in a place where no one suspects and the killer is off scot-free."

"Omigod!"

"What is it, Adie?" Cy touched my shoulder, concern on his face. "You look pale. Are you alright?"

Wolf called out, "Waiter! Water for the lady, *por favor!*" He frowned at Cy's hand.

"That thug," I said to Wolf. "Do you think there's a connection?"

"Adie was attacked at the movie theatre with a syringe."

"Not again! A man with a knife came at Adie outside my apartment last night. Thank God I was home."

Wolf lifted an eyebrow. "You helped Adie?"

Cy squeezed my hand. "I wish I could take credit. She took him down."

Wolf smiled. "She is good."

"If you," I pointed my finger at Cy, "weren't there, he

wouldn't have given up so easily. I owe you."

"And I appreciate you keeping my fiancée safe," Wolf said.

I shoved my plate away. "Enough about me, gentlemen. Listen, Cy. Whoever is behind these murders could have killed your father."

Cy's jaw was set. "Diego."

"Hey, I don't like him either," Wolf interjected, "but you think he'd kill his *own* father?"

15

"I don't *want* to believe it. No matter what, Diego is my brother."

Wolf shoved his soup dish away. "Prove his innocence then."

A drone from Wolf's pocket signaled a text. He dug the cell out and glanced at it. Was it business or had the viper summoned him?

"I have to go," he said poker faced, motioning for the bill.

"Put the drinks on my tab," Cy told Miguel when he came over.

"Thanks, Cy." Wolf laid some bills on the table. "For the tip." To me, he said, "I'll stop at the lab before it closes, babe. Pack up, I'll get you tonight."

"What are you talking about?"

"You're not safe at the hotel. I want you to stay at my cottage."

I glared at him.

"Is ten too late?" he asked politely.

"Wolf," I said calmly, "I'm not going anywhere."

Stooping down, Wolf kissed me quickly before he shot up to leave. "Don't be stubborn, my little mermaid. After what's happened, you can't be alone."

"I'll think about it."

Wolf's eyes teased. "And then say yes."

I sighed. "Good bye, sea god. Let me know about *any* test results you get."

In the crowd gathering for the show Wolf's tall figure and

blond hair stood out above the shorter tourists and locals. When I could no longer see him I had that feeling I get when my lottery ticket comes up a few numbers short.

"So he's your fiancé. Have you resolved your issues?"

"No. It's all a mess."

"You wanted to talk about it? Is that why you texted me?"

"Not exactly, but are you available tonight?"

Cy raised an eyebrow. "Isn't the Swede coming to get you?"

"I'll deal with that later. I have this idea."

"And you want me to help?" Cy grinned. "I'm flattered. What is it?"

"Pick me up tonight at eight. Wear black. I'll explain then."

"Alright." When he leaned in, his voice was different, husky and low. "You are an intriguing woman." His eyes flicked over my body. "Does this mean you'll be wearing something sexy and black?"

Men have a thing about a woman in black. "I meant T-shirt and jeans, not black tie." As the melody eased into lulling notes, I added, "There was another reason I wanted you to come here."

From the park right on cue, a lilting voice called out, "*Hola, amiga!*" In an off-the-shoulder fuchsia dress, Carmelita stood out like an orchid in a field of daisies waltzing through the spectators.

Dark sunglasses found their way back to Cy's nose. His jaw clenched. "*Mierda*! Why is my sister here, Adie? Is she the other reason you mentioned?

"Yup, I thought you should see her. Carmelita shouldn't suffer. She misses you terribly." I patted his arm. "And don't worry, she'll keep your secret."

"Right. Thanks for looking out for my interests." Cy shook his head. "It's bad enough you tell Du Lac. Well, I'm not taking any more chances." Pesos flipped on the table, Cy sprang up.

"Wait!"

"See you tonight, *cariño*. Eight." With a quick peck on my lips, he rushed to the entrance, brushing past his sister on the way out.

"Oo-oo! That one was in a hurry," Carmelita said in amusement, greeting me with kisses before she took the seat beside me. "Is he your dive instructor? I'd swear I've met him before, only," she said, her forehead furrowed, "I don't associate with the dive crowd. I'm probably the only resident of San Miguel who hasn't scuba-dived."

Feeling her pain, I squeezed her hand. "I don't blame you."

Carmelita frowned. "There have been too many deaths." In a flash, she smiled. "And of course, I'm too much of a fashionista." Signaling the waiter, she pointed at my goblet and held up a finger. "I see what you meant about all the hair on that man. He's quite the hippy." She glanced up at the gray clouds hovering overhead. "Strange how he wore sunglasses on a day like today, don't you think?"

"Like you said, hippy. Must have had a hard night."

The music started and our laughter was lost in the blast of salsa rhythm. When my drink was replaced, I sucked it in through the straw. My mind wandered. How would I approach this?

As the band took a break, Carmelita flashed me a smile. "Your dive master is athletic and tall, maybe even handsome. I'm seeing the potential. Mind you, he'd have to be stripped, shaved, and sheared. Speaking of men, how is your love life?" Her eyes glued on my ring. *"¡Ay, caramba!* Is that what I think it is? Adelina, you are engaged! It's beautiful!" She giggled. "I want one!"

"I know. Can't bear to take it off. Not just yet." The emerald sparkling alongside the diamonds was the same green as Carmelita's eyes. Those Bolivar eyes. If eyes were the windows to the soul, my bet was that Diego was not involved. He couldn't be romancing me one day and sending a hit man the next.

"Why take it off?" My friend met my gaze. "Neptune cheated on you? Already?"

"Cheated? Maybe," I said, shrugging, "maybe not. You remember Samantha at the party?"

"Um-mm, vaguely." Carmelita watched the waiter set goblets on the table. With the straw, she flicked salt from the rim into the goblet. "That was quite the bash. I had too many daiquiris. It's hard to remember much of anything. " She made a face. "Oh, yes. I was worried the reptile was getting too familiar with Fede."

"Fede wasn't her target. Samantha ruined my engagement."

"That's no surprise. The woman is evil."

"She's pregnant."

"Really? With Wolf? Do you seriously believe that?"

I nodded. "Why should she lie?"

"There's a story in this." Settling back in the chair with the margarita comfortably in hand, she said, "From the beginning, *amiga*," and looked at me expectantly.

"It all started when Wolf took me to Wet Wendy's after the party. The ring was in the glass."

"Oh, how clever of your sexy man."

"Caught me for a loop. I had no idea he wanted to propose."

Carmelita flashed her pearly whites. "Diego was a little upset after your beach excursion. Moping around…drinking. Now I know why."

Thoughtfully, I stirred the lime cocktail. "He mentioned it?"

"I stayed at his house that night. There was no way I wanted to set eyes on Fede after the party. Stupidly I didn't realize how much I loved Brock until it was too late."

She had my complete attention. This was exactly what I wanted to find out. "Did you know Larissa was killed that night?"

Carmelita's eyes widened. "No!"

"A stabbing. Inside Moray's Eel."

"*¡Dios mio!*" She crossed herself.

"Was Brock involved with Larissa?"

With a shake of her mane, my friend protested, "Brock was loyal to me. We were going to run away together to South America."

"Not Canada?"

"Brock wanted me to but I thought with all my money we needed to go somewhere warm. He was fluent in Spanish, you know."

"I didn't." But I had suspected in his line of work Spanish would come in handy. Wolf wouldn't hire someone without that skill. "Did he tell you why he was here?"

"Brock said he'd been hired for a bit of espionage."

"And you believed him?"

"Oh, yes." A tear trickled down her cheek. "He said I should never speak of it to anyone but I guess now it doesn't matter."

"What about when he flew in. Did you two talk?"

She bit her lip. "I phoned. Told him I needed time to figure out my marriage."

"How did he take that?"

"The poor darling was so confused. We met anyway and

ended up making love." She sighed. "I couldn't commit to him. He kept insisting I go to Toronto and I halfway agreed. But then reality set in. I'd have to divorce Fede." Carmelita's shoulders drooped as if she had the weight of the world on them.

"Do you have regrets?"

"Of course. I don't blame him. Why did I do something so stupid? I shouldn't have pushed him away. We could have had that night to work it out."

"You think you had a future together?"

"We might have if we'd talked. Communication is so important in a relationship."

So Brock and Carmelita had broken up. And then he had rebound sex with Irmgard. "Did you know he was with another woman that last night?"

Carmelita blanched. "He loved me. I can't see him doing that unless—"

"What?"

"He'd given up on me."

"What about your marriage?"

Shifting in her chair, Carmelita crossed her legs. "I'm beginning to think it's doomed. Fede was involved with Larissa. You saw the way they were making a public spectacle of themselves." The corners of her lips turned down. "It wasn't the first time. The man is scum. Absolutely no loyalty. Diego is right. I would be better off without him." She tossed back the margarita. "But to be honest, I have been equally guilty. We are both at fault. I tend to react after his infidelity. After confession, I resolve to make it work. Fede comes around and says he's sorry. Brings me chocolates and jewelry." Her eyes dropped to the slender diamond bracelet on her wrist. "See this? A trinket he picked up on our last falling out. I think he loves me in his own way. I'm his rock."

I shot her a look. "The Bolivar Alvarez rock."

She sighed. "Poor Fede is a Barrera de la Cruz. His family was one of the original Spanish families in Cozumel. Our story is not unusual. An old impoverished family marries into wealth. Papa saved his family's holdings and the Barrera de la Cruz family gained status. Our marriage was beneficial to both."

Carmelita stared out at the gray ocean where a cruise ship was docking. A glimmer of amber peeked between the scarlet edged rain clouds. Sunsets come early in winter. Today we were lucky the sun had appeared at all.

Her chin set, Carmelita continued the story, "After the hurricane, my papa started Royal Investments. Businesses were bought up and rebuilt. Papa made a killing on the misfortune of others." She shrugged. "But he was a good man. Make no mistake. Constructing condos and hotels helped the island. When he left for Mexico City with Mama, Royal Investments was given to my brothers. Amancio found real estate exciting but Papa had other ideas for him. He was told to leave everything to Diego and supervise the Cozumel end of Bolivar Imports and Exports."

"And that's when Diego and Amancio had a falling out?"

She crinkled her nose. "Why would you say that? It wasn't Diego's fault that Amancio had to head the Imports. It was the bigger operation. Papa thought it was best."

"Why?"

"Diego had women on his mind." She laughed. "It was hard for him to work more than an eight hour day, if that. My poor brother was always worn out from the clubbing and girlfriends."

"Wait a minute. When Amancio died I thought Diego took over Bolivar Imports."

"He became the new president but Fede kept his position as vice president and supervised operations. He positively glowed when he spoke of it. It was more successful than ever. Even Papa was surprised."

"So Fede had a good salary?"

"Diego was generous." Thoughtfully, Carmelita turned the diamond ring on her pinky.

"Do you think he set up Larissa? Gave her money to buy Moray's Eel?"

Carmelita's jaw dropped. "I…I don't know."

"Did Larissa have family money?"

"Whoring money, I'd think." Carmelita tossed her bangs back. "She arrived here from somewhere out west without a peso but it didn't take long for her to buy clothes and jewelry."

"And yesterday…was he upset?"

Carmelita gazed at me. "You think he cared about her?"

"Even if he didn't love her, don't you think he might be sad that she was murdered?"

She played with the napkin on the table. "I suppose."

"You did see him that day?"

"Briefly. I was staying at Diego's, remember? Fede came by to beg me to come home but Diego told him to leave."

"What about Diego? Was he acting differently?"

"You spent the day with him, Adelina. If he was withdrawn, it was because of your engagement to Wolf."

A headache was coming on. I rubbed my temple.

"Are you alright, *amiga*?"

Sitting back in my chair, I sipped my margarita then placed it back on the table. "Someone is trying to kill me."

Carmelita looked dazed. "What! Who?"

"I haven't a clue. First, there was a man with a knife outside my dive master's apartment and then, today, in the movie theatre, a man with a syringe."

"This has to do with the other murders, Adelina. It must!" Carmelita grabbed my hand. "I am afraid for you. You have to come back to Diego's with me. He has bodyguards. You would be safe there."

"I think I'm close to the truth. If I stay at Diego's now, the killer will be safe, too."

And if he wasn't the murderer, Hormonal Voice squeaked with excitement, you could take him for a test drive.

Put a sock in it! Logical shouted. Diego is ready to shut Adie up permanently.

"Now I am really worried, Adelina. You are so pale."

"Don't be. Wolf said he'd pick me up tonight. I'll stay there."

"Alright, if you must, but text if it doesn't work out. Remember, you have a serious player pulling out all the stops and she's after your man." Carmelita threw a few bills on the table and grabbed my arm. "Come with me, Adelina. I'll drive you back."

****

I was ready to crash and burn. My energy was so low I could barely peel off my clothes before crawling into bed. Just before drifting off, I set the alarm and then went out like a light.

Auburn-haired women with evil eyes threw me into the ocean. I sank deep into the salty brine. As my feet touched the white sand, I was sure death had me in its grip. "Never give up" was my karate mantra. I wouldn't let them kill me. I struggled against the current that fired me into sharp coral. With my last breath, I fought away from the spikes and pushed towards the cave. In the distance, two divers in black floated near the opening. Long black hair whirled around the female diver. The male was big and muscular. A perfect couple. Would they help me? As I caught up to them, they slowly turned. Flat dead eyes stared into mine. Brock and Larissa.

The beeping broke through the corrosion of my dream. A glance at the cell screen. I had time to get ready but my body was still in limbo. Shutting my eyes, I attempted to erase the images but they lingered like a dirty scum line in the bathtub.

Finally moving, I went through the motions of donning a black T-shirt, jeans and a pair of Nikes. With fresh lip gloss coating my lips, I headed out, pocketing my key card before clicking the door behind me.

Noises of a buffet dinner filtered up from the pool to the open air balcony. With entertainment to follow, I was free to find out everything I could tonight. I needed answers and I needed them fast.

The roar of the jeep pulling into the curved driveway sounded nothing like Diego's Ferrari. Cy's jet black mean machine coughed up smoke.

It stopped steps away from my feet. Hesitation filled me, but before I could cop out, my date hopped out and swung the door open with a bow. When I had one foot up, hands clinging to the frame, Cy gripped my hips to give me a boost me into the passenger seat.

"That was fun," he commented with a grin.

"I could have managed."

"Yup, but it's way more exciting when I assist."

"I can see you and Diego are more similar than you want to admit."

"Papa taught us to be men."

"But not gentlemen."

Cy laughed. "Oh, come on, Adie. That sort would bore you in no time." He turned the key, revved the motor and swerved onto

Melgar. "Where to?"

"Head towards the airport."

Diamond and souvenir shops illuminated the main street. Here and there, employees slid heavy glass doors shut as they closed for the night.

In the harbor, cruise ships flickered like spirits through the mist. Heavy cloud masses covered the night sky hiding the moon. My guess was we were in for some rain.

The Jeep's vinyl top gave us protection but someone had forgotten to zip in the vinyl windows. In fact, when I checked there weren't any.

"Like the air-conditioning?" Cy asked with a wicked grin.

"I was just thinking what an adjustment it must have been to assume a dive master's life after fast cars and big houses."

"It was. Something like camping. But I'm an outdoorsman deep down. I like casual."

"You mean no more tuxes or dinner parties?"

Cy's mouth turned down at the corners. "Those weren't always fun."

"Surely not all bad memories."

"No. Nothing in life is just black or white."

"But you're determined to see Diego as the bad guy?"

"Let's not be too serious tonight, Adie, hm-mm?" He glanced sidelong and checked me out. "I like you in black but what's the mystery? You had a goth party in mind?"

"Not exactly."

"Always the cryptic answers." His hands relaxed on the steering wheel. "I'd like to get to know you better, Adie. I have a feeling you'd be an interesting challenge."

I fluttered my eyelashes seductively. "So when are you shaving?"

Cy lifted a brow. "You mean if the beard goes you'd be interested?"

"And the shoulder length tresses."

Throwing back his head, he laughed. "Sounds girly. Your implication is I am too feminine?"

"Athletic and woodsy. You'd be a good candidate for *Survivor.*"

"Because of my unique physical powers?"

"I would hardly be the judge of that."

"Something you could find out about."

"I tend to take my commitments rather seriously."

"Oh?" Cy grinned. "You, maybe, but not your illusive Swede."

"Wolf is not up for discussion."

"Quite right. Why talk about your convoluted love life? This is our first date. Let's enjoy it. Where to?"

"Um-mm." When Cy headed past the Museo, I spoke up. "The Bolivar warehouse."

I braced myself as my date jerked the Jeep to a halt. In the dim light, Cy's eyes glimmered green like a cat's. "Just what are you up to, Adie Sturm?"

16

"I think you know the answer to that." I winked. "You're a bright guy."

Cy wore a bemused expression. "But not one prone to making errors."

One look at those lips curled up at the corners and I knew he was not taking me seriously. "Believe me, this plan will work."

"How so?" With a glance into the rearview mirror, he pushed back a lock of hair that had dared to stray to his forehead.

Who would have thought the hippy dive master was as vain as his brother? But it shouldn't have been a surprise. Amancio Edgar Bolivar Alvarez was probably as hot underneath all that hair as his sizzling brother. "It's been a while since you left Cozumel, correct?"

"Almost two years."

"So you're not familiar with the operation anymore."

Cy shrugged. "Bolivar Imports and Exports? No."

"And before? Did you know what was in the warehouse?"

"A bit of everything I imagine," he said vaguely, eyeing the street sign.

I had him nailed. Waving my finger, I said emphatically, "That's exactly my point. Were you looking into the inventory at the time of your accident?"

"I was new to it. Papa handled the Mexico City end and the rest of us worked on what we were sent here. I had a look around but that's about all." Cy's jaw tightened and he chopped the air with his hands. "Alright. I get it. You're right, Adie. We have to do this."

Shifting into first, he swung quickly back into traffic. Further away from the main street, the lights were few and far between. Dusk had surrendered to a misty night. I heaved a sigh of relief as Cy slowed down to let a wispy black cat cross the road. A man who likes animals is the only kind I can trust. And to me, the cat was a sign of good luck.

In the shrouded darkness of a moonless sky, an occasional house facing the street provided enough light to guide us to the next *calle*. The numbers of the narrow streets were barely visible yet Cy drove confidently through them.

As we headed away from the city central, the residential area faded into run down unoccupied buildings, sidewalks and gutters littered with garbage. Cy stopped in front of a boxlike house and parked. On one side peeling turquoise paint exposed the gray concrete underneath. A walled garden shut the property off from the street. Orange blossoms of a flowering hibiscus reached over a red tile roof, the tips hiding broken beer bottles lining an iron railing. Next to the house was an empty lot strewn with cans, cardboard boxes and plastic wrappers.

Coming around to my side of the Jeep, Cy whipped open the door and held out a strong hand to help me down. "Señorita, " he said with a smirk.

After landing somewhat awkwardly on the cracked surface of the road, I balanced myself as I spotted a bunker-like building ahead. A high ramp led up to an aluminum double garage door at the front. "That's the warehouse?"

"*Si.*" Taking my hand, he steered me across the street. "I figured we'd observe from the field."

Overhead, the gray sky was now cloaked in a soiled black. The lack of lighting made it difficult to see. "And how would we do this?"

He pointed to some bushes. "We'll hide there. Just ahead."

Twenty meters further along, we found a place between the banana trees. The warehouse stood directly in front of us.

"Will it be a long wait?"

Cy's eyes flicked to his Rolex. "Any minute now. If I

remember correctly, this is the last shipment for the night. We almost missed it," he said, then added with a mischievous glance, "So glad you finally filled me in on your plan, Sherlock."

I grinned. "Better late than never, my dear Watson. Master detectives tend to keep secrets."

"Crazy *chica*." Cy gave me a heavy-lidded gaze. "Let's sit down."

Lips pursed, I flicked him a doubtful look.

"Don't worry, *cariño*." He grinned. "I won't let the water moccasins bite your tender flesh." He laughed at my expression. "Joking. No poisonous snakes here in Coz."

Dropping down on the grass beside him, I couldn't help but think about mosquitoes. With the high humidity, I'd left my socks at the hotel. Fortunately, my jeans protected my legs while the Nikes did their best for my feet. I'd have to hope the little critters didn't figure out there was a buffet of skin in between.

After a few moments, I became painfully aware of the hard ground sparsely covered with grass. My problem was not enough butt fat. Some might say hard buns were a blessing but sitting that long was painful. Sneaking a glance at Cy, I wondered if he was any more comfortable. I leaned in and caught a scent of lime with a touch of musk. Mm-mm. Pleasantly arousing.

But it was from products. A man's natural scent is full of his DNA. The smell could make or break the deal. Of course, attraction gets much more complicated. If he passes the scent test, he has to have the face and body.

I'm not completely superficial. Sometimes a less than perfect male makes up for it with a mesmerizing personality. Or in the case of Wolf, his asymmetrical looks are really sexy. And something very important for me was his sense of humor, as long as he had a serious side. The best men are a complex mixture.

Life and love are complicated. The top twenty chart was loaded with sappy songs. If people didn't believe in love, the music industry would die. The fact is, "the one" has to surface by the time a woman reaches thirty, or she settles. The biological clock business has ruined many a logical woman.

Marriage has a forty per cent chance of success. And no wonder. As far as I could see, wet dewy romance slides under the table with babies and career. After that, boredom takes over.

Anything can happen when it comes to love. A man goes crazy over a woman or vice versa, and it's unreciprocated. My cheating jerk of a boyfriend had stolen my money as well as my heart before he took off.

I was back to square one. If only I could erase the sight of Samantha tarted up in skank wear. On that special night, her interruption had been a humiliating slap in the face.

Luckily for me, I had distracting options. Glancing at my companion, I admired his face. It was like buried treasure. From the photo Carmelita had shown me, it must be very handsome. More importantly, Cy showed potential. Firm rounded buns set off by narrow hips and wide shoulders. I pinched myself. Back to the purpose of this outing. "Are you sure there will be a delivery?"

"Sh-sh. Look," he whispered, eyes flicking back to the warehouse. "Over there."

A man stood outside puffing on a cigar. I hadn't seen him before as his dark khaki uniform blended into the surroundings, but now the sparks of the cigar seemed like so many fireflies. With a loud groan, the immense aluminum garage door rolled open to a couple of guards on the other side.

I peered through the bushes with a mosquito buzzing around my head. As it swooped, I swatted wildly.

"Don't move." Cy breathed in my ear. With a quick tap on my forehead, he squished the pest.

"Thanks."

Softly, a kiss landed on my cheek. "At your service, cariño."

Before I could process the unexpected caress, the rumble of a heavy vehicle broke the silence. I practically leapt to my feet, partially from shock. Or was it guilt?

A transport truck passed the garage and then began a series of maneuvers to place itself in the best position before the ramp. Through the noise, the men from the warehouse shouted rapid fire Spanish to the driver.

I studied my partner in crime from the corner of my eye. Passion forgotten, he was all business. The unloading of the goods had his full attention. I reminded myself that's all I should be concerned with as wooden crates slid down into the truck. After the last one had been hoisted up, the men fastened up the rear and disappeared inside the warehouse, leaving the garage door open. As I stood there wishing I knew what was in those boxes, Cy nudged me.

"Come on, Adie! Time to go. Back to the Jeep."

I couldn't believe he was ready to give up so quickly. Reluctantly, I followed. When he held the door open, holding onto the frame for support, I jumped up inside. He leapt into the driver's seat.

"Why leave now?" I had to ask. "Maybe we could check out the inside of the warehouse. This could be our lucky break."

Cy flashed me a grin. "You'll see, Sherlock."

It all became crystal clear when the truck rambled by and Cy stepped on the gas. The streets were empty so he took care not to follow too closely. As we reentered San Miguel, traffic on the Avenida slowed us down. A mass of pedestrians from the liquor and grocery store randomly crossed the road. Add to that an old man on a rickety bicycle weaving drunkenly through the shoppers. It was like a giant street party. Everybody and their brother was out tonight.

Luckily for us, the truck was in the same predicament. But before long, the crowd thinned and our target turned up a street, heading to Melgar. I had to admit, Cy was on the ball with this one. But if the truck ended up at the ferry dock, our assignment would soon be over.

When we tailed the truck past the marina, my excitement mounted. This could mean only one thing. "How did you know, Cy?"

"I didn't, but if everything was on the up and up, they would have headed to the ferry dock to unload the goods, right?"

I nodded. It was anyone's bet what their intended destination could be.

A good twenty minutes later, we were on the coastal road heading south. On the right, a road split to Chankanub Park and the exclusive El Presidente.

The island is approximately thirty-two miles in length, not as small as Isla de Mujeres near Cancun but it certainly wasn't anything as big as Cuba. It had one road that circled half of the island and another road that joined the west and east coasts. Travelling anywhere wouldn't take more than a few hours.

As we whipped by Playa San Francisco, I peered anxiously out the window wondering where they could possibly be heading. A good thirty minutes later, the truck slowed and swerved onto a partially hidden narrow dirt road. The open window swept a salty breeze in. The ocean scent made me think we were close to the beach. Cy pulled the Jeep over onto the grass under a coconut palm.

"Do you see that?" He pointed.

"What?"

"I'm not sure. But it might be a flashlight. Let's go have a look." Easing his door open, he dropped down and softly clicked it shut. By the time he strode around to the passenger side, I was in the process of sliding to the ground. He reached me just in time to steady my landing.

"Thanks," I whispered, thinking what a wild man he looked with a full beard and shoulder length hair tossing in the wind. "What about the Jeep? Won't they notice when they drive out?"

Cy nodded and pulled a few dead branches of a bush to hide the vehicle. The smugglers could easily pass by the black Jeep without giving it a second glance.

Together, we hiked in the direction of the ocean. The trees afforded some cover but we stayed close to the shrubbery just to be safe. With the force of the wind increasing, the rush of the surf became faint. A storm was moving in fast.

One of the men held a high-powered flashlight while the other two unloaded the crates. We were twenty meters away when the man swung around. I cried out faintly as Cy pulled us to the ground.

"Don't move," he whispered, his breath hot on my ear.

A fusion of fear and excitement tingled in my veins. Through the grass light blazed through, and then swept further. The man barked out orders. I had no idea what he was saying but the men scurried to retrieve cargo from the truck.

From the looks of them hauling the crate, the goods were heavy. When they disappeared out of sight, I cozied up to Cy. His shoulder was warm and hard. Mint and citron wafted from his hair.

I blew out a curl that had found itself into my mouth. "Let's go closer."

He shot me a look.

"We'll stay down. Please. It will work. They're way too busy to keep checking."

Cy nodded and put a finger to his lips.

I wasn't about to use the elbow approach. The grass was way too scratchy on my skin. But I was strong in my upper body and legs. One by one, hands and knees worked as a team. Ten meters is an eternity creeping through undergrowth.

As we neared the sea, gusts whirled my hair into a scarecrow coiffure. Holding it back, I peered into the night. Three men were busy unloading crates at twelve o'clock. A tall lean Ichabod-Crane was in charge. The other two assigned to freighting the crates reminded me of Sumo dwarfs, strong enough to heave box after box onto the sand. In all, it looked like six loads.

Now no more than ten meters away, their voices carried in our direction. If only my Spanish was fluent. Curiosity was killing me.

A sudden memory of Wolf's sparkling blues flashed before me. Gazing deep into my eyes, he would call me his little cat as his lips ignited my primal urges. Was all that gone forever? Curiosity didn't kill but loss kills a cat's spirit.

Cy squeezed my hand, startling me. He pointed. A flicker of light from the sea. As I scanned the bay, it grew brighter. A red orb shimmered in the night. The faint outline of a yacht appeared like a phantom, closing in slowly to the shore. Until then, I hadn't noticed the wooden wharf that was the boat's destination.

It was a struggle with the waves whipping high. The ocean's force shoved the boat away each time they tried to dock. Not an easy task for them to moor. Grass dug into my elbows and I squirmed uncomfortably. The waves viciously flung the yacht back. The wait was endless. After three attempts, I thought it wouldn't happen. Finally, the sailor hit pay dirt. He flung the rope out and secured the vessel.

When a dark figure jumped off the boat I became instantly alert. A sidelong glance at Cy and I knew he was as adrenaline-charged as I was. It was all coming to a head.

Tall, in a knee-length raincoat, his face too far away to

recognize, Darth Vader strode forward. Another man jumped off the boat, carrying an aluminum briefcase. From the trees, Ichabod and the Sumo dwarfs sauntered up to the beach like gunfighters facing off at high noon.

I shot up to get a better look. Cy shoved me down. A grunt flew from my lips. Cy's hand blocked the noise. He pulled me close and whispered, "Careful."

Realizing he was right, I watched a strange scene unfold. The head honcho from the yacht pointed to the crates. With crowbars in hand, the dwarfs pried open the lids. He took his time examining the contents of the cargo.

After every crate had been examined, Darth Vader motioned to his cohort and brought the aluminum briefcase forward. Ichabod peered at the contents of the case and took possession. They shook hands and the dwarves brought the crates to the wharf.

I squeezed Cy's arm to get his attention and jerked my chin in the direction of the Jeep. He nodded. On hands and knees, we crawled back. The howl of the wind hid the sounds of our retreat. Rain speckled us like machine gun fire as we jogged up the road. Thunder cracked the air. Lightning flashed a jagged scar in the armpits of the clouds. As the tropical storm struck, buckets of rain gushed down. Drenched through, we trudged against the gale to the vehicle. Together we shoved the palm fronds off.

Exhausted and dirty from the effort, I pulled myself up inside. A glance at Cy and I could tell he was feeling the same. Anxious. As he stuck the keys in the ignition, lights beamed on the dirt road.

"Duck!" I yelled, crouching down.

"Easy enough for you to say," Cy muttered, flinging himself over the throttle on top of me. The stick shift must have been painful, contorted as he was in an uncomfortable pretzel position. Neither of us dared look up. Light danced inside the vehicle as the truck edged by on the uneven dirt road. The headlights beamed flooding the Jeep with light. Time stood still. Sweat dripped off my brow. The truck's motor rumbled. And then it grew dark.

A while later we pulled into the driveway of the La Vida. Giving Cy a quick hug, I was ready to leap out but he was faster. Running over to the passenger side, he whipped the door open and held his hand out.

"Mama taught us how to be gentlemen," he said seriously. "Thank you for a memorable evening. Perhaps we can do it again?"

"Possibly." I winked. "See you tomorrow, weather permitting?"

Cy's grin was wide and white. "I wouldn't miss it for the world."

With a wave, I trudged up the stairs to my room and considered the investigation. A significant exchange had taken place. The briefcase contained a sizeable payment but what crates contained was still anyone's guess.

I couldn't wait to hit the sack but I was wound up tight as a kite. Once inside my room, I threw my clothes on the couch and padded to the bathroom. I took off the mascara using a cleansing pad and started the shower. When the water blasted a hot river, I stepped in. The cocoa scent from the bath gel wafted up in the steamy cubicle. All those feel-good hormones annihilated the negativity and my mood turned mellow. I got to thinking about the smuggling.

Darth Vader with the aluminum case had been too far away for me to ascertain the briefcase contents but I could guess. The crates held some very expensive goods. If Brock had knowledge of the contents, he'd written his own death certificate. And Larissa? What about her? How did she connect?

One thing was for sure. No matter what the motivation, I would find the killer. I was determined to right the wrong.

I made a mental check list. Fact one. llegal activity. Fact two. The gaunt man worked for Diego. Fact three. Wolf was right. There was no other explanation. I sighed. Diego had always been so sweet to me, it was hard to believe he put a hit on Brock and Larissa. But, I had to reconsider. Diego was Cozumel's godfather, not afraid of getting his hands dirty. Still, that was business. In my heart I knew Diego cared for me. He wouldn't send killers to off me. No, he was interested. Very. He wanted me more than he wanted any woman.

With a flick of my wrist, I switched off the shower and stepped out. The towels were white, economy-thin and barely adequate to wrap around. The towel end wouldn't stay tucked in.

Why did this look so easy in the movies? Finally, I threw it off and grabbed my products, spraying them on randomly. With the hairdryer, I fashioned the beach look. Satisfied, I gave my reflection a totally wicked smile. My life might be in chaos but I rocked. One of my favorite passions was deep sea fishing. Those men kept surfacing and my hook was ready. It was only a matter of time before I had the right one.

It was a cheap diver's hotel but I was fortunate to have a spacious suite. The bedroom separated from the living area by sliding doors. In the dark, I padded past the couch and into the bedroom. The bedside light was dim, casting faint light on the unmade bed. And it wasn't as if I hadn't tipped her. I sighed. Tomorrow I'd ask for fresh sheets. I was more than ready for sleep. Amazingly, the sheets felt crisp, smelling pleasantly of soap and ocean breeze as I crawled in and pulled them tight.

Laying back, I groped for another pillow and came in contact with the hard body of a man. My eyes widened. What was he doing here? Then it all came back how Neptune had threatened to come and get me at ten. I stroked Wolf's smooth back, my fingers trailing to his rounded firm ass. Could anything feel better? Oh, yes, that other part of him was equally enticing.

His breathing was so soft; no wonder I hadn't realized he was there. Leaning over, I took in his scent, my nose grazing the wild blond hair. What a gift to find a sexy man in my bed. Now it was decision-making time. Did I want to take advantage? I stroked his thigh. My lips turned up at the corners.

17

The storm had passed. Blue skies were fairy-dusted with golden light. Turquoise surf danced on the beach. Out in the bay, a catamaran's green striped sail puckered up with wind scooted across the waves as light as a feather. Pushing the curtains back, I slid the window open letting in the balmy breeze.

Last night's narrow escape had given me an unbelievable adrenalin rush. When I'd discovered Wolf in my bed I had the pleasure of pulling off the sheet that covered his hard, powerful body. A few well-placed licks and kisses and Wolf was primed. The ball was in motion. Sure, he was sleepy at first, but a virile man has needs. And so does a passionate woman. We were connected as only two people in love could be.

Hot lips mingled familiarly, our bodies entwined, moving in our own rhythm, slippery smooth with lust until the heat inside sparked and exploded. Wet with love juice, I sank back, happy and satisfied. Finally at peace, I'd fallen asleep. No regrets. If our relationship was to end, this was as good a way as any.

Outside the window, the lush green palm fronds swayed softly over the sandy white beach. My spirits lifted. A sunny day was the start of fresh beginnings. Good news was bound to come. Sam had men. Lots. Any one of them could be the father. She could confess and Wolf would be mine. My emerald ring flashed as if to wink and say, *You go, girl!*

A knock brought me rushing to the door. Wolf was back? My heart beat as rapidly as a captured bird's. Had he regretted running off to the construction site instead of staying behind to make love again? I smiled. My free morning would be his. Grabbing my silk robe, I slipped it on and rushed to the peephole. It was a teenage hotel worker, flowers in hand.

I jerked the door open. "*Hola.* For me?" I said, eyeing a bouquet of delicate pink flowers. "Beautiful! Who are they from?"

The boy shrugged. "From the flower shop," he mumbled. His eyes wandered down the hall.

"Wait." Dashing inside, I took out a bill from my purse and handed it to him. "*Gracias.*"

I couldn't wait to see the note.

"No problem." He pushed the flowers into my hands, pocketed the money and ambled down the hall in the direction of the elevator.

Left holding a bouquet of orchids, I brought them into the room and laid them down. I took a vase from the coffee table and headed to the bathroom to fill it. My pulse pitter-pattered at an alarming rate. The process of anticipation. The longer the wait, the more intense the satisfaction. Delayed gratification. I was a believer in that.

With such delicate pink flowers, the stiff wrapping paper could easily damage the bouquet. Carefully loosening the ribbons and tape, I sighed as they slid out. It took a moment to set the flowers in the vase, to arrange them amongst the ferns. Meanwhile, I thought of Wolf. His hands had touched every sensitive area on my body and his lips had set me on fire. Could anyone be a better lover? My smile held the proof.

A note had to be in the wrapping. Carefully, I peeled it away, searching layer after layer. Still nothing. When I gathered up the wrapping to look underneath, the little devil escaped to the floor. I sprang down on the tiles and snatched it up.

Brunch on my boat in twenty minutes. The driver is waiting downstairs. Wear something sexy and join me.

Besitos,
D

Hm-mm. Diego. I wasn't in a hurry to complicate my life but my rumbling stomach made the decision. Hotel food was much too blah and I was a girl with a healthy appetite. Brunch would be wonderful, especially if it was Diego's treat. That man knew how to live. As for the tour group, I'd see them for the dive later this afternoon.

The problem for now, was what to wear. Too bad I was here in Cozumel on a work assignment. Without the tour group, I could have stayed at that fabulous condo Diego had gifted me. Equipped with the latest designs from Carmelita's collection, there would be an endless selection of dresses. Here at the La Vida, I was stuck with what I'd brought in my suitcase. Not that my taste was bad but Diego was accustomed to women in Valentino, Versace or Stella McCartney. Most of my shopping happened online at Salina's Secret. Sensuous and on clearance.

After I slid the closet door open, I examined my wardrobe carefully. For his sake and mine, I had to eliminate the red dress. Too much fiery red in front of a red-blooded man can only signal *yes*. Diego would come charging like a bull in a ring. Sometimes this was a good thing but in this case...

Yet, it had to be somewhat sexy. Hanger after hanger, I eyed the potential possibilities. Then it struck me like a gold pebble in a stream. A form-fitting yellow mini dress with a hint of cleavage in the sweetheart neckline. Classy. It was perfect.

After makeup and hair touchups, I was ready to don the eye-opening lemon-yellow number. First try was less than successful, the zipper sticking in the middle. With a twist I pushed it back to front to zip it up. If anything would make Diego spill the beans, it would be a curve-hugging dress.

In the mirror the image of a slim athletic woman made me thank my wisdom in cutting down on chocolate cake. Two weeks of that had trimmed off my excess belly fat.

From my jewelry bag, a gold cuff bracelet to be the goddess he wanted. And then—there were the shoes. Cream platform sandals gave me a good four inches. For me, maximizing my height equates with charging my sexual allure. Take that,

Samantha Jurgens! The snake enjoyed towering over me with her model stature. Of course, she wouldn't be there. It would be just me and the richest man in Cozumel. That gave me pause to consider. The hit men he'd hired had been hugely unsuccessful. If he wanted to off me, a convenient accident overboard would do the trick. A karate weapon would have been nice, but the airlines were picky that way. Not only would they be confiscated but I would have been charged. So here I was, involved in a murder investigation without any protection. Not smart, but what choice did I have? It was up to me to find justice for Brock.

It wasn't easy to bolt down the stairs in platforms. Hanging tight to the railing, I managed a series of quick clicks, clopping along like a frisky plough horse let out to pasture. Luckily, no one was in the lobby to witness my sensational entrance.

Outside in the driveway I found a long black limo parked, motor running. Every time I saw Diego's limo, it reminded me of who he was. Not just your average dissolute aristocrat. Santiago Bolivar Alvarez owned this island and I had better step carefully or end up swimming with the fishes.

A familiar man in a black tuxedo popped out the driver's side and lunged to open the door.

"*Buenos dias,* Señorita *Sturm.*"

"*Hola,* Ernesto. Lovely day."

Peanut brown eyes twinkled. "It is," he said, as he assisted me into the back seat. "How nice you remembered me, Señorita Sturm. Usually Señor Bolivar Alvarez's lady friends keep their distance. It must be because you are a Canadian. Your country treats people equally."

I grinned. "The world is the same everywhere, Ernesto. Some are more equal than others. There will always be those who believe they are privileged."

The chauffeur nodded resignedly. While I sank into the plush comfort of leather, he strolled around to climb in the driver's side. Once in gear, the Mercedes purred softly like a contented cat. Tinted windows shielded my eyes from the bright sun. The smell of clean leather along with the cool air conditioning transported me into a world of luxury. I felt like a princess on a magic carpet ride.

The colors of orange, white, and yellow from the row of hotels blurred as the chauffeur drove along Melgar.

"Are you picking anyone else up, Ernesto?"

"No, Señorita."

So, that could only mean Diego and I would be alone. A memory of Diego on the beach flashed in my mind. How he'd whipped off his clothes so suddenly. The tanned hard body revealed in the skimpy fitted boxers. What confused me was his mood—not nearly as flirtatious as other days. I had to wonder if he'd hit on me today.

"Duh! How's the lobotomy going?" Logical snickered. "He'll get you in bed before lunch."

"So-oo?" Hormone growled. "The man's hot and don't forget she needs to check out his equipment. This way she can compare."

"You are worse than Adie. Just when things are getting back to normal, she should forget her soul mate and move in with the godfather?"

"No, of course not. Wolf is the King of Hearts but who's to say that Diego isn't the King of Spades? He's got money besides looks. Throwing that fish back into the sea would be downright stupid! She can test drive both!"

Why were they doing this to me? Hadn't I put up with enough BS to last a lifetime? "Stop, stop, stop," I muttered under my breath.

"Señorita Sturm? Did you say something?"

"No. Something caught in my throat." We neared the place we had docked in the storm the day Brock died. I gulped at the thought of the dismembered arm.

"Señor Alvarez said for you to help yourself to the liquor. He regrets he couldn't be here to pick you up but don't worry, he shall arrive soon."

"And where would that be?"

Ernesto's teeth flashed in the rear view mirror. "Señor Alvarez said it should remain a surprise."

I wasn't sure if I could take any more of those. Two dead people were enough for any trip. Involuntarily, I glanced at the sparkling green emerald, which was incredibly tight on my ring finger. The heat and maybe lack of sleep had swelled my hands. The last thing I wanted was for my body to bloat. It would hardly be attractive to a man like Diego. "Is there any water?"

"In the bar."

The wood grain disguised the lid of the box bar directly in front of me. When I opened it I was blown away by the variety of beverages. Every kind of wine, beer and liquor. The water bottles were hidden behind the scotch. As the limo rattled along the bumpy road, I managed to pour water into an acrylic glass without spilling more than a few drops. After drinking deeply I examined the landmarks for a clue as to our destination. We had left the town behind and headed south. In a few minutes, a narrow road took us past a sign for the El Presidente. Now I knew where we were going.

Amongst the fleet of boats anchored in the harbor, a large ivory vessel glistened magically in the sun. I had the feeling this magnificent boat would be the Bolivar Alvarez yacht. My arrival was as pronounced as a police car's siren. Hoots and bird chirps along with an occasional whistle from the crews on the neighboring yachts.

Diego leaned languidly against the railing as if posing for a photo shoot while cooling his mouth with his morning margarita. A white cotton shirt tucked into cream trousers and boat shoes in a neutral leather contrasted nicely to his tanned face and arms. It went without saying, the man was as delicious as chocolate mousse. And rich, too.

I have a curiosity about the privileged. Diego was a man who had everything from a Rolex watch to a yacht anyone would envy. My view was cynical. Relationships were tough enough without money screwing it up. I came from immigrant stock. Parents who had struggled to make their mark. It was doubtful that Diego and I could connect on all three levels. By that I mean the emotional, intellectual and physical. It was true, we had a spark and the banter was amusing, but an emotional connection took time. Too much trouble for a man like Diego.

No matter. That wasn't why I was here. If he had secrets I would get him to talk. *"Hola!"* I called out.

"Adelina!" The corners of Diego's mouth curled up as he set down his empty glass. "It is wonderful to see you."

"Thank you for the orchids! They are so lovely!"

Diego held out his hand to help me across the gangway. "Not nearly as beautiful as my Canadian flower," he said softly. "Whenever I see you, my heart sings. *Te quiero mucho*," he said, smooth as butter.

I looked up. The dark sunglasses hid his tiger eyes. I had to be on my guard. Diego was sugaring me up. Picking up his mood, I purred seductively, "And I am *so* happy you invited me to lunch. How did you know the hotel food was getting monotonous?"

"I wouldn't feed my dog that La Vida mush. Recycled goat meat. Disgusting stuff. " He grimaced. "My queen should eat only the best." He led me over to a deckchair.

Carefully holding the skirt of my outfit down, I sank into the cushion as Diego brought over a bottle and two snifters. "I thought you'd like to try this. Glenfiddich Havana Reserve. It's a controversial beverage," he said with a grin. "Outlawed in the US." From a dark bottle he poured a dram and passed it to me.

I shot him a saucy look. "Ah-hh. So illegal makes you want it?"

"I like a challenge." He poured the amber liquid into the other snifter. "Whether a commodity or a woman."

The scotch hit my lips with a bang.

Diego reached for a box on the table. "And to blend the flavors I have a Cohiba Esplendido, the finest cigar from Cuba. Some say the Montecristo but I prefer this. Smell."

I detected a faint scent of manure from the end of the pale brown cigar. "Hard to obtain?"

"The authentic ones…yes. It has a process of taste. Cedar, spices and finishes with a delicious chocolate mixed with peppery flavors."

"That would be nice but when do we get to the chocolate part?"

"In an hour and a half." He laughed at my expression. "We won't smoke it all, *mi amor*. We have other experiences to savor."

I wasn't keen on having cigar breath. "To share?" I asked tentatively.

"Of course, my lovely Adelinita. From my lips to yours with a touch of scotch in between."

I was up for it. With both of us smoking, the bad breath

problem would be eliminated.

Diego snipped the end and brought it to his lips. Like magic, from below deck, his bodyguard appeared to light the cigar. While Diego puffed a moment, the man stood patiently waiting.

The twins were identical, like bookends. From the smile tossed in my direction, I assumed it was Churo, the friendlier of the two. I was certain it was he when the bodyguard said, "Good morning, Señorita Sturm. The oysters are ready, Señor Diego. Should I bring them?"

"*Por favor.*"

After Churo disappeared down the stairs and the sounds of his footsteps faded, Diego's gaze traveled over the cigar. "These are Fidel's favorites, *cariño.* In fact the scotch also has Cuban origins," he said solemnly.

"How so?"

"It was stored in rum barrels. It softens the bitterness with the sweet taste of rum." He brought his glass to mine. "To us. May we have many more lunches together." He grinned. "And breakfasts."

I clicked his glass thinking that seeing him across the table would perk up any morning.

"The nose is one of the richest you'll find."

Sampling the amber liquid, I detected oranges and a hint of toffee. "Smooth."

"The rum finish blends seamlessly with the malt and doesn't stand in front as one might think."

I flashed a smile. "Chocolate and vanilla."

"And?"

"What else? Hm-mm." I laughed. Diego was so predictable. "Tones of dark chocolate. So delicious." Even if it was scotch and not my favorite beverage, quality speaks for itself.

Taking his sunglasses off, Diego set them on the table, and pulled his chair closer to mine. "Would you like a taste?" he said, holding out the cigar, his brandy eyes glimmering suggestively.

I ran my fingers up its length and brought it to my nose. "Mm-mm."

"It is fresh and very strong," he said, watching me.

When the cigar entered my mouth, I breathed in.

"Harder, Adelinita. It will go out."

Under watchful eyes, I gave it my best but it needed more.

"No problem, my beauty. I shall light it again." Diego flashed me a Hollywood smile, letting the flame of his lighter fire the tip. "Now suck hard."

This time the end flared up red.

"Bravo! You are doing it justice. Have a few puffs and then go back to the scotch, Adelinita."

"You're afraid I'll finish it?"

"Not at all." Diego's voice trailed off as he reached to run his fingers in my hair. "So soft. Your hair is lovely." Closing in, his mouth pressed on mine.

I felt myself melt into the kiss. Lightly caressing, soft lips moving urgently, I found myself sinking back in my chair, the cigar and scotch forgotten.

"Er-hm!" Churo coughed behind us. "The oysters."

Diego's lips twisted. "On the table," he barked.

"I am sorry to interrupt." The bodyguard placed a covered silver platter down along with linen napkins and small forks.

Diego stared. "What's done is done."

"I apologize, Señor Diego."

"It is essential you do better, Churo. You must be aware of the comfort of my guest. Bring the champagne, *por favor*. And pace the next appetizer."

Churo inclined his head and I'd swear he backed to the stairs before he turned to go down. In karate, the Japanese say walking backwards shows respect for the master. Apparently, Diego's bodyguard agreed.

"Well, shall we?" Prying open an oyster, Diego dipped it into the wine sauce and brought it to my lips." When I hesitated, he added, "Let me assure you Churo is an excellent chef."

"Yes, he is an artist, I agree." I pushed my bangs back. "It's not that. You were a little rough on him."

Diego smiled indulgently. "Such is the role of the employer. It has to be done that way. When you move in with me, you will have to act the part of the mistress."

I grinned. "The mistress?" He was hardly thinking of marriage.

"Hah. Funny girl. I'm glad you didn't question the part about moving in with me."

I put my hand to his cheek and let my finger trail down very slowly. "But I do," I murmured. "Unfortunately, we are not ready for that."

Diego's tiger eyes stared with intense hunger. "Eat, my darling. Perhaps it will enhance your longings." He brought the tiny tidbit of oyster up to my lips again and this time, I swallowed. The buttery sauce made it heavenly.

A shuffle of feet and Churo reappeared with a bottle of Dom Pérignon chilling in a bin.

"Excellent! That is perfect pairing." He fed me another oyster as Churo popped the bottle and filled the glasses. The champagne bubbled to the top.

"To you." Diego paused as he clicked my glass. "My lovely one."

"And to this day." I smiled flirtatiously. "With a very attractive man."

Giggles and a groan from the stairs.

"You are such flirt, Diego. *Hola*, Adelina!" Carmelita, wearing a flowing white semi-transparent robe, traipsed over and slung herself into a deck chair exposing one long slender leg. "Why didn't you wake me and tell me about lunch?" she demanded of her brother.

"I thought you'd like to sleep." Diego turned to me. "Seriously, *mi amor*. Excuse this rude interruption. I hardly thought…my sister was sleeping like the dead. I had no idea she would wake up at all." He stage whispered, "Carmelita passed out last night not long after she staggered on board. I thought, in her state, she'd stay below and nurse her hangover."

"My head will be just fine unless you make me laugh again," Carmelita muttered, picking up a glass and pouring herself some champagne. "What do they say? Hair of the dog." Tilting her head back, she drank deeply of the sparkling liquid. "You know where that adage came from?" Not waiting for an answer, she continued, "Back in the middle ages when wild dogs roamed the streets of Europe and bit pedestrians. I'm sure the majority died but the rest got drunk." With another swig of the sparkly, Carmelita leaned back in her chair, adjusting the sunglasses that had slid down the bridge of her aristocratic nose.

"So this is your version of black velvet," Diego said dryly.

"Black velvet?" I looked at Diego in confusion.

"It's a hangover cure. Guinness with champagne, but my sister is ultra-sophisticated."

"No need for the beer." Carmelita wiped her forehead. "Why ruin a vintage Dom Pérignon?" She noticed the look of confusion on my face. "Let me explain, Adelina. Drinking champagne for a hangover cure was also called Royal Velvet. The Prince of Wales drank it the morning after."

"Um-mm, alright." Personally, I doubted there was any cure for a hangover. But it brought to mind a question. "There was a party last night?"

"A paltry pity party." Diego snickered. "Carmelita was having trouble adjusting to Fede's absence. She found out I was on the boat and crawled over in the middle of the night."

"No, not crawled—danced!" Carmelita giggled. "Juan Carlos was with me. You know the rest."

"I can just imagine," Diego said, rolling his eyes.

Carmelita tossed back another glass of bubbly. "He's so jealous, Adelina. Doesn't have you and wants no other woman. How is your sea god by the way? Gone back to that *puta* or has he put a hit out on her?"

"It would be malicious of me to suggest she meet with an accident, but," I grinned, "I'm not an angel."

"Really?" Diego draped his arm around my shoulders and teased my lobe with his tongue. "You are to me, *mi amor*. You come to me that way in my dreams."

Carmelita snickered. "See what I mean?"

Diego shook his head and pointed his finger at his sister. "You need to get your life together."

Suddenly, his sister's eyes closed. When she reopened them, tears welled up and spilled onto her cheeks. "It's not so easy when I've lost the only love of my life."

"What?" Diego picked up his cigar from the ashtray and lit it. "Surely you're not referring to that lazy good-for-nothing leech?"

"You wouldn't understand." She wiped a tear away, then stared meaningfully at me.

Rushing over, I took Carmelita in my arms and gave her a reassuring hug. "I'll find his killer. You will have justice."

Diego glanced from Carmelita to me. "Ladies, what are you talking about? If you want something done about the bastard, come out and say it. A man that displeases my sister doesn't have to see tomorrow's sunrise."

"No! Don't talk crazy. It is just as much my fault that our marriage is such a mess." Carmelita gazed mournfully at the sea sparkling brightly with yachts. "But I do wonder. Does he even know I wasn't home last night?"

"I'm sure he had a nice warm body to comfort him and didn't miss you in the least. So that makes me question your reasoning. Sadly, dear sister, you need a psychiatrist."

A yell from the other side of the gangway interrupted the conversation. Speak of the devil. In a fitted ivory suit, a darkly handsome Fede strode purposefully over to the yacht.

"Oh, no," Diego groaned. "Why is he here?"

"*Hola,* everyone!" Fede said cheerfully. "So Diego, you have found the lovely Adelina again. This time you will need to charm her to stay with you longer, eh?" Seeing his wife, he remarked, "Perhaps you might want to get dressed in something more attractive, *mi amor*. Guests are expected." Fede flung himself in a leather deck chair. "Oh, and do something with your face."

"What the hell are you talking about?" Diego grumbled.

"I was just in town lunching. Having a beer. Told a few ladies I met up with to come and enjoy the sun on our boat. Don't worry, I told them to procure some more champagne on their way."

"This is not an opportune time, you idiot. Can't you see Adelina is with me for luncheon?"

Fede flicked an imaginary piece of lint off his suit. "You always have some woman. So what? Now there will be more. You and Adelina are not engaged, are you?"

Diego looked longingly at me. "No, not yet. I need some time with my goddess. Surely, even an imbecile like you can see that?"

Fede stood at the railing, eyes glued on the shore. "The ladies were eager for an invitation to the yacht. Believe me, Diego, it will be a delight to see such a bevy of beauties. You will thank me. Three of them said they would love to come." Fede frowned.

191

"Unfortunately, we will have to share them with another gentleman. A pleasant man. A Canadian. You might know him. His company constructed an addition to one of our import buildings and I told him to bring the papers and join us for a drink."

Diego frowned. "I see. So it didn't occur to you to check with me about any of this?"

Fede guffawed. "When your father passed his will bequeathed all of us this yacht, remember?"

Diego tipped back the champagne. "Senile old man. Always screwing up." He gave me an apologetic look. "I'm sorry for this situation, *mi amor*."

"It's alright but watch what you say about your father. You're upsetting Carmelita," I whispered, placing my hand on his.

But the warning was too late. Jumping up on her feet, cheeks flushed, Carmelita spat out, "You are both despicable!" She grabbed Fede's arm. "What will it take for you to honor me, your wife?"

Fede wrapped his arms around her. "These women mean nothing, my queen. It is you whom I love."

Pushing him away, she pointed a finger at Diego. "And you. He was our father. Have some respect!"

"I know, I know," Diego muttered. "Did he ever let us forget that?"

"Carmelita, be realistic," Fede remarked casually with an even Colgate smile. "It was a sad occurrence but the old must die." He lifted a glass and examined it in the light. "Look on the bright side. Your father left us well provided for. Let's celebrate that today." Reaching for the bottle, he filled it and with a quick *salud* slung it back.

A look of disgust on her pretty face, Carmelita swept past Fede and raced down the stairs.

"I hope she remembers to change into something decent before she returns. It's embarrassing the way she walks around like that, looking like some slatternly *hausfrau* instead of the well-known model and designer that she is. These women coming here will see her and talk." He shook his head. "Sometimes I wonder where her head is at." Fede gave the oysters a once over. "*Bueno!*"

With a fork he speared one, contemplating it a moment before slipping it into his mouth.

From the coffee table, Diego lifted a silver bell and shook it. The tinkling sound was loud enough to carry down below deck. In moments, Churo's heavy footsteps resounded up the stairs. He appeared holding a covered plate in his hands. "Shrimp," he said solemnly, setting it on the table. "I will get more champagne, Señores."

"Two bottles. There will be more guests." Diego took my hand, gently stroking my palm. "Prepare a fruit tray, and caviar, *por favor*." Churo nodded. "And bring more seafood appetizers?"

"Mm-mm," he murmured, his eyes taking on a dreamy expression. "Did I tell you how beautiful you are, Adelinita? The yellow is perfect for you. Although, I have to say, you look equally enticing in red, maybe more so." Leaning over, Diego kissed me. Softly at first, pressing on my lips lightly. As I let myself relax, the tip of his tongue stroked my lip, triggering a tingle.

"These shrimp are superb. Your man is gifted in the kitchen," Fede said approvingly, swallowing a shrimp. "Look! I think the girls are here. Now it will be perfect. A blonde, a brunette and a redhead. Of course, Adelina is yours, but for me, maybe, the others. And if Carmelita needs a man, she can have the contractor." He chuckled.

Diego glanced over at the women coming through the parking lot. "They look familiar. Who are they?"

Fede's eyes lit up as eagerly as a dog's seeing a tasty steak on the barbie. Waving to the women standing on shore, he ignored his brother-in-law. "Over here, *chicas!*" he shouted, rising to his feet. "*Caramba!* They still don't see me." Fede raced to the gangway waving his hand. "Girls!"

The brunette in a black skin-tight dress changed direction and sauntered over, hips swaying to a silent rumba beat. In black sequined outfits, the blonde and redhead stalked her like ninja body guards. The dazzling sunlight backlighted the women, offering an image similar to an intro scene to *Charlie's Angels*. When they got closer, I saw who they were. My stomach cramped up as if invaded by rotten fruit.

Striding forward holding a champagne bottle tightly by the

neck, the brunette sashayed over the gangway first. In staggering five-inch red platforms, she was not quite as tall as the other two but she walked the walk tossing back her long locks, a snarly smile on her engine red lips. "*Hola*, Diego!" she called out in a sultry voice.

"I am so sorry for all this, Adelina," Diego said in an undertone. "As soon as we can, let's escape down below."

"No you don't, bro," Fede warned him. "These women were dying to come here. You are the main attraction." His cocoa bean eyes flicked to his brother-in-law. "So what's the problem. Are you afraid they will speak to Adelina and tell all?" He grinned. "Have I let the cat out of the bag?"

"Diego!" The redhead tottered on board, gold stilettos wiggling dangerously. She approached her host first.

"Samantha, how lovely you look." Diego smiled before they exchanged kisses. "So glad you had time to visit."

The viper flashed her fangs. "Fede was very thoughtful to invite us all." She grabbed my friend's two-timing husband by the shoulders and kissed his cheeks before she spotted me. "Ah-hh, I see you have your little friend visiting."

If only Diego had pushed Fede overboard. I'd come here to relax and wheedle information, not to exchange snipes with snakes. But Diego was cool, not at all perturbed by the cobra. "*Mi amor*, you remember Samantha?"

My gut had told me to wear heels and it was right on. Samantha was eye-level with the men and they were tall. The last thing I wanted was to look up to someone who ate men for breakfast. But at least, Diego, with his arm slung around my shoulders, compensated for that. He did everything he could to protect me from the malice of the witches.

This was literally a ghost ship. Spirits of my past and present had returned to haunt me. Daniella, the petite brunette, was from Venezuela. A real estate agent with a heart of steel and a brain that maneuvered like a chess master. She had bedded Diego and I could hardly forget her plan to seduce Wolf. Unsuccessfully.

And then there was Samantha. Pregnant with Wolf's baby? Maybe, or maybe not. The woman had any number of lovers and plenty of money to support her lies.

But it was the third that caught me off guard.

Diego helped a tall blonde on board. "We met before, correct? At my party the other night."

"Such a lavish and entertaining affair. Thank you so much for including me." He fluffed his waves as he murmured, "How sweet. You remember me?"

"Of course. How could I not? The model from Toronto."

The transvestite offered his hand. "Ronnette. And, yes, I am a dancer and model." From the bow to the stern, his heavily made up cat eyes examined the heavy mahogany built-in deckchairs and table. "Might I say the yacht is magnificent? You are a man of exquisite taste."

"You flatter me. Please." Diego poured a glass of champagne and handed it to Ronny.

Ronny's pink lips twitched. He took a gentile sip of the bubbly. "Excellent, thank you." A quick glance. "Oh, my dear Adie. How wonderful you are here also. We haven't spoken since the party. It was kind of my new friends to bring me. I hesitated but they said you would not mind, Diego."

"Of course not, *mi amor*. Did you ever speak to my sister about modeling here?"

"No. I would like to."

"Then this is your opportunity. She will be joining us shortly. Do help yourself to *the hors d'oeuvres*." He turned to me. "Would you like some shrimp, Adelinita?"

I nodded and received one gently thrust between my lips. Whatever had Churo done to roast these creatures to perfection? The man was gifted in the culinary arts besides being a formidable bodyguard.

"Well?"

"Oh, Diego." I sighed. "They are incredible."

"Chilies." His eyelids lowered and his voice became husky as he whispered in my ear. "The best aphrodisiac." Then, grabbing a bottle, he capped my champagne. "*Salud, mi vida*." To the others, he said, "Welcome!"

Daniella sidled up and clicked his glass. "Did you know Diego was once my fiancé, Aggie?"

"It's Adie, and yes, I did know. Wasn't it you who decided on marriage?"

"That's the way I remember it." Diego laughed. "One day you were my girlfriend and the next I heard you had invited guests to our wedding. Mama was not too thrilled to be on the phone for hours canceling."

Arrows darted from Daniella's coal black eyes in our direction. "It was hardly like that. I admit it was a trifle premature."

"All is forgiven, *mi amiga*. Your business is successful and we are both happily single." He smiled at me. "Free to find romance."

"So amusing you are, Diego. You find the most intriguing women to date." Fede gestured to a chair next to him. "Sit, my dear Samantha. Relax. Have some champagne."

I was a little surprised to see her take the offered glass and tip it back. Didn't she think about the health of the baby?

Diego had the same thought. His head tilted as he checked out Samantha in her clingy red dress. "Oh, I forgot. So sorry. How are you feeling? We could get you something non-alcoholic. There is no need for you to drink liquor." He reached for the bell. The tinkle brought Churo running up the stairs.

"*Si,* Señor?"

"A non-alcoholic beverage for the Señorita, *por favor.*"

Churo nodded and thumped back down.

"That isn't necessary, Diego. I won't have much."

"Oh?" Daniella said with an arch of a brow. "I didn't know you had a problem."

"Not that sort of problem, darling. Not alcohol," Samantha snipped.

The brunette frowned, eying the redhead's stomach. "My condolences. I suppose you won't be needing those Louboutins." Daniella stared at Samantha's glittery platforms. "Those big feet of yours will bloat, *amiga*." She giggled. "I would have been pleased to take them from you but my feet are so much more delicate and small."

"Yup, just like your brain, pygmy." Samantha stared pointedly at me, venom in her eyes. "You know the father, Daniella. He's both handsome and rich." She patted the brunette's head. "And much too tall for you, short stuff."

Her dark eyes lit up. Daniella was sharp as a tack. "Wolf? You are one lucky woman. That man is *muy caliente,*" she paused, looking thoughtfully at me, "but I thought he was with Aggie."

From my seat, I examined Samantha for a baby bump but saw only an iron flat stomach. I flashed the emerald. "He is."

Daniella's eyes darted from me to Diego before she casually sauntered over. She checked out the ring and snickered. "Shame on you, Diego, luring Wolf's fiancée away."

"I learned everything from you, *cariño*. You are the mistress of deceit," Diego drawled, offering her the oysters.

I laughed.

Daniella smiled. "I have my ways, it is true, but pregnancy is the oldest trick in the book." She kissed his cheek. "One that I never pulled on you, *mi amor*," she said softly.

"No trick here, darlings," Samantha said smugly. "I have the blond Adonis in the palm of my hand. He was dying to have children when we were married but," she shrugged her shoulders, a disdainful sneer on her lips, "I was in no rush. Yet he knows as well as I that independent types like Aggie are not ready for family. So," she curled her lip, "I would advise you to give it up. If you play your cards right, perhaps Diego will let you move in with him."

"That would fulfill his dreams," Carmelita said from the stairs. "Why don't you, Adelina? It would keep my naughty brother out of trouble."

"It's Fede you should be worried about, Carmelita." Daniella laughed. "Trouble follows him."

"I can't stop having fun," Fede remarked dryly.

"But you can discourage women and make my sister happy," Diego said, his eyes narrowing.

Carmelita tittered. "Now, now, dearest. Fede means nothing by his flirtations."

Plopping herself rather heavily into a chair, Samantha stretched out her legs. "We must all do what is good for ourselves. Life is too short."

"At the detriment of others?" I asked.

"Wolf and I are perfect for each other. It's you that doesn't fit into his life."

"She does live here now remember, Aggie," Daniella added. "And with this baby due, isn't it time for your ship to move out of port?"

"I think since you could never capture Wolf's attention you want him speared and served on a platter for your friend, but, Daniella, that's not how it works." Carmelita poured herself another glass and grabbed a juicy shrimp. "Men do have some say. In case you haven't noticed, Adelina can have any number of men. By the way, Churo has outdone himself, Diego. I am so hungry, I'd swear I was pregnant."

Fede's ears perked up. "That would be wonderful, *mi amor*. A little heir for us."

"Oh? Let me understand this. I should stay home in the kitchen frying sausages," Carmelita laughed, "while you have a harem of women?"

Fede sighed. "You know it is you I love forever. The ladies are mice compared to you, my lioness. How many times must I say I am sorry before you return to our house?"

"Perhaps if you were on your knees and said it with sincerity." Carmelita lost her train of thought as she spotted someone on the shore. "*¡Ay, caramba!* What is going on? Did you invite him, Diego?"

"Who?" Diego's voice trailed off as he gazed at the shore.

This was Fede's doing. The construction company in charge of the warehouse addition? I should have known. I tipped back my champagne. Cowardly strength derived from a bottle of fizz. What the heck? Wolf was my fiancé but you wouldn't know it with the buzzards circling.

Quick as a flash, I tore down the stairs. Diego raced behind me calling, "Adelina!"

This man did his cardio. In a few strides, Diego had caught up and taken my hand to his lips. "Believe me. My apologies. Forgive me, *cariño*. I had no idea." Pulling me close, he wrapped his arms around me. "Once again, that bastard has put a stick into a hornet's nest. I swear he lives for drama. Come." Taking my elbow, he steered me down to a room near the stern of the yacht. "Why don't we go in here?" he said, swinging open an opulent oak door.

Fourteenth century French furniture, including mahogany

chairs upholstered in yellow silk damask, had been grouped in front a similar couch. On the other end was a desk and a very large four poster bed draped with silk curtains.

"There is no need to be concerned with Du Lac or the *chicas.* Let them have their own fun. I invited you for a quiet romantic lunch and you will get one. Now what would that be without a fine wine?"

Diego helped me into an ivory love seat, soft and luxurious with the rich scent of leather, then sat himself next to me. From the ceiling, a knotted tasseled cord hung within reach. A tug brought about a faint tinkling sound, which resonated to another area of the yacht. Within a minute, Churo appeared at the doorway. "*Si,* Señor?"

"Make sure you replenish the food and drinks upstairs but Señorita Sturm and I will remain here. It is most important you bring us the lunch first."

Churo inclined his head, leaving us alone in the maharaja's den or should I say the fox's lair. Diego was as handsome as a fox and as wily. I wasn't at all sure as to how I could find out anything more. "Diego…"

"Yes, my lovely?"

"I was wondering—"

"Wait." Back on his feet my host waltzed over to the crystal decanter. Pouring an ample amount of medium ruby wine into each glass, he made his way back with a charming smile on his shapely lips. "You will love this wine, Adelinita. It will be your favorite Syrah. Steve Tanzer's from California. "

"Really?" I gazed at him from beneath my eyelashes in a flirtatious fashion.

"To us," Diego toasted, clicking my glass. Holding up his wine to the light, he let it form legs before he brought it to my lips. "Let us be French, if only for a romantic moment."

"Alright," I said slowly, lost in the shimmering green of his eyes. My arm reached around his and brought my glass to his mouth.

As I tasted the spicy chocolate nectar, I was mesmerized by the perfectly symmetrical features in front of me. How could any man be so drop dead sexy and be capable of murder? Well, that is a fact. There have been many handsome killers. I shivered thinking of the Canadian serial killer who had lured women to their deaths. Like a devil in disguise. Was the man sitting in front of me one of those?

"I remembered the shiraz you enjoyed and found this Syrah."

"Chocolate flavors."

He checked the air. "You pass." Sitting back in the couch, he laughed heartily. "You are my favorite student."

"Of?"

Diego leaned in and brushed my lips. "Love. And I am of yours." Reaching over to stroke my leg, his fingers suddenly froze. "What happened here?" His finger centered on the dark bruise on my calf.

"The other night I went to see my dive instructor. Outside the gate a man came at me with a knife."

"What!" Diego took my hand. "Cozumel is a safe place. I know you, Adelina. You must be involved in something dangerous."

Was he playing cat and mouse with me? "I am looking into something."

Diego's eyes narrowed. "Leave it alone. Someone wants you dead." He took my face in his hands. "Seriously, *mi amor*, you must desist."

"Not going to happen."

"Why? What would be so important you would risk your life?" Diego gazed into my eyes. "It has to do with that fellow in your tour group, right? The man who met with the dive accident. What was his name…Brett?"

"Brock. I found out he was involved with numerous women. It could have angered their partners."

"Where are you going with this? You don't think I had anything to do with his demise?"

Staring into those brandy eyes, I wondered about their depth of deceit.

Diego shook his head. "Believe me, I hardly knew the man. Like I said, if I'd trusted him, I would have hired him to investigate something for me. He suddenly straightened up. "You would never believe what I came across." With a quick smile, he reached over to a box sitting on the bookshelf. "One of our imports. I thought you might like it. It's rather powerful I was told. Maria, my maid, believes in them." Diego laughed. "So did Papa. Strength, fertility and this one should even help defend you from attacks. " He leaned in and whispered in my ear, "Better still you need to move in with me, hm-mm?"

"Is this object something to do with your father's belief in the power of the Atlanteans?"

"You hit the nail on the head. The Bolivars were from the Basque region. Thus, they had superior knowledge." With the tip of his finger he took a strand of my hair. "I admit I hadn't looked into the exportation of these until you," he said, trailing his fingers down a strand, "pointed out I knew too little about that aspect of the business. And again, my sweet, you were right. I shouldn't rely on the wisdom of lackeys." He handed me the box. "For you, my darling Adelinita," he said softly. "May it do everything it's meant to do."

"I don't know about fertility." I laughed, but inwardly I was pleased that Diego wanted to protect me from danger. The brightly decorated box with Mayan warriors marching on the lid opened easily. Inside was a dark green shiny object at least four inches long and three inches in width.

Diego smiled lazily. "Siberian jade. An excellently carved piece."

The skull was smooth and cool. When I turned it towards me, the sunken eyes stared back. Dark holes. They put me off but I continued to examine the rest. Finely detailed from the indentations in the forehead to the tear-dropped shaped nostrils and straight square teeth. In my hands, the stone warmed as if responding to my energy.

"You feel anything?"

I heard his voice as if from a distance. Surprisingly, the jade skull was taking on a personality of its own. "The eyes are turning darker." It was as if the skull was responding to my question— *Is Diego innocent of the murders?* The force of the skull was powerfully hypnotic. The eyes glowed with an eerie red light.

"Adelina? You are picking up on something, aren't you?"

My grandma had told me to always listen to my intuition. Fine tuning my ability was the challenge. I was beginning to think the skull was transmitting a message. Blocking out Diego, I focused on the object and searched for answers. A voice told me where I needed to go. With newfound relief, I breathed freely.

"What is it, *mi amor*? You look pale." Diego took my hands. "Did you pick up on anything? Maria says she does."

"I did." I placed the warm skull back into the box. "It's hard to explain." I wished I had never met Wolf. I just wanted to forget all the drama with Samantha and let Diego take care of me.

"Listen. If Samantha has Du Lac's child, you are free to be with me, correct?"

He was drop dead delicious and right now all I wanted was for Diego to meet my needs. No more brain waves. I think he was taken aback when I climbed on his lap and started to kiss him. But the man was no fool. Soft lips caressed mine while his hand stroked my breast. Under the clothing, my nipple responded.

 Somewhere in this process, the straps of the dress slid off and he kissed a trail from my neck to the valley between my mounds, sending intense sparks to my core. Everything was forgotten as I stood. Diego undid my zipper and my dress slid to the floor.

"What the hell…get your hands off her!" Charging in, Wolf gripped Diego by the shoulders.

Diego might have been caught off guard but he was able to put his lust on hold. Hands went up, knocking off Wolf's hold. The six footers stood head to head. A cock fight ready to happen.

"Stop it!" I yelled.

Just then Fede barged in through the door. Right behind him, Churo took action and stepped between the men. A massive barrier no one wanted to contend with.

"She's not yours, Du Lac. Ask her," Diego sneered.

Wolf glanced at me. "Adie is confused."

"No, I'm not. This is none of your business, Wolf. You gave up that right when you had that night with Samantha and got her pregnant.

Wolf's cool blues ignored me. "You plied her with alcohol, Alvarez. She's not into you. Adie loves me. You could never be man enough for her."

From behind Churo, Fede leered at my lacy duds. "This is

definitely the most interesting place on the boat. I had no idea that Du Lac was your fiancé. I can see why you are a threat to the redhead. Even the brunette is green with jealousy. Hm-mm. *¡Dios mio,* you are a fine looking woman! I can see the allure she has, gentlemen, but seriously, you must be logical. A woman with great tits and ass is still only a woman."

With everyone's eyes on my skimpy attire, I snatched up my dress and stepped back into it with as much dignity as I could muster.

"She's her own woman, Du Lac. If you screw around on her, you can't expect her to stand by you, can you?"

"There was no way in hell I willingly had sex with Samantha Jurgens." Wolf took my hand. "You must believe me, princess. She is one skillful manipulator, much like Alvarez here."

Diego smiled lazily while flicking a speck of dust off his shirt. "Miss Jurgens is hardly in my league. For your information, I have genuine feelings for Adelina and until you resolve your situation, it behooves her to stay clear of you."

"I am sending the DNA results to Canada. There isn't a lab I can trust around here to come up with the truth. Adie, you need to believe in me just a while longer." He brought me close. "I really do love you," he whispered.

Involuntarily, the neurons in my earlobe shuddered with the warmth of his breath. Its promise of pleasure sent my pulse racing. If only this was a dream. But then it would be a nightmare. First the murders and then Samantha. I wished I could wake up as if none of this had ever happened. With a glance at the emerald, I turned to Wolf. "I need time."

"You'll have it. And I'll fight for you," he glared at Diego, "if I have to."

"You can bet you will have a fight on your hands, Du Lac, no matter what the test results," sneered Diego.

"Come now, gentlemen," Fede broke in, chirping happily. "There are papers to sign. Let us forget this unpleasantness. Remember, regardless of your enmity, you fellows work well together and," he said emphatically, "our project is near completion. If you will, Diego, Señor Du Lac requires a continuance and your signature is needed." He strode to the desk and picked up a pen. "Diego, if you please."

The more I heard from Fede, the less I wanted to be here. In fact, the idea of being on this boat was rubbing me the wrong way altogether. I spotted the box. "Diego, thank you," I said, taking the present.

He shot me a look. "For?"

"Everything." I smiled mysteriously, squirting by Churo on the stairs. Brushing past the trio of women on the deck, I traipsed over the gangway.

His back against the shiny white limo, Ernesto stood smoking When he heard the tapping of my heels, he came to attention. "You are leaving now, Señorita?"

"Yes. You can drive me back?"

"Certainly." Ernesto tossed the cigarette on the dock where it fell sparking between the boards. Whipping the door open, he held his hand out to assist me. Once the door closed, the limo became a cool air-conditioned haven. Finally, I had time to think about the message from the skull.

A tap on the window and a heavily made-up face stared in. "Can you give me a ride, honey?"

18

Ronny's pink-trim wet suit was zipped down, exposing a narrow, hairless chest. His hair was slicked back with gel and he grinned from ear to ear as he sat on the wooden bench, head tilted back, basking in the afternoon rays. I was in my bikini, contemplating when to don my wet suit. Beside me, my dive master was unusually quiet. His wild black hair blew in all directions as he tugged on his beard. I wondered if Cy had come up with a new plan of attack but from the time we'd gathered at the dock, there hadn't been a moment to question him.

We were on the *Sagitario* heading out for a single dive. Nothing deep, no more than forty feet this time. No cause to worry, therefore, but a sense of dread filled my core. The last dive had been doomed with Brock's murder being much too pat. There was no way it had been an accident.

The bright sunny day cheered me up a little. Fluffy white clouds like giant whales shifted ever so slightly in the cerulean blue expanse of the sky. At the stern, a frothy trail of water splashed up in the wake, spraying the divers. Nobody seemed to mind. Humidity was heavy. We'd hit the high eighties a couple of hours back.

"Lookin' good, mama." Larry grinned evilly at Mary, who'd poured herself into a black one piece. With the spillage over the top and high cut below, his thinking was actively below the belt.

Mary Battrock tossed her red mane like a frisky foal ready to let loose in the pasture.

"I found a great l'il cantina in town." Larry leered at the freckled valley between the twin peaks. "How's about we chug a few down after the dive?"

"Yeah, alright." Mary's eyes glinted. "This will be a great dive. I think celebrating will be just what I'll need." She stretched her hands behind her head, locking fingers. "Later," she agreed, with a happy smile.

Funny thing was, I didn't think she liked the firefighter much. Most of the time she bit his head off about anything and everything. Not that I blamed her. What woman in her right mind would like that army gorilla? But there was no use figuring out Battrock. The woman was weird as hell.

Across from me, Irmgard sat as stoically as a nun, hair tightly clasped in a bun, chugging water like it was the last drink on earth. Today, Daniel was her boyfriend. He was fussing with her mask, cleaning it with a tiny squeeze bottle and rubbing it with his finger. Every once in a while, he'd leer at Irmgard.

Frankly, I didn't care as long as the boss lady was chill. I was much too tired to deal with Irmgard the drama queen. If he put a smile on that prune face—no objection from this woman. There was no question in my mind where I'd be after this dive. A nap in my room—alone.

I shouldn't have been drinking at lunch today. Diego's generosity with the booze had sabotaged my subversive investigation. But I shouldn't blame him for what fate threw at me. Fede had invited Wolf. The letter *S* for stupid must be stamped on my forehead. The whole incident had been so embarrassing and there was no one to blame but myself.

Right now another problem needed attention. Dehydration. I groped in my dive bag for my water bottle but came up with nothing. I could kick myself for forgetting. The wretched dry throat I had would only get worse with breathing through a reg. I couldn't think of a more uncomfortable feeling than that. Sometimes it's like there's no saliva left to gulp back. It would be endless torture until I resurfaced.

Spotting a tub filled with water bottles, I was about to ask Mary to toss me one when she waved around a bottle in the air. "Is this anyone's?"

I perked up. "Must be mine. Probably rolled out."

After I chugged it down, I glanced at Cy. What was with him anyway? The guy looked like he'd lost his best friend.

"Did you see my brother?" he whispered in my ear.

Thoughtfully, I ran a finger over my lip. "He invited me to lunch."

Cy's eyes turned a thundercloud gray. "A liquid affair, I'd bet."

I patted his arm. "Don't worry. I'm fine to dive. Slept a couple of hours when I got back." I glanced at the dust consultant and yelled out, "Mary, could you pass me another bottle, please?"

With an annoyed expression, the stocky woman dug into the bucket. Flaming red hair blew into her eyes, whipped by the wind. She took a moment bending down before she threw it over.

I passed this one to Cy. "Here." When he stared spaced out at the bottle, I added, "Drink it." What was he in a funk about anyway? Men were so strange. Take the gorilla. A guy like that would be in rage all day if he cut himself shaving but took a bullet no problem. Now with Cy, I'd think it had to do with something more primal.

"And Du Lac?" His mouth tightened into a straight line. "Are you still engaged?"

I had this vision of a tall strong Neptune emerging from the water—totally nude. I sighed. The perfect cover model for Men's Health. Much too good for that slinky snake. But still, I was disappointed. Why hadn't he called her out on that lie? Wolf was dragging his tail. Hardly the decisive man I once knew. It served me right, falling like a fool. I should be conniving like the vultures he hung with—waiting and ready to feast on my man. Women who always got what they wanted.

I glanced at my hand. My finger was bare. I'd left the emerald ring in my hotel room. No need to attract barracuda. I didn't want to end up like Brock.

"Well?"

How could I answer that? It all came down to trust. Once that was lost, it was easy to look at other men. There was no doubt Diego made a delightful dessert. A chocolate mousse feast. With a taste of him, all my frustrations would vanish. Yet once again, fate had intervened. The godfather was still untouched territory. Maybe it wasn't meant to be. I rubbed my forehead. Always so close and no cigar. My life was one convoluted mess.

Cy took a swig from the bottle. "Adie?"

I shrugged my shoulders. Time would decide that. "Not exactly."

Apparently, that wasn't the right answer. Jaw clenched, Cy turned away to check his equipment.

"Cy!" our dive master called out. Balanced on solid tree trunk legs, he rocked like a tugboat in a storm as he trekked in a wide gait towards us. The wind was strong and when the boat hit the wake of a passing speedboat, Usiel swayed unsteadily. His leg knocked my open bottle out of my hands. Last I saw, it rolled aft spilling on the deck. Call me a coward but with that bitchy look on Battrock's mug, I wasn't about to ask her for another.

As Cy and Usiel exchanged boy talk, I glanced at the boss lady. Irmgard was coping well with Brock's death. In fact I'd say from the smile on her lips, Daniel was starting to get in her good books. Sex had improved her demeanor. She was almost pleasant. And helpful. There was this dopey, glazed-over, lustful gleam in her eyes. Could it be she was having too much sex? Was that possible? Nope, no way. Sex revitalizes and increases longevity. Better than super vitamins. Which made me wonder why it was someone like Irmgard who got whatever she wanted.

No, I take that back. Sex wasn't the be all and end all. I knew it in my brain if not in my heart. I had higher ambitions. My goal was love. It was cliché but the man of my dreams had to connect with me emotionally and intellectually, not to mention sexually. Someone like Wolf. He did it all for me.

"Say, Adie. That was some lunch, eh?" Ronny shouted over the roar of the motor.

I nodded, feeling a little uncomfortable about it. Cy stopped talking to Usiel.

Ronny leaned forward, his blue eyes animated. "The Alvarez family must be loaded, eh? Champagne and oysters. Would I ever love living like them!" Ronny studied my body. "Lucky lady! Looks to me like it's in your cards. Diego is yours for the asking. And no wonder. That dress you had on. Wow! Nearly knocked my socks off!"

Cy's eyes were burning a hole in my side.

"You were back at the Bolivar Alvarez house, Adie?" Irmgard asked. "Good for you! Diego is dead delicious." She frowned. "But you must be conflicted."

"Hm-mm?

"That blond superman of yours sizzles. I met him at the Alvarez party, remember?" Her forehead crinkled. "What was your guy's name?"

"Wolf." Ronny interjected, a smile on his lips. "He was there for lunch, too. On the yacht not the mansion. You should have seen him. That tight black T-shirt showed off some great guns. Not to mention those powerful shoulders," the transvestite groaned, "and iron-board flat abs to die for."

"Yes-ss." Irmgard flicked her tongue over her lips. "Wolf. A perfect name for an alpha male like him. Yummy!"

"Totally," Ronny squeaked.

"Oh?" I tried to be casual but I was seething inside. I hated talking about my situation. It would have been different if I knew Wolf was mine but I didn't.

"I'm sure he's got a good business head but I'm looking at him like your friend and boss. He's buff and there's—" Irmgard grinned.

"An undercurrent." Ronny said helpfully.

"Yes!" Irmgard blurted. There's a smoking hot vibe coming from that man."

"Hm-mm," Ronny murmured. "Definitely an éclair. Chocolate coated with a thick creamy filling."

"So-oo delicious," Irmgard agreed and seeing Daniel's glare, added, "as is my honey here."

Ronny's jaw dropped. "Daniel is an éclair?"

"Well, no." Irmgard examined the valve on her BCD. "Daniel's more like a donut with sprinkles."

That stretched the imagination thin. Donuts were soft tasty comfort food. Daniel was a skinny sexless beanpole. But as far as Wolf was concerned, she'd hit the nail on the head. The sea god was creamy rich and sinfully delicious like a chocolate feast. And he was man enough to make me purr like a cat in heat.

"But wait a minute. You were with Diego," Irmgard pointed out. "He's hot for you. You can't deny that. How was lunch with Mexico's Enrique Iglesias?"

"It was lunch, Irmgard. And we were definitely not alone. His sister and brother-in-law were there. Not to mention a few guests, including Ronny." Why was I making up all these excuses? I needed a reality check. Samantha was pregnant. What was stopping me from ditching Wolf and going for bodacious Diego Alvarez? *Nada,* absolutely nothing.

Irmgard screeched in laughter. "So funny! Both of those beefcakes on the yacht with Ms. Adie Sturm." She glanced at Ronny. "Say, you were lucky to get an invitation, buddy. What I don't understand is why Diego would mess up his chances by inviting Wolf."

"Business."

Irmgard giggled. "Monkey business. Wish I'd been a fly on the wall. So spill, Ronny. Tell Auntie Irmgard what Adie was up to."

Luckily, we were approaching the dive site and he wasn't able to fill her in. The boat rocked as the motor slowed down. With a hand on the railing, Usiel stood and brought his hand up in a stop gesture. "Folks, we are almost there. Does everyone remember the signals?" When Ronny looked confused, he went through the drill once more. "Check your equipment. The crew will be around to help." He waved. "I'll see you all below."

Nervously, I glanced at Cy who took my hand and gave it a firm squeeze. "Relax, Adie. We'll go down after them. I'll take care of you. Don't worry. If you feel panicky, just sign." He pointed his thumb in the up position.

With a nod, I picked up my wet suit. I could trust him but it was hard getting past the fear. The Cressi suit gave me a fight, sticking to every part of my body as I tugged it up over my legs. Some people coat themselves with oil before putting on their neoprene suit. Not a bad idea. Definitely would have helped. I needed to wisen up in more ways than one. Finally, with the zipper at the back tightening the slack, I pulled it up to the nape of my neck. Next, I clipped on the weight belt. When that was done, a crew member lifted the tank on my shoulders. Heavy—almost like having a small child sit on my shoulders. With me being a one hundred and ten pounder, the weight was an uncomfortable workout. On the up side, I couldn't wait to see the hidden wonders of the sea.

After everyone stepped off the stern of the boat, one by one, I waited. Finally, I followed Cy, feeling like I was walking the plank on Blackbeard's ship, hungry sharks waiting below for breakfast. Again, a crew member pushed me off the edge. Hitting the water, I dropped about twenty feet before the inflated BCD shot me to the surface. Condensation. With the help of spit spread over the fogged area, the mask was ready and back in place.

Cy's head popped up twenty feet away. One hand cleared the water as he signaled going down. I felt panicky. After a few deep breaths, I talked myself into relaxing, plugged the reg into my mouth, and released air from my BCD.

My descent was slow. I equalized my ears with a pinch to my nose every two feet. It takes time but I kept to the routine. With each puff of air, I drifted lower. At the coral bottom, the sand was powdery white, like ground up diamonds. Far above, the surface shone like glass. Bright blue tangs swam by on their way to the fan coral ahead. A massive amount of knobby yellow brain coral towered a few meters away. I felt like the Little Mermaid in a magical sea world. Everything was just right. Even my throat was normal. I had this tremendously relaxed feeling flowing through my veins.

My mask didn't allow for peripheral vision but it hugged my narrow face and I'd bought it. So far I'd gone through too many, all ending up loose and leaky. Bad equipment can ruin a dive. The fit was the deciding factor besides the fact it matched the Cressi suit. When I looked around, I didn't see my dive instructor. For a moment I thought I'd been abandoned. Then I felt a nudge from Cy and turned to see him. He was close, his green eyes magnified by the depth, a message in them that I couldn't read.

Ahead, divers from our boat floated in behind the coral. All the black suits looked alike. It was hard to tell who they were from a distance. In pink neon edging, Ronny stood out like a spotlight parrot fish. Usiel examined a giant yellow barrel sponge with an opening of more than six meters. Hovering at the site, Larry pressed in between Daniel and Usiel. Camera in hand, the army man closed in for a photo op.

Mary Battrock and Irmgard edged in for a look. Spooked by the attention, a nine foot shark escaped and scooted away to the overhang where it disappeared from sight. The mouth at the bottom of the gray creature made me think it was a harmless nurse shark.

The sand whirled up by the divers clouded the visibility. A push from behind alerted me to Cy. His hand signaled forward.

I tried to sign but a queasy wave took over my body. My brain was out of sync. I kept telling my fins to go but my feet propelled me at a snail's pace. A giant turtle whizzing by turned and grinned a toothy smile. Strange. It was like falling though ice. A chill oozed into my veins. All my energy was gone. My stomach somersaulted. Was it the spicy oysters from lunch? The light-headed feeling made me stop and float.

The ocean shifted in shades of emerald and aqua, layer after layer revolving in a spiral. I tried to make it stop. If only I could steady myself. The whirling fan coral waved like a demented purple spirit tortured by demons. I wanted Cy to slow down but he continued at a relentless pace. Panic set in. He was leaving me behind down here. Brock's face loomed between the branches of coral.

Like a maverick horse at a rodeo, my gut bucked wildly. I tried to force the bile back but it gathered momentum, spilling out my reg like dust in a storm. Brown specks flew into the water. Passing striped grunts gulped up the undigested rejects. Big yellow eyes so close to my mask. Unspoken messages from the fish. *Go back to the boat.*

The grunts were right. I tried to get Cy's attention but my fingers froze, refusing to do what my brain commanded. Something was wrong. Cy's movements looked odd, as though in slow motion. He turned to me as we entered the cave, his eyes large and bulbous, gleaming red. Squid-like purplish tentacles waved from the mask. I recoiled. This couldn't be Cy.

The monster turned to me and signaled up. Afraid, I pedaled my fins as quickly as I could, swimming into the dark cave. From behind, a hand grabbed my shoulder. Fear filled my heart. The sea blinded me. Salt stung like nettles as my mask was torn away. With my eyes closed I shot forward lost in a black abyss with no way out.

****

Voices. I could feel myself lifted onto the deck. I couldn't see. My eyes burned painfully.

"Adie?" A far away voice. "It's me, Cy."

"What happened?" I croaked.

"Your mask was gone. Did it catch on the coral?"

I shook my head and retched. Quick as a flash, he handed me a pail. He waited while I heaved. When I sat back Cy passed me a water bottle from the tub. I took it but couldn't bring it to my lips. Steadying my hand, he held it while I slowly sipped. I took a last glance at Cy confirming it was really him before I passed out.

****

This time I woke up in a strange bed in a room with a water-stained white ceiling, but the cotton sheets were fresh, crisp and clean under a thin, fuzzy tan blanket. I looked around. Behind me a woven turquoise, black and white blanket with an eagle in the center of a striped design hung above the wooden bed board. All warm and cozy, with a big heater against my back. Only it was way too solid and human. When I tried to move, I couldn't. A strong hand clasped my hip in a solid grip.

"Wolf," I said tentatively. My eyes widened. The dark hairs on the forearm were not the sea god's. Gently, I pushed the heavy arm away and turned.

Omigod! Who was he? I took in dark hair, even features, a nose a little long and hawkish and shapely lips. I had picked up a random stranger? How could this have happened? I wasn't a sex junkie. I believed in making love, not getting my rocks off with good-looking strangers.

I twisted my body around to fully face him. He was familiar and rather sexy. I reached out and stroked his cheek. Black lashes fluttered open to a pair of brilliant green eyes—Bolivar Alvarez eyes. The light in my brain clicked. "Cy?" I whispered.

"Adie." His lips tilted up at the corners. "How are you feeling?"

The light-headed feeling was gone. My stomach wasn't gurgling. "I'm okay. Why am I here?"

"We were in the hospital. You were kind of out of it. Once we got to my place, you fell asleep."

"I can't stay." I pulled up on my elbows to get up and then paused, wondering what I was wearing. I peeked under the sheet and felt relief.

Cy held my arm and brought me back down. "Wait."

"But the tour group!"

"They're flying home as scheduled." He tapped the tip of my nose. "But you're staying."

I gripped the sheet nervously. "But I have to go with them."

"There's no way you can fly. Don't worry. Irmgard is taking over."

"Oh. Why? What's wrong with me?"

"You've heard of the bends?"

"I have it?"

"Let's say the doctors are playing it safe. You ingested something and weren't breathing properly in your ascent. I brought you to the surface without a decompression stop. I was afraid you'd stopped breathing. We got to the boat in the nick of time."

"How did this happen? Was it the drinks I had at lunch?"

"I don't think so. Probably they didn't help any, but with the stuff you were coming out with, I think someone drugged you."

"What stuff?"

"You were talking about squids coming out of my face. That's just before you vomited. After you passed out, I had the captain stop at the nearest dock. We took a taxi to the clinic. I wasn't feeling so good myself. They checked us out."

"I remember you were swimming really slowly before you signaled to go up."

Cy touched my cheek. "Why didn't you come?"

"I panicked."

"That's why you swam into the cave?"

The devil image replayed. "Did you come after me?"

"Not right away. I was dizzy. I thought it would pass but when I thought you were in danger, I went in."

"The burning." I blinked. "My eyes. They're dry as dust."

"Salt water. Someone tore your mask off down there."

"Omigod." There was nothing more painful than salt. I'd seen people diving without a mask in sea water but for me, a few seconds was murder. "I don't know how you got me to the boat, but thank you."

Cy shook his head. "I'm blurry on that, too. I was feeling a little light-headed. That's why I signaled for us to make an ascent."

"Do you think you were drugged?"

Cy nodded.

"Someone on the boat." I scanned his face. "Is that why you shaved? You want to go to Diego. You know he's not behind your car accident."

"Hardly." A slow smile spread on Cy's face. "I thought you might like it."

"Oh. Is that why we're in bed together? And I'm wearing a towel?"

"Well, you were soaking wet in the bikini." He frowned. "Didn't think I should take your clothes off."

"You thought right about that."

"Don't be angry. We were exhausted. I was no danger to you." Cy's eyes gleamed a soft emerald. "Nothing happened."

My dive master was not the hippie I once knew. With the shorter wavy hair, I saw how similar he was to Diego. Only his eyes were different. The light changed them from green to gray. Still sexy. I bit my lip and asked myself why I was in bed with this man.

"Really. It's true. Nothing happened. Just relax." He put his fingers on my shoulders and massaged the stiff muscles joining my neck. I sighed and sank back into the pillow. "But it takes supreme will power not to kiss a tempestuous woman like you."

"Is that like intriguing?"

He grinned. "Fiery, dazzling and hypnotic."

I giggled. "You Latinos sure know how to flatter."

"It's all the truth." He fingered his chin. "Look at me."

When I met his gaze, I blushed.

215

"Like it?"

"Looks good, dive master."

"I like the sound of that," he said, brushing his lips on mine, "being your master."

My core responded with an excited tingle. Realizing, where this was going, I sat up. "Only in the water, Cy." These guys. All that they wanted was recreational sex. "Did you bring my bag?"

Looking at me in amazement, he nodded.

"If you don't mind, I'd like to take a shower and change. We've got lots to do."

****

I came out to the smell of bacon and eggs. My stomach couldn't have been happier.

In the kitchen with an apron tied around his narrow waist, Cy stood at the stove flipping an egg. The bacon was sizzling in another frying pan. Bread popped out of the toaster.

I went straight to the fridge. "I like my eggs over and hard," I said over my shoulder. Was that a chortle I heard?

"What are you looking for?"

"Ketchup. Got some?"

A brilliant smile reached his eyes. "Yup. Set the table, my queen. Dishes over there." He jerked his head towards the cupboards.

Just as I put the finishing touches on the table setting, Cy brought over our supper. Beans had been added to the meal, as well as a bottle of red wine.

"Well done, King Cy. You wouldn't believe how hungry I am."

"I would. I saw you feed the fish with your lunch."

"Let's not think about that. What's the wine?"

"Shiraz. Australian. Nothing expensive but not easy to get here. A dive buddy brought me this one. Reminds me of you."

"Oh, why?"

"The name. *Cat Amongst the Pigeons. Nine Lives.* You've used up three lives in this last week but you're still the all-powerful cat." He poured the deep red liquid into our glasses. "It hasn't had too much time to breathe."

I clicked his glass. "To more lives."

Cy laughed. "For both of us."

It may not have been a hundred dollar wine like the ones Diego had, but this purple wine was rich. "Got any chocolate?"

"Maybe."

A man of mystery. Just my type. What was I thinking? First Wolf, then Diego, and now Cy? I was a serial dater with no conscience.

"Eat your eggs and then we'll satisfy your other needs."

"Smooth talker," I said, in between mouthfuls of eggs and beans.

"I am," Cy said, a twinkle in his eyes. "How about chocolate for dessert?"

I nodded. "I have a plan."

"I have a feeling you're not just talking chocolate."

I took my last sip of wine. "My investigation is coming to a head. Someone is seriously gunning for me. If I don't act, I'll be the next dead body." Half a glass of the red elixir would be plenty. This operation required an alert Adie Sturm. "The warehouse. We've got to go back."

Cy handed me a chocolate square. "And why would that be?"

The skull had given me a distinct message. It had been downright freaky the way those eyes had glowed red before telepathically communicating the plan. "The warehouse has the answer."I popped the square in my mouth, savoring the rich sweetness.

Cy raised an eyebrow.

"Seriously. It will clear up everything."

"And you know this because?"

"If you knew why, you'd think I'm nuts."

Cy shook his head. "I already know that and don't hold it against you." He smirked. "Maybe I should."

"What?"

"Hold it against you."

I rolled my eyes. "Well? Are you going with me?"

He sighed. "Okay, *chica*."

"Thanks."

"What's your plan?"

"First, I want you to drive there with me but I'm going in alone."

"How do you get by the guards?"

"Do you know anyone that could help?"

"Will they be in danger?"

"No. Just a diversion."

Cy grinned. "A couple of ladies owe me a favor."

****

Dusk had settled in. From behind shifting clouds, the moon hung low in a cobalt blue sky. Cy passed me the binoculars. Thankfully, the two men sitting on the stoop came in bright and clear with the night vision magnification. Baseball Cap flicked his ashes on the sidewalk. He was a good foot shorter than Bozo, his buddy. The clown was a weightlifter. All neck and shoulders. From the width of him, I'd say he ate steroids with his burger.

The gloomy street between us and the guards was in need of repair. Pot holes and cracks were everywhere. When I scanned beyond the warehouse, I spotted a beat up black vintage VW Beetle in an otherwise empty parking lot. From the looks of the buildings on either side, they were abandoned office or storage places. Nobody would be in a hurry to build out here.

After dinner I'd dug out the duds from my dive bag. Black jeans and T-shirt, which I always kept in there just in case. Not nearly enough protection. I wished we'd thought of a blanket. My elbows had indentations from the twigs and stones. I suppose we were lucky there was any grass at all.

As usual the mosquitoes buzzing around my head were out in full force. The shampoo attracted them, or was it my spicy man-bait perfume? I ran my fingers through the silky strands. No products to give it volume or shape but I'd done the best I could with a brush and hair dryer. Mascara and liner made me feel feminine again.

Makeup didn't really matter. My skin with its golden hue, tanned easily in the tropical sun. Must be my mixed heritage. It prepared me for all types of weather. Personally, I preferred hot places. I sighed. So many places still to see. The bends had given me an extra two weeks in paradise, but who knows if I was getting paid? It wasn't beneath Irmgard to renege on the contract. Chintzy woman wouldn't care if I died on the plane as long as her business was booming.

The scent of lime and pine woods drifted to my nose. Masculine but not too powerful. It suited the clean cut and very handsome Amancio Bolivar Alvarez. I had to tell myself to pay attention to the guards because I was getting a strange vibe from this guy—something I wasn't prepared for. I refocused, aiming the binoculars back at Baseball Cap, and saw him take a swig from a mickey before passing it to Bozo beside him.

Alcohol takes off the edge from a stressful day. Maybe they needed it. They could be the ones shipping out the stolen goods to the mystery ship. I wish I knew who the smugglers were. There had to be a connection to the murderers. Skulls were cool and probably in high demand but I had a feeling there was more to this picture. It would be an hour before the warehouse closed. The plan was in place. I hated the wait. Just as I was feeling pain in every part of my body, the women showed up.

Judging from their outfits, they could have been hookers or just regular islanders in tight spandex. A bouncy brunette in a flaming red dress swished her hips and stopped directly in front of Bozo. If her words didn't distract him, an eyeful of cleavage did.

Baseball Cap was sloshed but not too wasted to finish the bottle and throw it in the gated property next door. With Bozo weighing an additional hundred pounds, I was a little worried he was way too alert. The mickey was nothing to a tank like that. Apparently, the girl in black had the magic potion—a bottle of tequila she was generously sharing.

"You told them to bring liquor?" I whispered.

"It occurred to me that we didn't want the guards standing around when you went in."

"Right. But they'll lock the door when they leave."

"That's where my women come in. Watch."

While the lady in red got the dudes drinking, the tiny girl stuck something into the door catch.

"Smart," I muttered.

Cy pointed to his temple. "I'm not just a pretty face, *chica*."

I cocked my head. "So you think the new look is sexy?"

"Your words not mine." At his smug expression, I sharply poked his arm.

In answer, he wrapped his arms around me and latched on to my lips in what became a very sensuous kiss. I withdrew, slightly breathless.

"Er-rr, Cy."

He put a finger up against my lips. "Don't say anything. Everything will work out."

I doubted that. This was a royal screwup.

19

The security guards left with the women. I felt sorry for the bait. The men were losers. If I were in their shoes, I'd bring them to a bar, get them drunk and leave through the back exit. Cy must have done them some big favor.

"Here's the crowbar, Adie." Cy placed his hands on my shoulders and searched my face. "You sure you want me to stay here? It won't take me long to pry open a box."

"I know but it's my problem."

Cy lifted an eyebrow. "Really? It's my brother that tried to kill me and he's running these smugglers."

"You don't know that. Hand me that crowbar, please."

Cy shook his head resignedly. "Okay, you've got twenty minutes max. Then I come in. Now are you sure you can handle it?"

Almost three feet long with a double hook on one end and heavy, I wasn't sure if weight lifting had prepared me for this. And no, I wasn't sure about any of this, but ever since Brock's arm had floated by, his murder was on my shoulders. The key was the smuggling.

Inside, dim lights lit the place. Pulleys and cranes sat forty feet away. Nearby boxes were stacked at the far end of the building. Crates that were either on their way in or out had been piled near the middle. I examined the labels as I walked down the aisle. The first stack was marked *Cigarros*. *Ron* was lettered on the boxes in the next row. Only when I reached the third aisle did I come to a chest with a sketched skull and *Cráneos* printed on it in black ink.

I froze. My gut screamed—*open this one!* Carefully, I wedged the crowbar into the gap between the boards. The board loosened and flew off. With all my strength, I broke off another board. A wide enough gap allowed me a view of jade skulls in the straw. When I moved them, I had a moment of truth. Something lay underneath.

With the crowbar, I pulled aside the straw and hit a hard object. A long brown barrel. I'm not an arms master but I'm not stupid. Clearly, Diego was shipping weapons illegally out of the country. That's where the profit was, not in the skulls. Idly, I pushed away the straw. The weapon didn't look like any rifle I'd ever seen. My guess was some sort of terrorist weapon. From the size of the crate, it held ten or more. I stepped back and looked around for other skull boxes. Just then, I heard a click. A glint of light. Inches from my fingers, a bullet punctured the crate.

My knee jerk reaction was to swing around and pitch the crowbar. The gun fired again as the shooter hit the cement. An adrenaline rush hurled me into survival mode. A kick into his chest kept him down. Another to the head made sure. The Glock slipped out of his fingers.

I bent down and tore the ski mask off his face. The crowbar had struck hard. Blood poured over my fingers. "Mary," I gasped, my voice hoarse.

Another shot cracked the air. A bang so loud, it hurt my ears. Mary jerked on impact. A circle of blood spread on her chest. A man's laughter echoed from the back of the warehouse.

When I whipped around, I found myself looking at the business end of a Smith and Wesson.

"Stupid bitch. Can you believe it?" Fede sighed. "Couldn't manage a clean kill."

I got up slowly, hardly trusting my eyes. "You're behind all this? You killed Brock?"

"*Sí.* But not me personally. I hired Battrock for the job. For once, she was successful. I'd bet you wouldn't ever guess she's a hired assassin, would you? The manners of a hillbilly and an ugly gene to boot. It was kind of me to kill the incompetent cow."

I shook my head, not quite believing what had just happened.

His eyes met mine. Cold flat eyes. Killer eyes.

"One of Canada's best, they'd told me." He snickered. "Not that good if a little tart like you can take her down."

"You caught me by surprise."

He beamed. "I am good, aren't I?"

"You sure are." The crowbar was on the ground a few feet away. I had to keep him talking. If I could distract him maybe I'd have a chance.

"*Escúchame*, Adelina. I am much more intelligent than any of those Bolivars give me credit for. Did they tell you how they think they came from Atlantis? Ridiculous craziness," he spat. With a wave of his weapon, he added, "It all ends tonight. Each loose end will be tied up—firmly. You will see." Fede stared. "Or maybe not."

"I doubt if anyone would guess you were the mastermind in either the murders or behind the sabotage. You certainly pulled a fast one." I had to gain time. Let him talk. "So you were shipping arms out of the country for a profit?"

Fede smiled. "Indeed. A huge profit. Millions for me. I see you recognize my genius. A brilliant plan, was it not? The pirates paid for rocket-propelled grenades, not to mention those RPG-7. The Colombians gave me a deal."

"But why kill Brock?"

"He hacked into my computer. There were bank accounts in the Turks for my share of the profit and I'd set up a Swiss account for the pirates. Duval knew too much. When Battrock told me that Du Lac had hired him, I knew I had to put a stop to it."

"And if you hadn't, your house of cards would come tumbling down."

He pointed the Smith and Wesson at my face. "Exactly. As they say, a witness is a liability."

"And Diego? Was he in on this?"

"That pompous prick wouldn't consider any of my ideas. The Bolivars are delusional."

"They're not stupid."

Fede nodded. "I give them that but their perception of reality is off. Take that older brother of his. I doubt if he caught on to the brake malfunction. The idiot was living in a fantasy. He was full of Zen philosophy or some other such spiritual garbage. I doubt if he clued in unless he had a fleeting reality check before his dive accident."

"You messed with his brakes?"

"Of course not."

He grunted at my look of disbelief. "Eduardo did that. He hated the family as much as I did after what my esteemed brother-in-law did."

"Diego's hit man?"

"Ex hit man. I think he resented his toes being crushed on numerous occasions before he was finally given the boot. It would have been smarter to have terminated him permanently. Loose ends screw up a good plan." He stared significantly at the limp body on the cement floor.

"And your plan was to take over the company?"

Fede nodded, a distant look in his dark eyes. "Francisco co-operated so well."

"How did you kill him?"

"After our afternoon tequila. It was a hot day. Francisco liked to put his feet up. He was getting old and lazy. In fact, the old man was so relaxed he nodded off. It was easy enough to inject him with digoxin."

"Is that like digitalis?"

"*Si*, a medication for the heart. He was taking it in pills." He grinned. "But this was an injection between the toes. A little too much digoxin brings on a heart attack. It was all easily accepted by the doctor. And believable. He'd had a heart attack a couple of years back. It was a perfect plan."

"And what did Larissa do wrong?"

Fede laughed. "That selfish, demanding whore? She wanted into my world. There was no way in hell I'd let her break up my marriage. Carmelita is ten times the woman."

"You liked being part of the Bolivar Alvarez family, eh?"

"Who wouldn't? And now I will be head of the family. The entire family. Francisco is gone and after Diego bites the dust, Carmelita gets it all. That means I will be running the empire." He glanced at the floor. "But first, there is a little matter of life insurance—Battrock. Interesting, I see her twitching. *Por favor*, Adelina, I'll let you do the honors. You can take her out." He smirked. "Oh, wait. I forgot, I've got the gun. Guess I'll do it for you."

He raised his weapon but he was too slow. Mary had the final say. Rising on one elbow, she aimed the Glock and fired before he could scream *Dios mio.* The blood trickled from Fede's mouth as he hit the cement.

Mary slumped back. Getting on my hands and knees, I crouched close. "Mary? You killed him."

The dust buster groaned. "Bingo." I'd swear I saw a trace of a smile on the ghostly white face. Her mouth worked before the words came out, "Diego. Car bomb. Hurry."

From the entrance of the warehouse, Cy called out. "Adie! Are you alright?"

I pulled out my cell and texted Diego.

Don't get into your car. It's wired.

Cy looked at the two bodies on the warehouse floor. "What happened?"

I rapidly explained as I pulled him along to the Jeep. We hopped in. He revved the engine and stepped on the gas. White knuckled hands on the steering wheel, he drove like a bat out of hell. In moments, we were on Raphael Melgar heading north to the mansion. I retrieved the cell from my pocket. No texts. I voiced a silent prayer.

In my head, I had a vision of Diego on the yacht. Handsome in white like a Calvin Klein model. Only he was a real person and needed help. We had to get there. We just had to.

Cy's eyes flicked to me momentarily. "Why did she tell you?"

"Being called an incompetent cow didn't go over well."

"So she decided to screw up his plan." He shook his head. "I was too late. Some backup I turned up to be."

I patted his arm. "The first shot was fired with a silencer."

"I don't know why I didn't see those two."

"They came in from the back."

We'd made it to that section of the road before the north island hotels. The mansion was close. At the entrance gate, the barrier was lowered. "This is an emergency," I shouted out to the guard. "I need to see Señor Alvarez. I'm Adie Sturm."

From the mean look on the guard's bulldog face, I wasn't surprised when he barked, "Señor Alvarez requested your presence?"

"I'm his friend."

He snickered. "That's what they all say."

Cy put up his hand. "Check your computer for Amancio Bolivar Alvarez or better yet, phone the house and tell them I've come back."

This time the bulldog's jaw dropped.

"Tell them!" Cy yelled.

The guard shot him a look but returned to the gate house to raise the barrier. The Jeep shot down the road to an interlocking brick semi-circular driveway. The six car garage was just ahead. A red Ferrari sat in front.

I breathed a sigh of relief. "We're on time."

But Cy wasn't listening. He jumped out of the Jeep shouting, "No-oo!"

The Ferrari's engine roared as it started, seconds before it exploded before our eyes. Sky high flames. Metal bits blasted in all directions.

We ran towards the car. An inferno blazed from the trunk of the Ferrari.

A man and a woman ran down the driveway from the house. At the car, Diego froze. Mesmerized by the fire, Carmelita stood silently, eyes riveted on the flames.

Another woman I recognized as the housekeeper rushed out shouting, "I shall call the fire department, Señor Alvarez," and headed back to the house.

Diego's eyes flicked to the car and then to us. "Stand back everyone." With a sudden urgency, he tore off his T-shirt and wrapped it around his hand before he flung the car door open. Flames shot out from the back.

Cy sprang in to help his brother. "Pull on his legs," he said urgently. "I'll get his shoulders."

Together, they dragged the three hundred pounder out.

"Bring Luis over there," Diego indicated a tree with a jerk of his chin. They carried him a good forty feet away and placed him gently on the ground.

Carmelita and I went along. It was hard to tell if Luis was alive, he was so badly burnt.

"He went out to bring the car," Diego murmured. "I was busy with a conference call." A shadow darkened his eyes. "It's my fault."

"No, Diego," I said, trying to calm him. "You had no idea this would happen. None of us did. I just found out about the car bomb."

Diego stared at me. "And that's why you're here?"

"I tried to stop it. I texted you."

"Damn it! I didn't see it. My cell was charging," he muttered, staring at the unconscious bodyguard on the grass. "Luis needs to get to the hospital." His eyes flicked up the road, searching for an ambulance before his glance set on Cy. "What the hell?"

"*¡Dios mio!*" Carmelita spoke slowly as if in a trance. "I heard the strangest message from the guard. I could not believe what I heard. It *is* you!"

Cy caught her before she fell to the ground.

Diego looked confused. "You are alive! How?" Suddenly, he pointed a finger accusingly. "You had something to do with this explosion, didn't you?"

"Of course not, Diego," I stepped in between them. "Cy came here to save you."

Diego stared at his brother. "You did?"

"Yes." Cy looked regretfully at the burning car. "But we were too late."

Carmelita smacked Cy's cheek. "You should be ashamed! After all this time, you come back? Don't you have any feelings for your family? Do you realize we had a memorial service for you?" She glared. "Mama has been in mourning all this time."

"Please listen. It was not by choice that I went into hiding. Things happened. I had to find out who tried to kill me."

"Someone tried to kill you?" Carmelita grabbed his hand. "Who?"

"It was a mystery. I only had suspicions. When enough time passed, I decided to come back to find out."

"And you couldn't confide in me—your only brother? I would have helped," Diego said stiffly.

Cy met his gaze.

"I see. You thought I was plotting against you, planning to usurp your position in the company."

"It's more complicated than that."

"*Basta!* Stop arguing!" Carmelita shouted. "I want to know

why this happened. Amancio, tell us!"

The horn of the fire truck drowned out Cy's reply. On the driveway, the firefighters hosed down the car. A tremendous rush of smoke shot into the air.

Diego stared hypnotically at the car. "*Tranquilo*. We'll talk in the house," he said, before he strode over to the captain of the brigade.

Flashing lights, the wail and yelp of a siren. An ambulance tore up the driveway. Attendants rushed out and placed Luis on a stretcher before loading him into the ambulance.

Diego returned just as a police car flew down the road, heading to the mansion. When the car parked beside the ambulance, a plain clothes man and two officers got out.

"Hernandez is here. I'll deal with them,"Diego said to us. "Everyone go into the house!"

Cy had a stubborn set to his jaw.

"It's better that we leave, Cy. We don't want to explain now," I said, looking significantly at Carmelita.

****

Embers from a log glowed in the fireplace. A cluster of plush cream leather furniture was positioned on either side. From the heavy oak coffee table, Carmelita picked up a decanter, poured a golden liquid into snifters and handed them to us before seating herself. I took the love seat but Cy decided on the leather chair next to his sister. Carmelita was in tears. "I don't understand any of this, Amancio."

In the leather chair, Cy crossed his legs and sat back. "I'm sorry. Believe me it was a necessity. I had to find out who tampered with my brakes."

"You actually thought I would put a hit on you?" From the doorway, Diego stood gazing evenly at Cy. "I know we've had our differences but you are my brother and I love you."

"I know. I love you also. It was foolish of me to conclude you were behind this but Fede convinced me you wanted me out so badly that you would go to any means to take over Bolivar Imports and Exports. In addition, Francisco wouldn't allow me to make the final decisions on the business. It was becoming frustrating, especially once he started to listen to Fede."

"Don't blame Fede, Amancio," Carmelita said hastily. "He was way more interested in the business than either you or Diego. I know he can be callous and conniving but he wanted to learn more about our family enterprises. Surely that wasn't bad?"

I exchanged a look with Cy that Diego caught.

"There's something you're not saying. It has to do with that scumbag, doesn't it?" Diego asked, his tone demanding.

"Yes. He's involved in this."

"That doesn't surprise me," Diego said solemnly. He tipped his snifter, reflectively staring at the liquor. "What I'd like to know is what exactly is the connection between you and Adelina?"

"Your brother is my dive instructor," I said hastily. "We discovered Brock's body together.

"Oh my!" Carmelita exclaimed. "You were at the square yesterday. The hippie with the beard!" She knocked the heel of her hand to her temple. "I was stupid not to recognize you. I had this nagging feeling."

"There is something else," I said quietly. "You already know Brock and Larissa were murdered but today I was nearly killed."

Diego rushed to the love seat and took my hand. "Are you alright?"

"I am. It was a fluke I wasn't shot."

"Adelina needs to stay with us, Diego." Carmelita refilled her drink. "This is serious. I insist you live here." Then she added, "And you too, Amancio. I don't care what you do as far as your job but this is our family home. You belong here."

Cy put his hand up as if to stop her from saying anything else. "Hear me out. Today we had a dive that nearly killed us. Someone drugged our water bottles."

"It looks like someone is after our family," Diego said, accepting a glass from Carmelita. "Stefano will find the people behind this."

"No need to. The worst of it is over. But there is something else." I gazed intently at Carmelita. "Cy and I went to the warehouse tonight to see what was being exported."

"Why did you do that?" Diego gripped my hand. "You couldn't have asked? What possessed you?"

"The other night we followed a truck from the warehouse to a beach. Some of your people are smuggling goods. Tonight I opened a crate of skulls and found weapons. They look like terrorist attack arms."

Carmelita stared at Cy. "What do you know about this?"

"It's true."

Diego's gaze swept the room thoughtfully and stopped at his brother. "Are you sure?"

Cy nodded.

I gripped the stem of my glass. "Inside the warehouse, a woman fired a gun at me. She missed but when she tried again, a man shot her."

"Who were they, Adelina?" Diego squeezed my hands. "I need to get Stefano on it. He can bring them in."

"It's too late," Cy said. "The hitwoman is dead. She told Adie about the car bomb before the man killed her. And as for the man, you both know him. He was the one behind the explosion and the attacks on Adie."

"And the murders," I added.

Carmelita's eyes widened.

"Brock's murderer?" Diego kissed my wrist. "Don't worry, *mi amor*. I will make sure he doesn't get away with this."

"He can't any more. The hit woman killed him," I said tightly

"*Bueno!*" Carmelita smiled brightly. "It's all over then."

"Not for Luis." Diego tossed back the rest of his drink.

"How insensitive of me, Diego. I was just glad that horrible man died. How dare he threaten Adelina?" Carmelita stared forlornly at me. "And my poor Brock. The man deserves death."

Cy shook his head. "I don't know how to tell you, *cariño,* but you know him."

Carmelita placed her glass on the oak table. "What are you talking about? I know who? I don't know any killers!"

His jaw clenched, Cy took his sister's hand and said quietly "The man is... Fede."

Carmelita froze. "Fede? He is the man who murdered Brock?"

Cy nodded. "Yes, he hired a woman from Adie's tour group to do it. She tried to kill Adelina in the warehouse. Fede shot her and then decided to kill Adie. Luckily, the woman had enough strength left to shoot him first."

"I'm sorry, Carmelita, but your husband is dead," I said.

Emotions worked Carmelita's face. A tear escaped the corner of her eye.

I hugged her close. She shook like a leaf, sobbing.

Finally, she pulled away, a strange smile on her lips. Jumping to her feet, she took a last sip of tequila before flinging the snifter on the fireplace. The glass shattered. "To the Bolivars—*salud!*"

20

Clear blue skies. In the distance, the hazy white shoreline of Cozumel. The breeze blowing through my hair lifted the weight off my shoulders. Prepared with a bag packed with bikinis, shoes and necessities, including the Ixchel candle and skull, I was more than ready for this adventure.

It had been a sudden decision but one that was necessary. I suppose we were lucky Diego took care of the mess we'd left behind. Stefano and his men cleaned up the warehouse. I didn't want to know what they'd done with the bodies. I had the feeling they wouldn't be found for a while. Carmelita would eventually be declared a widow.

The ferry headed at a steady clip to Playa del Carmen. Passengers had filled the deck chairs but I didn't mind standing. We'd be there soon enough. A Jeep was waiting on the other side. Exhilaration made my pulse race.

Isla de Mujeres was a fantasy island. Where else but in a dreamland could I forget Wolf and his pregnant ex wife? And I wasn't alone. A man stood with me—a sinfully delicious man like chocolate. He wasn't creamy white milk chocolate like Wolf or a smooth dark cocoa like his brother. Cy was a mixture. Dark rich chocolate on the outside and a frothy lighter mousse on the inside. It made me wonder. What would it be like to idle away the days on an isolated beach, under the sun and its heat, with Amancio Bolivar Alvarez?

*****

AnastasiaAmor.com

Anastasia.Amor@hotmail.com

http://anastasiaamor1.blogspot.ca

www.ingramcontent.com/pod-product-compliance
Lightning Source LLC
Chambersburg PA
CBHW071145260626
47162CB00003B/925

* 9 780099 180623 2 *